A Girl's Guide To Turning 50

Jo Gardetta

For Jack

and in memory of Lilli

ACKNOWLEDGMENTS

I am very grateful for the unstinting support of my friends who have, over many, many years, tirelessly encouraged me to write and for allowing me to borrow from their lives. I am also especially grateful to be allowed access all areas in Le Jardin de la Mothe, my perfect writing retreat.

Chapter 1

'The Big C?'

'Yep,' said Sally, 49 years old and palpably disappointed after yet another failed attempt to re-launch her romantic life, 'and he wasn't 'up to it'.'

'Understandable.' said Will, Sally's gay-best-friend.

'It's not him who's got it,' said Sally, her mobile phone pressed hard against her ear, 'it's his 'friend'. Or imaginary friend. I don't believe him, no one who is distraught starts a text with, 'Howdy!"

'You don't know that.' said Will.

'I do, he's dumped me,' said Sally, 'before the date.'
She peered into the magnified bathroom-mirror, scrutinizing the face of the unknown woman looking back at her: the lines etched beneath her eyes that no amount of sleep could now erase, the deep furrows on either side of her mouth rendering her expression in repose that of a glum clown, and the two dents between her eyebrows, the pinched-inverted commas denoting the '7 signs of ageing'. This was trench warfare on a grand scale, the lines of battle had been drawn up while she wasn't looking. Who was this old woman in her bathroom?

'It might be true,' said Will, although he was having doubts, 'think of it as a good thing, shows he's caring. And concerned. And…'

'A text,' said Sally, 'on the day.'

7 signs didn't come close to covering the aging process, she thought, swapping the phone to the other ear. What about the sagging, bagging and aching? The loss of memory, eyesight and sleep? The high anxiety, low energy and confusion? The spots? She had acne. Again. No one had told her about that.

'He's tall,' said Will, 'got a good head of hair. Don't give up on him, not yet.'

'A text. On the morning of the date. Not even a phone call.'

There was a lot she didn't seem to know anymore, like what to wear? She wasn't ready for a twinset and pearls, unless that twinset was a Vivienne Westwood. But she was well aware it was a thin line between Kristen Scott Thomas in skinny jeans and mutton dressed as Lady Ga Ga. Sally had thought growing old would equal growing up and knowing whatever it was she was supposed to know. But just when she'd thought she'd made enough mistakes to learn a few tricks, her hips ached, her back hurt and she couldn't find her glasses.

'Wait till next week,' said Will, 'then text him.'

'But…'

'But what?' Will hyperventilated, 'He's got a flat on Portobello Road.'

'A studio.' Sally corrected, 'Above an Office.'

'So? It's a shoebox above a shoe shop, who cares? It's Porto-fucking-bello.'

'But Will…'

'Does it matter? He's got hair, teeth, his own place. And he's tall.'

'I don't care about that,' said Sally, 'and I certainly don't care about Mark.'

'What about someone else on the site?'

Will was running out of steam.

'What S slash D?'

'No, not him.'

'Most are more like cellmates than soulmates,' said Sally, 'I wouldn't want to share a lift with half of them let alone my life.'

'Just text Mark next week,' Will counselled, 'it's the 21st Century, you can ask him out now.'

'But I don't want to ask him out. He didn't even offer any alternative dates.' she whined, 'Why couldn't he have called me? I don't want to be texted or tweeted or Facebooked, I want to be face to face with a real man who I really like, who really likes me. A proper man, like Cary Grant or…'

Sally's love of old movies was bordering on obsessive.

'Now…' said Will.

'Gregory Peck or…'

'We've discussed this before…'

'Jimmy Stewart…'

'You're obsessing again. That's the movies not real life. Gay, balding, bad breath, men standing on boxes, women in holes, that's the truth about Hollywood.'

'A proper man in a hat.'

'Relationships are not like riding a bike,' Will continued, 'you will forget. You don't have to marry him, just text him, have some fun.'

Sally massaged her French face oil up her neck, under her chin and around her jaw line, as described in a magazine she'd found left on the bus. She couldn't remember exactly what she was supposed to do next, so after a few strokes she abandoned her new beauty procedure. She wasn't looking for another husband but she did feel she'd spent enough time being single. She'd stopped arguing with Ed-the-ex-husband long ago but now that their two kids were grown-up, in the eyes of the law at least, what she'd like was a bit of love and affection. Will was right, she thought, she did need to have some fun. Before it was too late. She didn't need someone to pay her mortgage or donate their sperm. She just wanted someone to share the rest of the adventure with and possibly the remote control. And a boyfriend wasn't just for Christmas, he was good for going on holiday with too. Sally liked sharing her life, 2-for-1 worked better with two. But whereas a bachelor may be in high demand at every dinner or party, a single woman was often perceived as a social pariah: the odd number perched on the corner of the table, a potential mistress on the lookout.

On the advice of others, Sally had gone against her better

judgement and online. It had been a disaster: the fat one, the bald one, the one with the dodgy teeth, the angry one and the hairy biker. She'd made sure the 'dates' had been in daylight hours, as Alice, her married-best-friend, had suggested. There had been absolutely no alcohol, as Jaz, her single-best-friend had advised, not after the quick coffee had turned into wine and she'd ended up in bed all afternoon, wondering what she was doing with an out-of-work-newly-divorced-banker who shouted 'fuck her' while he was in fact fucking her (see the angry one). So now she made appointments to interview the owners of various new restaurants and cafes for her column, *Snacks and The City*, directly after her meetings with the men she knew she would never see again.

'Come to the party.' said Alice.

'No.' said Sally.

'One date disaster does not mean you have to stop going out altogether.'

'One?' said Sally, 'What about the D slash S debacle.'

'Only you could think D slash S meant dinner or supper,' said Alice, 'you obviously didn't read fifty shades.'

'Well now I've got cancer-boy, I've had enough of on-line dating. Any dating.'

'Forget him.'

'I was looking forward to it. I'd had my legs waxed.'

'Then come to the party, don't waste the waxing. No, Stan stop it, I mean it. Basha…' bellowed Alice, 'could you? Sorry Sally, just come, you'll have fun.'

Sally could hear Alice's twins in the background: Stanley and Olive, IVF, four years old and perfect in every way, fighting somewhere in Alice's cavernous open plan kitchen-diner.

'I hate parties.' said Sally.

She had recently decided she wasn't a party person. They used to always start with such high hopes, plump with the promise of fun and frivolity and who knew what might happen. But that theory only held wine when she was 19, not 49. Now, it had sprung a leak; now she knew exactly what would happen: the evening would end in a drunken slur and the absolute certainty of an expensive taxi ride home. Alone.

'Don't be silly,' said Alice, desperation rising in her voice, 'we'll both have fun.'

'We won't.' said Sally.

'I need you to come.'

'Why don't you just not go?'

'I have to go, social politics,' said Alice, 'even if Ben is away.'

Her husband was inconveniently out of town, making a documentary in Reykjavik, and she very much wanted Sally to go with her. Her argument had been tenacious.

'Babysitter?' said Sally.

'I used that excuse last time.'

'Food poisoning? On the day?'

Sally searched the shelves of her bathroom cabinet, stacked high with lotions and potions, creams and unguents.

'Time before that.' said Alice, 'I know she can be a bit… and I can't stand him but they're our friends. It'll be fine. If we go together.'

'But…' said Sally scanning the shelf where her son Max, the boy who'd turned his gap year into a lifestyle choice, kept his Lynx and the razor he hoped to one day fully deploy, 'I won't know anyone.' She reached for the twisted curl of an old tube of spot cream.

'That's a good thing.' said Alice, detecting a chink in Sally's party-pooper armour, 'I'll pay for the cab.'

'It'll be full of Booker long-listers and people who know Richard Curtis. And Alan Yentob. I'll have nothing to talk about.'

At one of Alice and Ben's parties Sally had once famously asked Alan Yentob if they'd ever worked together because she felt sure she recognised him. Ben never tired of repeating the story.

'You can pretend to be anything you want, you'll never see any of them again.' said Alice, chipping away, 'And you never know who you might meet.'

But Sally did. She was sick of talking to men who spoke in the vernacular of a single person from the land of me, myself and I, allowing her to wonder: could she fancy them despite their lack of height? Hair? Sense of humour? Allowing her to ask questions about their tedious work while wondering what dinner together might be like. Or laughing at their stale one-liners while imagining them naked in bed together. Or rejoicing in their mutual love of Marrakech until eventually a woman would appear from nowhere and place a proprietary hand upon her partner's arm, grin a bare-toothed smile of ownership, and he would look round, give her the reassuring hug of one caught in mid-flirt, and try to introduce Sally, who would then drain her glass and tactfully turn, waving the now empty beaker in an amusing-must-get-a-drink manner and reverse into the crowd, allowing him to make good his mistake.

'I don't want to meet anyone,' she said, 'ever again.'

'You could get a column out of it,' said Alice, who wasn't giving up, 'top tips on how to survive a party?'

'But…'

'You're always saying you need more fun in your life.'

'Ok,' said Sally, squeezing out a blob of gel, 'I'll think about it.'

She applied a dab to the promising new spot on her chin.

'Great,' said Alice, 'what are you going to wear?'

Sally did not text Mark the following week, but she did say yes to Alice and set about making elaborate calculations involving pounds-per-day she would like to lose before the party, against pounds-per-day she could actually lose before the party. Despite her misgivings her spirits were definitely on the up as she began to plan her outfit for the evening; she was even nice to Kirsty-in-accounts when she failed to pay her expenses, again, made a coffee for Tricia, her office nemesis, and a special effort with special-Jenna, the idiot intern. She even contemplated writing the two articles that were way past their deadlines.

Sitting alone in her pink kitchen, filing her nails, Sally was just pondering whether to go for Naughty Nude or Aubergine Noir polish when her phone bleeped into life. It was the errant son, Max, texting to say not to bother about food, he wasn't coming home. She turned off the simmering pot of slow cooked lamb with lentils she'd lovingly prepared to feed her boy. She certainly wasn't going to eat it, horrified at the thought of the unnecessary consumption of all those calories before her party. She'd only cooked it because he had said he'd wanted it.

Resisting the urge to be an angry, old bird and send a 'but you said…' reply, Sally wandered into her bedroom hoping that the exercise of movement might lighten her now darkening mood. Clothes spilled from her frayed laundry basket, its wicker worked so long ago that tufts had sprung free and the pregnant bulge of too much unwashed washing was making it list dangerously to the right. Perhaps, she thought, she might put on a wash? Or, she thought, gathering up the discarded newspapers by the bed, leftover from several Sundays, she might clean. The dust on top of her chest of drawers was thickening around her jewellery box, several rings and random earrings lay scattered amongst the discarded mascara, sticky lip gloss and sundry make-up mistakenly bought because someone somewhere had said that orange was in or glitter was back. The mirror, from which several strings of beads and chains of tarnished silver hung, was reflecting in soft focus through its dusty veneer. Perhaps, she thought, the looking glass was best left that way.

She put the top back on a charcoal eye pencil that was older than her son, and gathered up the rings, returning them to their individual velvet nests. She un-toped the bottle of Pomegranate Eau de Cologne, hoping the heady aroma of her favourite scent might raise her flagging spirits, and sprayed it towards her neck but the bottle was all but empty. She pumped the atomiser violently, and a squirt splashed her chin, mingling with the now dusty air, making her sneeze. Even her perfume had run out on her. And now, despite not wanting to eat supper, she was hungry.

Top tip: perfumed oil lasts longer than Eau de Cologne, try Jo Malone's bath oils massaged in small circular movements, behind your ears and down the neck towards the heart, smell fabulous and aid the lymphatic congestion that can develop into bags under the eyes.

CHAPTER 2

On the morning of the party Sally set off early to her yoga class, walking and thinking, smiling up at the cool blue sky and fluffy squirrels like some latter-day Snow White, waiting for the day her Prince would come.

'Let your neck go,' said Fenella, the yoga teacher, as she adjusted Sally's posture, her own straight back and flat tummy enviable at any age let alone at seventy-three, 'relax your shoulders and… breathe.'

Sally exhaled. She was the youngest member of her yoga class, the rest of the group being in their sixties, seventies and beyond.

'Tuck the elbows in.' said Fenella, 'Release the tongue.'

Most of them had been meeting up regularly to do their practice for the last forty odd years.

'Don't allow your thoughts to wonder.' said Fenella.

Sally tried hard to 'be in the room' and 'stay in the now' but she was mainly back in her bedroom going through her wardrobe, imagining what she would wear that evening.

She had recently read in a magazine that the aging woman should in fact exercise six times a week. This, she felt, was completely impractical but she had upped her yoga class to twice a week and was attempting to walk to any destination she could reach within half an hour. Weather permitting. She made sure she walked to work that morning and eschewed all the biscuits and cake Tricia tried to force on her and drank nothing but orange and carrot juice all day, in the hope that she could shed another few pounds before nightfall. And finally, she received a response to the message she'd left for her daughter, now studying at Uni to be… something, two days previously.

'Darling,' said Sally, leaving her desk and moving into the office kitchenette, 'How are you?'

'Yeah good…' said Poppy, '… yeah fine.'

She listened to the pause in conversation.

'All… fine.'

She couldn't help feeling that Poppy was actually doing something else whenever she rang her.

'And the course?' Sally asked.

'Yeah…'

Sally was positive she could hear the tap-tap of keys on a keyboard being… tapped.

'All good.' said Poppy, distractedly. She was studying knitwear design this term, having abandoned interior design last term. She had at least managed to move out but only as far as the next borough, and now lived with her boyfriend, Habib, in his studio flat.

'Why don't you come over on Saturday, have a proper catch up?' said Sally, 'I'll cook…'

'Yeah, great, actually,' said Poppy, perking up, 'yeah, Saturday evening we're going to see this flat, can you drive us?'

'Oh,' said Sally, 'you're moving?'

'Yeah, I know, landlord shit. So that would be great, if you could, and you know that black top with the sleeves?'

'My Marc Jacobs?'

'Yeah… the one that doesn't really fit you.'

'It does fit, it looks great with my jeans…'

'Yeah… but it's a bit tight, anyway, can I borrow it tonight?'

'Well, I was going to wear it, to a party,' said Sally.

There was another pause.

'I've lost weight.'

Silence, but for the faint tapping.

'I mean it's nothing special.' said Sally, filling the void.

'You're going to wear it,' said Poppy, finally, 'with your jeans?'

'What's wrong with my jeans?'

'I just really wanted to borrow that top. Please.'

'But,' said Sally, 'I mean I suppose…'

'Please?'

'Ok…'

'So, I'll just come round and get it, yeah?'

'Ok.' said Sally, feeling derailed by her daughter and big-bottomed in her jeans.

'And we can catch up in the car,' said Poppy, 'when we go to look at the flat, yeah?'

Standing in the bathroom, dressed only in her underwear and a pair of ratty-furred slippers, Sally stared into the jar of expensive mud-pack she'd been saving for a special occasion, now dried to a hard, sun baked, Sahara crust, fit only for the bin. Party preparations were not going well. She padded back to her bedroom and discarded the jeans her daughter had been so rude about and put on a dress she never usually wore.

The party was already in lively mode when she and Alice arrived, the stoop packed with the smokers spilling onto the pavement despite the chilly night air. Inside, Cold Play played, their big sound emanating from tiny speakers, guiding them if not home then towards the kitchen table, festooned with bottles of red wine and flanked by buckets of icy-water in which bobbed bottles of foil-wrapped Prosecco and cold beer. And people, so many people. Sally immediately knew she'd made a mistake, she should not have come, she was in the wrong frame of mind, the wrong dress, the wrong body.

Glass half empty with ice cold Prosecco, she talked to a director who'd moved to Los Angeles, about how much he loved driving through the streets where the Hollywood sirens once swanned. And then to his screenwriter wife about how tricky it was to have your son be in a fist-fight with James Cameron's son in the school-yard. She told them she assessed the work of a major charity and had just got back from an arduous month in Pakistan.

Then she talked to a man about what his responsibilities were, as a member of BAFTA, to the future of British film and what a great guy Colin Firth was. And then to his husband about whether the accidental pregnancy of their Labradoodle meant he might get into puppy breeding and what a great guy Colin Firth was. She told them she was a nature photographer and had just completed a coffee table book on the changing polar landscape with a forward by Sir David Attenborough.

Sally was actually quite enjoying herself, now listening to a tale of woe from a TV producer who had recently been dumped by a hand-written note put through her door.

'What is that?' said the woman, 'Is that a romantic thing? Or is that just a weird thing? I mean, he'd written it with a pen. On a piece of paper. Just folded it in half and put it through the letterbox. What's that about? Who writes anything on paper these days? Is that a stalker thing?'

Sally then embarked upon a story of novel writing: her in the middle of writing an historical thriller set in the art world, and the immense amount of research she'd had to undertake and how hard it had been getting permission to search the archives at the National Gallery, when the TV producer said:

'You should talk to Peter, he's in the arts, got ins everywhere.'

'Right,' said Sally, distractedly fishing about in the recycling tub full of ice for yet another foil-topped bottle, 'it'll be awhile before I get to that bit.'

She looked around for a tea towel to help her free the cork from the Prosecco.

'Can I help you with that?'

Warm and deep, like salt caramel over toasted pecans, the accent was American, east coast, dry-witted, cultured and confident.

'That's ok...' said Sally, who prided herself on her abilities to open a bottle, any bottle, 'I'm good.'

She held tight and turned to discover the stranger was a tall man with a full head of gently greying hair and dark, kind eyes, crinkled at the corners by the broad smile of a mouth that had clearly seen a lifetime of excellent dental care. Bowled over by his striking resemblance to her perfect man, she loosened her grip and the cork burst from the bottle and whistled past his ear while the Prosecco splashed over his trousers.

'Fuck.' she said, pawing at his crotch with the damp tea

towel, 'I'm so sorry…'

'It's fine,' he said, taking the tea towel in one hand and the foaming bottle in the other, 'it's drip-dry.'

He smiled his slightly lopsided smile, turning a tiny scar at the corner of his mouth into a dimple, dipped a finger in the splash on the table and dabbed it behind each ear.

'And I love Prosecco.'

'I don't know how…'

'May I?' he said, pouring her a glass and one for himself. She smiled and raised her drink in a gesture she hoped might suggest, 'yes you may, please join me for a drink and perhaps the rest of my life.'

'I know you,' he said, with a quizzical look, 'members' bar at the V&A?'

This man, this gorgeous man, was he flirting with her?

'No.' she said.

'Tate Britain?'

'No.' she laughed.

'We don't know each other?' he said, his brow furrowed in thought.

'I don't think we do,' said Sally, 'I know a lot of people but I think I would have remembered if…'

'Oh, I am sorry,' he said, picking up his glass and turning to move away, 'my mistake.'

'Quitter.' said Sally.

Now she was flirting.

'This is Peter.' said the TV producer, 'Sally's a writer.'

'Not a wine waiter then?' he said, 'Maybe we should step away from the bottles, just in case.'

They moved to a quieter corner, away from the producer.

'So, you're a writer?'

'Well,' said Sally, checking his slender fingers for a ring, 'a sort of writer.'

'Really?' he said, taking a sip of his wine, 'And what do you sort of write?'

Sally laughed. He was lovely, really lovely and to think she'd nearly taken his eye out.

'No, seriously,' she said, 'I do write but….'

'Oh don't say seriously,' he said, pulling a stern face, 'the older I get the less I want to hear that word. I especially don't want you to be serious.'

'Ok.' she said, as they sat down on the sofa together.

Sally told him about the magazine she really worked for, her various features, columns and the top tips she wrote. He listened and laughed in all the right places and refilled their glasses. He told her about the changing world of art and how much he believed it meant to the future of civilisation, the long running, PBS television show, *The Art Of Life*, he'd co-created, and the educational arts programme he'd started for disadvantaged kids and young offenders, in New York, which had been used as a template across the country to start similar projects.

'Bill and I go back,' he said, 'so funding was never an issue then.'

'Oh,' said Sally, 'of course.'

'Bush was trickier, but I won him over,' he laughed, 'in the end.'

Well, thought Sally, who wouldn't be won over?

'And Barak loved it.'

Of course, of course Barak loved it. Who wouldn't love it? Bill? Bush? Barak? Who was this man? She waited for the feminine hand of a female to appear on his shoulder, but none arrived. Instead, they laughed about their mutual mistrust of Facebook and lack of application with Apps.

'I'm more of a face to face kind of guy,' said Peter, 'I guess I'm too busy enjoying the experience, is that selfish?'

'No,' said Sally, 'not at all.'

It's not selfish, it's brilliant, she thought, she wasn't the only person left on the planet who wasn't living the tweet life.

He told her he lived in Manhattan but was regularly in Europe for work. She told him she loved the Chrysler Building and waited for a man to appear at his side and say it was time for them to go walk his dog, but none came. Instead, he asked her if she'd like another drink. Was he actually single, she wondered, this lovely, gorgeous, proper man? Sally didn't want the conversation to ever end. She didn't want the evening to ever end. Peter was funny and interesting and appeared to be interested in her. She couldn't remember the last time she'd met a real live man who she genuinely liked. She didn't want…

'Sally,' said Peter, glancing down at his watch, 'I'm terribly sorry but…'

Here it comes, she thought, my wife, my girlfriend… my husband…

'… I'm going to need your phone number.'

'Oh.' Sally beamed.

'For the dry-cleaning bill, my suit?'

'Ah.' Sally's face dropped.

Peter laughed.

'No really, I have to go now, early flight tomorrow, but you should see your face.'

Damn, she thought, he was taking the piss. She was an idiot.

'But it would be lovely to see you next time I'm in town, if you'd like to...'

'Sure,' said Sally, trying not to punch the air, he did like her, 'I mean…'

She tried to calm her excitement.

'Unless,' he said, draining his glass, 'you fancy a night cap. Now?'

'Yes.' said Sally.

'I think you should say yes.'

'I said yes.'

'You said yes?'

'Yes.' said Sally, 'I said yes.'

Top tip: if you've lost the willpower to lose weight cast aside your smock tops and leggings and instead squeeze yourself into your tightest jeans and create your own gastric band.

CHAPTER 3

'I thought you said you wanted to see the flat?' said Poppy, 'And catch up.'

'I did,' said Sally, 'and I do.'
She pulled the duvet up and hunkered down amongst the pillows.

'But you don't,' said Poppy, 'because you're not.'

'Not this time,' she said, grabbing the phone as it slid from under her chin, 'something's come up, I can't do it today.'
Her head hurt. She needed water.

'It's Saturday,' whined Poppy, 'what's come up?'
Water and medication.

'What are you doing on a Saturday?'

'I do, do things on Saturdays.' said Sally.
Water and medication and coffee.

'But you said.'

'I know,' said Sally, she could hear the blood whooshing in her ears, 'But now I can't.'
What Sally was actually doing was having a serious hangover.
'Can't we do it tomorrow?' she said.
She wasn't sure if she felt sick. Or hungry. Definitely hungover. Maybe it was a good thing Peter had left before she'd woken up, at least he hadn't seen her like this.

'No, it has to be today.' said Poppy.
Oh god, she wondered, was she snoring? There was a knock

at the bedroom door.

'Look,' said Sally, levering herself out of bed, 'I have to go, I'm right in the middle of something.'
She pulled a large, white waffle robe about her, and padded over to the door.

'Great, how are we going to get there if you won't drive us?'

'Tube?' said Sally,

'But it's miles from the tube.'

'Bus?'

'What?'

'Well maybe it's not the right place to be moving to,' said Sally, exasperated, 'if you can't actually get there.'

'I can't believe you're doing this,' said Poppy, 'I'm going to be homeless.'

Sally thanked the waiter who'd delivered her breakfast: a pot of coffee, eggs Florentine, pain au chocolate, croissants, cherry jam and a sausage, she hadn't been able to make up her mind and Peter had said to order whatever she wanted from room service, in his 'thank you' note. And so she had. She sat back in bed, with her coffee and eggs, and ran over the fuzzy details of the night before. It was all crystal clear up to a point but the ending was a bit of a blur. The food was making her feel better but she still couldn't quite remember quite how they'd left things, other than Peter had left her, alone, in a hotel room. It had certainly come as quite a surprise, the invitation to a sleep-over, and one she'd felt would be churlish to refuse what with the fact that she'd just had her legs waxed and couldn't remember the last time she'd had sex, or sex worth remembering. She certainly wouldn't forget Peter though. And so what if she never saw him again? He lived in New York, she didn't, he was hardly date material. But it would be brilliant, she thought, if when he was in London… She re-read his note, it was polite but succinct. He'd apologised for having to leave so early, thanked her for a wonderful night, said he would call. Well, thought Sally, starting in on the pain au chocolate, it wasn't as if he'd left a fist full of cash on the dresser. She was feeling quite emboldened by her nocturnal outing. And it was an excellent breakfast.

Back home, her hangover was moving into phase two: self-loathing and depression, as she poured a bag of Omega 3 mixed seeds into the coffee grinder. Maybe, she thought, she shouldn't have slept with Peter. Maybe she should have been more aloof and alluring and played a little harder to get. She'd practically had her coat on before he could say 'my place'. The seeds spluttered and splurted out of the bag, filling the grinder and cascading onto the kitchen work surface. Maybe Peter wouldn't call. Fuck it, thought Sally trying to scrape the escaped seeds back into the bag. Did the supposed good this mix actually do, really outweigh the amount of trouble they caused, she wondered? She had read in a Sunday magazine, that grinding them into a powder was an excellent way to consume their wellbeing properties, 'mixed into soups, sauces and cereals'. Right now, they were simply mixing in with the crumbs around the back of the toaster and the dust on the floor. Maybe this was not the thing to be doing, with a hangover. Maybe she should take to her sofa instead, watch one of her old movies. And maybe Peter would call, she thought, blasting the grinder into action, she needed to be ready or at least awake She could hardly hear her phone above the din, lurching to grab it while switching off the machine. Maybe it was him?

'It's not funny,' said Sally, trying to get the lid off the coffee grinder without spilling the newly ground seeds, and failing.

'Oh yes it is,' said Will, 'it's hilarious. You're like a teenager.'
He could not stifle his mirth.

'It's a reaction,' said Sally, abandoning her seed grinding, 'to being dumped before the date. I thought I should seize the day.'

'And seize Peter's...'
The rest of the sentence was lost in Will's laughter.

'Thanks.' said Sally, flopping onto her sofa, unimpressed by her friend's hysterics.

'But a hotel,' he said, regaining himself, 'he took you to his hotel, god, how louche, I want to date Peter. How was the sex?'

'I can't.' said Sally, 'It's too… personal.'

'Oh great, you give up all the boring minutiae, all the hours of what might-might-not-does-doesn't-happen stuff and now you've got some actual good, clean dirt to dish I get none of it.'

'Good is all I will say.' said Sally.

'Good? What good is good? You haven't done it for ages, of course it's going to be good. A night in watching a Javier Bardem movie gets you off. Even *No Country For Old Men…*'

'Ok it was very, very good. He's good at it.'

'So lighten up and don't think so much. It'll all be fine, it's better this way,' said Will, 'you had a great time, a great breakfast, he says he'll call, you're already a head of the game.'

'S'pose.' said Sally.

'That's practically a relationship for you.'

'Yes, but,' she said, 'it all feels a bit *Butterfield 8* now, what if he's just another loser? And I slept with him. I'm done with losers. I'm too old to waste any more time with anymore lying…'

'Don't be too quick to judge, you don't even know him yet.' said Will, 'And maybe you won't get to, so stop projecting. The man has hair, teeth, a proper job…'

'But suppose…'

'Suppose nothing,' said Will, 'open mind, open heart.' Sally knew he was right. Sane, sorted Will was always right. Well, sometimes always right.

'So,' she said, 'what about you? Any love looming on your horizon?'

'Still getting random emails from the stalker-formerly-known-as.'

'Daniel?'

'Ah ha.' said Will, 'He's a freak.'

'But he was so sweet.'

'They're all sweet to start with before they become axe-murderers.' he said, 'He had no ambition, no drive.'

'He'd been a waiter in a hotel for five years, English was his second language,' said Sally, examining the chipped varnish on her toe nails and wondering if Peter had noticed, 'should have given you a bit of a clue.'

'Quite, maybe I should have got to know him better,' said

Will, 'before I slept with him.'

Top tip: once the breakfast of horses, Oat Bran is now the breakfast of menopausal champions when mixed with a couple of spoonfuls of ground Omega 3 seed mix and oats; lowers cholesterol and sets you up for the day, and night, ahead... a healthy aid to halting middle age spreading any further.

CHAPTER 4

Sitting at the far end of the long zinc bar, Peter finally abandoned his unfinished New York Times crossword and resumed drinking his Gibson, a sure fire cure for his jetlag, at least that's what he liked to tell himself. He was sitting in one of his favourite bars in Manhattan, the wood panelling and tiled floors, high ceilings and low lights, were unchanged. Apart from no longer being smoke-filled, the place was just as it was when the bar had first opened back in the forties. A corner of old New York that would forever stay the same he hoped, as the sound of a jackhammer ratter-tatted across the road from another new development. It was the kind of place Sally would enjoy, like stepping back in time, he thought, like being in one of those old movies she loved so much. He smiled to himself as he reached for a handful of bar nuts, remembering their night. Sally had been an unexpected surprise; unexpected and delightful. When it came to romance he'd never been particularly taken with the British and to be honest, she was a little older than the women he was used to dating. But she was sexy. And funny.

He checked his watch, Karen was late, nothing new in that, but the thought of another high maintenance blonde was beginning to lose its charm. His phone beeped into life. He retrieved it from his inside pocket as the barman placed a second Gibson in front of him.

I've changed my mind sorry

It was Karen.

I appreciate your honesty
Call me when you're divorced xxx

Oh well, you win some, thought Peter, raising his glass, you lose some.

'He's romantic.' said Sally, 'old school.'

'Old school?' said Jaz, as she and Sally waited in line in the steam-windowed café to order their coffees, the air thick with damp coats and woolly hats.

'Yes,' said Sally, 'he left me a note. And he bought me breakfast.'

'After inviting you back to his room hours after he first met you,' said Jaz, surveying the clientele, 'very old school.'

She pulled a face and continued studying the baroque-framed-blackboard listing cappuccinos, lattes, Americanos; tall, skinny, grande, hanging on the wall above the tall, skinny, gorgeous bloke behind the counter. They'd met for a coffee so Sally could talk about Peter and Jaz could spy on the competition. She may be an airhead in certain areas of her life, but Jaz was always on trend and a shrewd businesswoman. After living in New York some years ago, where the cupcake had ruled, with a man who'd said he was an artist but who Jaz had called the wanker, she had finally returned home armed with an American cookbook of baked goods. At that time in Britain the cupcake was more commonly known as a fairy-cake, but Jaz had set about creating her emporium of all things sweet and iced regardless and had been one of the first on the cupcake scene with her own café: *Cake.*

'And he said he would call.'

'Really,' said Jaz, eyeing up the buns, 'and you slept with him?'

'Yes.' said Sally, peering at the meringues, macaroons and cupcakes piled high, pretty, pink and cherry-topped like a Noddy and Big Ears tea party.

'Mmm...' said Jaz, 'romanced you right into bed.'

Cake had been an instant success so Jaz had opened a second café, a little further east, a little more trendy, bang on time, *Eat Me* had lines out the door from day one. It sold Middle Eastern and Mediterranean delights served on small plates, designed to be shared with good friends, just when it became popular to share your food. It had the added novelty of recycled charm and every stick of furniture, vase, picture, knick and knack was up for sale along with the odd bit of vintage Ozzie Clark or silk-screened T-shirt created by the latest, local Tracey Emin wannabee. In fact Tracey herself came in and breakfasted on occasion.

'It was wonderful.' said Sally, 'He's wonderful.'

'Sounds like a smooth operator.' said Jaz.

'D'you think?'

Jaz rolled her eyes.

'If it sounds too good…'

'Ok,' said Sally, as they shuffled towards the head of the queue, 'but it went really well. I think. I was a bit drunk. I've never slept with a man that old before.'

'You've never been this old before,' said Jaz, 'when you've slept with a man.'

'True,' said Sally, 'he has this way of… he made me feel very… comfortable. But sort of sexy comfortable, you know?'

'Or maybe,' said Jaz, 'you're more comfortable in yourself.' Jaz beamed at the tall, skinny, gorgeous bloke and ordered two skinny lattes while flirtatiously commenting on his Ramones t-shirt.

'I definitely have better sex now than when I was younger.' she said, over her shoulder to Sally.

'Anything else ladies?' asked coffee boy, clearly not so keen, 'The tart is delicious.'

They eschewed the carbs and found a table by the window.

'Ladies,' said Sally, 'I hate that. All he sees are a couple of middle-aged women.'

'I keep forgetting I'm probably old enough to be his mother.' said Jaz, still eying him up from afar.

Sally shouldered off her coat and sat down.

'Hair looks good.' said Jaz.

'Thank you,' said Sally, catching sight of her post-coital

bob reflected in the glass of the large framed, black and white photo of Bridget Bardot on the opposite wall, 'I asked for about ten years off.'

Sally gave herself a wide, toothy-grimace and smacked her softening jaw-line with the back of her hand.

'Have you lost weight?' said Jaz.

'Since I've found my libido,' said Sally, 'I've completely lost my appetite.'

She smiled and thumbed the gap between her shrunken tummy and the waistband of her skirt. Outside the rain-splattered trees whirled into a fury and rags of cloud scurried to the corners of the sky.

'They want me to go in for a smear test.' she said.

'Ahh,' said Jaz, 'nice. I haven't been for years.'

'Really? Why not? You must. Apparently once you get past 50 you only get one every 5 years.' Sally continued, 'I need to make an appointment before it's too late.'

'So now it's official,' said Jaz, 'you really are an old cunt.'

Coffee boy set their lattes down between them and backed away at speed. Sally smiled at the handsome, young man.

'You know you're getting old,' she said, 'when you think: your mum must be so proud. As opposed to: cor aren't you gorgeous.'

She took a sip of her coffee.

'So,' Jaz spooned sugar into her cup, 'has he called, this Peter Perfect?'

'Not yet.' said Sally.

'Why hasn't he called?' said Jaz, pulling a face, 'Skyped? A text?'

'It's fine,' said Sally, she took another sip of her coffee, 'I'm not worried either way, if he doesn't he doesn't. It was a brilliant night and if that's all it was, so be it.'

'Really? You're fine with that?'

'I may not have any choice.' said Sally, 'I really liked him but he lives in bloody America.'

'Mmm, it is a bit of a commute.'

'Typical, I meet someone I like,' said Sally, 'and he lives on the other side of the world.'

'You can get some really cheap deals...'

'A call would be good right now,' said Sally, 'jetting off to

New York can come later. I'm under no illusion.'

'Really?'

'It's just… he is the best thing that's happened to my love life… and,' she paused, 'of course I hope he calls. I'm sure he will.'

She reached for her coffee, trying hard not to be under any illusion.

'No more internet dating then?'

'No.' said Sally.

As a serial-girlfriend, Jaz was Sally's dating coach; no kids, no interest in kids, independent and up for it. But even she was beginning to find that being firm of breast and buttock post forty was a hollow victory if you're single. If no one actually feels your inner thigh is it really firm?

'Maybe keep it in reserve,' she said, 'it'll take the pressure off the whole Peter thing… just in case he…'

'What? The two liars, one weirdo and a pervert.' said Sally.

'Liars?'

'Under six foot is not tall and over sixty is not forty-five.' Jaz spooned up the froth from her coffee.

'The weirdo?'

'Still lived with his mother.'

'And the pervert?'

Sally tapped open the text on her mobile phone from D/S man and thrust it at her friend to read.

'Oh!'

'Yes,' said Sally, 'I'm keeping it in case I have to show the police.'

'Right,' said Jaz, nodding sagely, 'of course.'

'The thing is,' Sally continued, glancing around the café just on the off chance, 'the difference between the women of a certain age on the Internet and the men is palpable.'

'It sounds like most of these guys,' said Jaz, 'are single for good reason.'

'Exactly,' said Sally, 'but Peter's not like them. As I said, he's old school, he plays it straight, I can just tell.'

Jaz did have a point though, surely if he were interested in her he would have found time, made time, for one quick missing you call. He was in America, not the eighteenth century.

Unable to recognize the caller ID without her glasses, Sally had answered the phone half asleep and totally confused.

'Hello Darling.'

But the voice was instantly recognizable: warm and deep, like salt caramel over toasted pecans, the accent…

'Peter?'

'Did I wake you?'

'No,' she lied, propping herself up with a pillow and trying to sound awake, 'I was reading… it's fine.'

Exhausted by the new intern at work, Sally had gone to bed early. It was barely eleven but she was tired, constantly it seemed these days. Recently her sleep had been broken by anxiety attacks and night sweats, all part of the perimenopausal merry-go-round.

'Sorry to call late,' he paused and she heard the ice chink in his glass as he took a sip of his drink, 'I just needed to talk to you.'

'That's ok.' is all she managed, delighted he'd called at all but wondering what was so urgent.

'The thing is…'

'Yes?'

'I don't think I've been very fair to you.'

'Fair?'

'Yes, what with all my coming and going, well mainly going so far and…'

Here it comes, she thought, she had been beginning to wonder if their affair was not going to be one to remember and now he was calling to end it before it had started.

'Yes?'

Thinking fast, she planned her breezy fine-yes-you're-right-transatlantic-relationship-how-ridiculous response.

'I'm not coming to London anytime soon…'

'I see.'

'But I do have to be in Italy for an arts festival…'

'Italy?'

'Yes, and I was thinking of stopping over in Venice, do you know it?'

'No.'

What was going on now, she wondered?

'Great, we can explore together.' said Peter.

'Explore together?'

'Yes.'

Sally could hear the smile in Peter's voice.

'I thought you might like to meet up. In Venice.'

'Meet up in Venice?'

'Yes, I wanted to book you a flight.'

'A flight?'

'You know there's a terrible echo on this line darling, should I call you back?'

Sally laughed, it was the only response she could muster, the shock of his suggestion having robbed her of her words. He didn't want to dump her, he wanted to date her and on an International scale. No one had ever booked Sally a flight before. No one had ever organized anything for her before. She was always the one who'd had to trawl the Internet, cross-referencing the cheapest budget options, departing and landing at the worst possible times, and now she was going to fly to Venice and meet Peter at Marco Polo Airport. And stay in a beautiful boutique hotel overlooking the canal, according to the hotel's website from which he now read to her while sitting in his study at the back of his New York apartment, while she lay in her bed in her London flat. It wasn't going to be easy, she realized, having a relationship with a man who not only lived in a different city but a whole other time zone. Not easy no, but a long distant lover was an exciting prospect.

'And,' said Peter, pausing to take a sip of his drink, 'there's something else.'

'Yes.' said Sally.

'Yes,' he said, 'the thing is, I haven't been entirely straight with you.'

'Straight?'

Barely listening, Sally was already wondering whether she should unleash her credit card on a whole new wardrobe for her trip.

'No,' he said, 'and I want to be straight with you.'

'Good,' said Sally, feeling her throat closing around the word as she re-engaged with what he was now saying, 'I want you to be straight.'

'I don't want you to be misled.'

'No.'

'You must know Sally, how much I like you, but…'
'Yes?'
'I'm married.'

Top tip: with the ever increasing changes in middle aged lifestyles, and the over 40s flooding the dating scene, STDs are on the increase in the old. Take care, be aware and go for regular check-ups.

CHAPTER 5

Standing on her yoga mat, feet hip width apart, Sally folded forward and dropped her hands to the floor.

'Let your head go,' said Fenella, twisting her silver grey, corkscrew curls back into a knot, 'there shouldn't be any tension in the neck.'

Since Peter's revelation, Sally had felt nothing but tension.

'Relax the shoulders.'

He had explained that he and his wife were separated but had remained married quite simply because she did not want to be divorced, something to do with the children and being a Catholic. He hadn't wanted to cause any further distress to her or their family and so he had taken an apartment in the city when they'd split up while Lee, the wife, and their two daughters, had remained in their upstate home.

'Left arm across the right leg, turn… and breathe.' said Fenella, adjusting Sally's posture.

At the time Sally had been a bit shocked. A bit pissed off. A bit disappointed. She had listened calmly as Peter had explained how Lee's father had given him his first job in the art world, teaching him everything he knew and how, for reasons he didn't really go into, their good marriage had gone bad. It was all over a long time ago.

'Deep breath in through the nose,' said Fenella, 'twist on the out breath.'

Sally exhaled.

'Keep breathing,' boomed Fenella, 'release the shoulders.' According to Peter, for the most part it was an agreeable arrangement with his wife, and if Sally was agreeable, he would very much like to see her when he came to London, or Europe. His work kept him traveling so they would have plenty of opportunity to spend time together.

'Could you darling?' he'd said, 'Would you darling, still want to see me under these circumstances?'

'Keep your mind in the room…' said Fenella.

Sally closed her eyes and tried to get her thoughts into the Now but it was a fruitless task.

'… and relax.'

The class was smaller than usual as many of the older participants were away on their Spring break.

'Pam's in Bhutan,' said Joan, pulling on a fleece and winding a brightly coloured scarf about her supple neck, 'and I'm going to Japan and then New Zealand.'

Despite their advanced age, most of her yoga class's senior moments seemed to be spent gadding about the planet on springy knees, and new hips, spending their kids' inheritance. Sally wondered at their energy, she could barely make it through the week, would she be like them at their age?

'Hill walking and a glass of red wine,' said Mary, a sprightly ninetysomething, when Sally had asked her how she did it, 'champagne if you can get it.'

Was it a simpler time when they were growing up and growing old, Sally wondered? Or was a post-war life something they had learnt to cherish and live without fuss? They certainly didn't seem to have let the slings and arrows take them down.

'So,' said Will, stabbing thoughtfully at a piece of oily tomato cloaked in a basil leaf, 'what did you say?'

'No.' said Sally, slicing off another corner from the slab of Pecorino with peppercorns, crumbling it onto the wax paper.

'What?'

'I said no and he said don't say no, say you'll I'd think about it.' said Sally, 'so I said I would.'

'What's to think about?' said Will, refilling their glasses, 'It's the 21st century. What does it matter to you?'

'He's married.' said Sally, reaching for her glass.

'In name only.' said Will, authoritatively.

Sally had thought about it. It didn't really change anything so did it really matter? But then she'd thought: maybe his wife thought they were happily married. Maybe he was lying.

'Isn't that just what he's not doing?' said Will, 'Why would he go to the trouble of telling you about his wife if what he's said is not true? You'd never have found out about her, you're not even living in the same country. Why not just not tell you?'

'Good point.' said Sally, still not convinced.

'Sounds like an ideal situation to me,' he said, 'he turns up, he's pleased to see you, you're pleased to see him, he wines you, he dines you and before it gets boring he fucks you and fucks off. Win, win.'

'But…'

'And you're free to loll on your sofa in your pants, watching whatever, whenever you feel like it.'

'I really like him, but it's not going to work.' she said, looking out of the window at the melty wetness of another damp, Saturday evening.

'Because?'

'Because,' she said, 'I've never been out with a married man, I don't think I'm up for it.'

'Really?'

'Where can it go?'

'Venice for starters.'

'But is it right?'

'This,' said Will, 'from the woman who thinks finishing her drink means playing hard to get?'

He picked up the tub of hummus and gestured to Sally.

'No, you finish it.' she said, helping herself to more onion and tomato salad, 'I'm addicted to the stuff these days.'

'Hummus?' he said, dipping his flat bread into the pot, 'Interesting, chickpeas are very good for people like you.'

'People like me?'

'Old women,' he smiled, 'supposed to help ward off osteoporosis and minimize hot flushes.'

'Really? Well you're the doctor, you should know. I have developed quite a habit,' said Sally, 'I'm probably doing a tub a week. More.'

'Make your own,' said Will, 'it's easy, Daniel-the-stalker did it all the time.'

'He did?'

'Mmm,' said Will, 'thought he was Otto-bloody-lenghi.'

'How long has it been?' she asked.

'14 months.' said Will, 'I'm over it. Next.'
He reached for the bottle.

'If there ever is a next. You know I think I'd be happier straight. This whole gay thing isn't really working out for me.'

'Isn't it a bit late now?'

'I don't know, I'm only 45, I can still get married, have kids.'

'Live a lie. Commit suicide.'
Sally took the rhubarb and almond crumble cakes, still warm from the oven, and put them onto two plates.

'It's all lies.' said Will, raising his glass, 'That Oscar Wilde has got a lot to answer for.'

'You need to embrace your homosexuality.'

'I am embracing my homosexuality thank you very much. On a regular basis.' said Will, sitting back in his chair, 'All I've got to embrace is my homosexuality as it happens. Thanks for reminding me.'
Sally took the tub of crème fraiche out of the fridge.

'Why does it have to be so complicated?' she said, 'Why can't Peter just be single and…'

'It's life,' said Will, 'you're old, he's old, you're going to have baggage. Be weirder if he didn't.'

'Suppose so,' said Sally, 'but…'

'What?'

'He's married and he's not getting divorced anytime soon and…'

'And why don't you just fall in lust,' said Will, 'and forget the love this time?'

'But…'

'Love can be very overrated,' he said, tucking into his cake, 'in six months, you'll have gone off him anyway.'

'Maybe.'

'Six weeks then.'

'Maybe not.' said Sally.

Still unconvinced she should embark upon a relationship with Peter, long distance or not, Sally was yet to call him back. She put the lid back on her Persian chicken soup with pearl barley and checked her phone again; still no response from her son despite her texting twice to check when he was coming home for supper. Should she call Peter, she wondered? A trip away with him would be wonderful but she had never dated a married man before, was she going to start now? She'd always wanted to go to Venice but were married men her only choice left? If his marriage wasn't really a marriage then… the sound of someone coming through the front door crashed through her romantic imaginings.

'Max?'

'Hi Sal.'

It was not Max. It was Ed, ex-husband and father of her children. He stood in the doorway, thrusting a bottle of wine in her general direction as if it was something he'd made at school.

'Thanks Ed,' she said, putting the bottle on the worktop, 'how are you?'

'Good, great, how are you?' he said, taking off his coat, pocketing his keys to her front door, and sitting himself down at her kitchen table, 'The kids?'

He glanced over at the bottle of wine.

'I don't know,' said Sally, 'have you tried asking them?'

'Well, you know,' said Ed, looking up at Sally and then back at the bottle, 'Poppy's always busy at Uni and well…'

He glanced towards the pot on the hob.

'Something smells good.'

He beamed at Sally but she said nothing. When Sally and Ed had split up it was not because of another woman. It was because he had said they had out-grown their relationship, he had changed, they had changed, that although he loved her and their children he didn't love living with them. He needed to find himself, which would, in the end, be better all round. For everyone. Ten months later he'd met and moved in with Tamsin, who became instantly pregnant, and so he'd mainly been finding himself in Mothercare.

'Glass of wine?' he said.

Sally had not opened the bottle and poured two glasses as she usually did, she didn't really want to spend her evening listening to Ed go on about his newer, younger wife or his two terrible, newer, younger, sons.

'Well…'

Ed approached the bottle himself and twisted the top.

'Got room for one more?' he said, reaching up to the shelf for two glasses before Sally could answer.

Baby Billy was barely off the breast when along came baby Frankie and somehow Ed had got into the habit of dropping by, popping in, just to say 'Hi', see his 'big' kids, and complain about his thin wife and how she expected him, at his age thank you very much, to get all down and dirty with their boys while she went off with her girlfriends for spa weekends or mini-breaks in Ibiza, leaving him in sole charge of their children, as apparently being a stylist meant she earned a lot more money than him and therefore the right to do whatever she wanted.

'I'm starving,' he said, 'we can have a chat.'

'About Max?' said Sally, perking up at the prospect of Ed taking onboard his role as father to a man-boy who appeared reluctant to grow up and leave home, 'because frankly I'm at the end of my tether with him.'

'Well, yeah,' said Ed, filling his glass, 'we can talk about Max. Where is he?'

'Out.' said Sally.

'Great,' said Ed, 'I mean great he's out. And about. With his mates. I mean that he's got mates. Is he out with his mates?'

'Don't know.' said Sally, 'Don't care.'

'Tamsin said she could get him some work,' said Ed, 'nothing definite but maybe. What's he done now?'

He went, with alarming familiarity, to the drawer to find cutlery while Sally ladled out the chicken and barley, flavoured with lemon and turmeric.

'Nothing, that's the point,' said Sally, sprinkling a handful of chopped coriander over the dish, 'he's done nothing. He does nothing except play games, watch DVDs and get stoned.'

'And goes out.' said Ed, tucking in, 'This is delicious Sal. You know you really are a great cook.'

Ed paused to savour his delicious supper and smiled the smile of a man who now lived with a woman who didn't even shop let alone cook.

'Look how worried you were,' he said, waving his spoon aloft to make his point, 'when you said he didn't have any mates at school. Well he's got mates now.'

'And they all sit round here, playing games, watching things and getting stoned.'

Sally refilled her glass.

'But he's got friends at least.'

'Yes, but I don't want him to have these friends.'

Ed sat back and took a sip of his wine.

'He's ok, he's just trying to find himself.' he said.

'Really? Well he's mainly finding himself in my potential spare room.' said Sally.

'He's 21.' said Ed, 'What were you doing at 21?'

'Nearly 22, and I was at college.'

'And getting stoned.'

Ed helped himself to a little more from the large pot on the stove.

'But not in my parent's home.'

'It's different for kids now,' said Ed, licking the handle of his spoon that had slid beneath the pearl barley, 'harder for them to move out, and I remember when your mum found…'

'Harder? What because not every room comes with a flat screen?' said Sally, 'If he can't find his own place then he can go and live with you.'

'I'd love him to live with me,' said Ed, topping up their glasses, 'of course I would but I've got the boys.'

'At least he used to stay with you at the weekends.'

'We just don't have the room, Sal.'

'You've got four bedrooms.'

'Well,' said Ed, 'to be fair, one of them is my study.'

'Really?'

'Look it's hard for me too you know. I'd have him like a shot, of course I would. But Tamsin, you know, it's not easy with the kids, Billy's ADHD and we think Frank may be dyspraxic or dyslexic or…'

'What?'

37

'It might be an intolerance, he's being tested but Tamsin thinks…'

'Well now I'm intolerant,' said Sally, trying to steer the conversation away from Ed's world and back to Max, 'he isn't even trying to find a job.'

'He was working.' said Ed.

'Three weeks stopping strangers in the street and trying to make them handover their bank details for charity, does not a career make.'

'Oh right,' Ed chuckled, 'well tell him he's got to pay rent.' He sat back, satiated.

'Get a job or get out.'

'Throw him out?' said Sally, looking at her ex-husband.

'Yeah,' said Ed, 'I would, if he was living with me.' He finished his wine and left without helping to clear up.

Sitting in her office, Sally stared out of the arched-window, out through the small, square panes of Spring-rain spotted glass. Once the window of an old tea-warehouse, it now looked in on several floors of open plan, flat-packed offices, home to furniture solutions and web-innovators and, *The Right Stuff,* a consumer and listings magazine caught between the big, bad world and the worldwide web, where Sally had accidentally worked for far more years than she cared to remember, writing about which washing machine and what gas company were the greenest in the land, or ten top tips on how to keep toddlers and teens happy on family holidays or how to make the box room look like a big room, along with reviews about new cafes and fast-food emporiums, sandwich shops and ethnically-squeezed juice bars, for her weekly column, *Snacks and The City.*

She was finding it very hard to focus on her work. Had she been a bit hasty in saying no to Peter? If his marriage was over who would she be hurting? How often did a man like him come along? How often did any man come along? And what was she going to have for lunch? Despite it only being 10.24 am, Sally was wondering if it was going to be a protein day? A meat-free day? A fasting day?

'Coffee?'

Horrid Tricia broke through her reverie.

'Looks like you could do with one.' she smiled.

Sally could most definitely do with one but she didn't want to have to accept this act of kindness from Tricia. On the other hand she didn't want to have to get up and make it for herself.

'Black,' she said, 'please.'

Maybe, she thought, it was going to be a pretend-to-be-French day. Tricia smiled and adjusted the gold-threaded scarf artfully looped about her neck. Sally had accidentally made friends with her when she'd first started working at TRS, mistaking her smiley, can-do helpfulness for friendship instead of cunning manipulation. Too late, the damage was done over after-work drinks when Sally had said too much and Tricia hadn't said enough. Tricia's glass was not so much half-full as her cup runneth over and Sally had a deep mistrust of the perpetually perky.

'There you go.' said Tricia.

Sally tapped her keyboard and the screen flicked from the online tabloid she'd been scanning for celebrity gossip back to her work emails. She wasn't quite sure what it was that so irked her about Tricia: her we-weathered-the-storm husband, Jeff, that she was forever flaunting or her one-at-St. Andrews-the-other-volunteering-at-a-refugee-camp daughters? Or her thumb ring?

'Got you a biscuit too.' she said, carefully placing a Waitrose Essential chocolate-chip cookie next to the mug of hot, black coffee.

Or was it because she was a feeder?

'Is it Max again?' Tricia asked, through a pinched smile.

Either way, Sally rued the day she'd confided in her about her children's shortcomings. Tricia had that way of luring you in when your guard was down and getting you to spill the beans. Over the years Sally had let slip much she'd wished she hadn't.

'No, no… no,' she said, 'he's fine, I'm fine. It's all fine.'

She flicked her screen back to reading the latest beauty news about anti-aging procedures.

'Everything's fine.'

'Got you this.' said Tricia, thrusting a thick, glossy covered magazine with the words Tango, Italian, Computer, Photography, graffitied across the front in clashing colours.

'Remember?'

Sally stared blankly.

'I told you? About my cousin? The one who did belly dancing? Started doing Italian? Met that man?'

'No.'

'Adult education?'

She waggled the prospectus in Sally's face.

'Oh right.' said Sally, taking it off her before she lost an eye.

'Thought you might like to have a look. Never know who you might meet.'

'Thanks.' said Sally, thrusting it deep into her bag and wondering whether she should just go to the kitchenette, find the sharp knife and stab Tricia. Or herself. Or both. She imagined a Tarantino moment as the room ran red with the blood of Tricia and the interns.

The bottle of wine she had accidentally finished by herself, while catching up on catch-up TV, had rendered Sally sleepless and thought-fuzzy. Will did have a point, hadn't Peter proven himself to be a good guy by telling her the truth about his situation? She didn't want to do Italian classes or a photography course to try and meet a man. She didn't want to go on looking. It may not be perfect but she didn't want it to be over with him. Not yet. It was just baggage, she thought, who wasn't going to come with a couple of Louis Vuittons at their age? She had planned to wait a little while before declaring she was up for it but it was hard to play hard to get with a man who was hard to get hold of. She reached for the phone, what time, she wondered, was it in New York?

Top tip: based on Otttolenghi's recipe, hummus is delicious, easy and excellent for women of a certain age.

A can of chickpeas … who has time to soak?
Couple of cloves of garlic peeled and crushed
10ml lemon juice
50g of tahini paste
Good pinch of salt

Drain the chickpeas but keep a couple of tablespoons of the liquid. Put all the ingredients in a blender and blitz, add the chickpea liquid a bit at a time depending on preferred consistency. Add salt to taste. Chop in half a red pepper if you fancy it and go crazy.

CHAPTER 6

Spring sunshine had begun to leak into the lengthening days, the trees were starting to bud and leaf and the sky seemed somehow higher. Or maybe it was just Sally's mood that was elevated.

'I've decided,' she said, 'I'm going to be Peter's lover.'
She was feeling emboldened by her new status.

'What?' said Alice.
They were sitting outside a café, in the shade of the lime-green awning, trying to take full advantage of one of the few and far between, sunny days that had so far been missing from the season.

'And he's going to be mine. My transatlantic lover. Doesn't that sound grown-up?'
Alice gave her friend a look.

'Let me get this straight,' she said, 'you're going to take married Peter as your… lover?'
When Alice Newby had first met her husband, Ben Tate, he was a married man, so she knew only too well the agony and the ecstasy of being a lover.

'Exactly, he's in and out of Europe all the time.'

'In and out of you too, now.' said Alice.

'And,' said Sally, ignoring her friend's remark, 'we're going to Venice.'

'Venice spluttered Alice, pomegranate juice spackling her

chin, 'he's taking you to Venice?'

'Yep.' said Sally, smiling the smile of the over-excited.

'Bit quick,' said Alice, wiping the juice from her face, 'you just met.'

'And we're going to stay in a beautiful hotel,' said Sally, 'overlooking the canal.'

'There is no such thing as a free lunch,' said Alice, 'or dinner. You do know that?'

Sally ignored her friend and dug into her salad.

'He's just being flash with the cash,' said Alice, 'he wants something.'

'Yes, he wants me.' said Sally, defiantly.

'Probably looking for a nurse. Like Ben, he knew he'd need someone younger to take care of him in his old age, all his aches and pains and knees.'

As a young researcher on the award-winning documentary series, Last Look, back when Ben's star was on the ascent, Alice and he had spent several weeks together bivouacked in the Brazilian rain forest in search of rare-plant smugglers; things had got more than a little hot and steamy. At the hotel in Rio, Ben had booked them into the honeymoon suite where they'd stayed on for three extra days, racking up a room service bill to rival the national debt. Alice had not known Ben was a married man when she'd sat opposite him in the London office. He did not wear a ring. But she knew all about Mrs. Tate and their two sons by the time her head hit the pillow on the king-size, back in Rio de Janeiro.

'That's Ben,' said Sally, 'Peter is not in his sixties.'

'Not yet. And neither was Ben.' said Alice, 'Then.'

At the time of their affair she'd believed Ben's marriage was anything but happy because that was what he had told her. And what Alice was, was a thirty-four year old woman who'd spent the past few years planning the rest of her life around, and supporting, Tim-the-brilliant-photographer, because she'd thought she was going to spend the rest of her life with him. Except he had gone to live in Los Angeles without her. And then she'd found out that he'd not only left her holding the bills but also moved in with a really-lovely-American-girl called Amy. And Alice had been heart broken. So she'd had casual sex with random drunks and random sex with casual

44

drunks. And an abortion. She was not in a good way when she'd met Ben, sixteen years older than her, a proper grown-up who'd made a fuss of her.

'I'm going,' said Sally, 'and it's going to be brilliant.'

'Just be careful.' said Alice.

'Peter isn't free but he is serious,' said Sally, poking about in her watercress and orange salad for the ricotta, 'about me, and I just want to have some fun. Like you said. Before it's too late.'

'But where can it go?'

'Venice for starters.' said Sally, reaching for her glass of tap water.

Alice had been under no illusion, it was, she'd believed, a blame-it-on-Rio fling. Until Ben had explained his divorce was imminent, just as soon as his youngest was off to Uni. Even then Alice had still only ever seen it as a stopgap on the road to Mr. Right.

'Why do I have to define my relationship?' said Sally.

'You don't,' said Alice, 'but do you accept the mistress contract?'

'The what?'

'Worst case scenario, if his marriage is more demanding than you believe, you have to be less demanding. No Christmases, missed birthdays. But if you're cool with it…'

'It's not a proper marriage.' said Sally, 'I'm going to be fifty, doing things the way I've been doing them hasn't really worked out for me. I'm going to do things differently now. Move the goal posts.'

'Even fifty year-olds need boundaries,' said Alice, 'like kids.'

'Why? Without boundaries I can have more fun. I want to have a life. It'll great.'

'That's what kids think,' said Alice, 'that's why they need boundaries.'

Alice's fling with Ben may well have stayed just that had she not left documentaries and started working at a talent agency. When Ben was nominated for his first BAFTA she was delighted but sadly tickets were limited to the production team only. Alice had secretly gone with Tabitha, who ran the agency, with the intention of surprising Ben. Fortunately, or unfortunately, Ben won but when Alice had stood to applaud she was surprised to see a very attractive women, clad head-to-toe in designer kit, draped about him in congratulatory ecstasy and even more surprised when she discovered the woman was his wife. Far from being in the death throes of a blighted marriage, they'd looked very happy. Alice had got very drunk and planned a great many vengeful scenarios, finally throwing Ben's possessions into black trash bags and having them delivered to his home with a large bouquet of flowers and a card that read:

Congratulations... Bloody Asshole Fucking Traitorous Asshole

Home alone in a basement studio in Whitechapel, having been thrown out by the wife, it took Ben just six weeks to win Alice back. North of 35, she had been swayed by the not-getting-any-younger camp. And Ben offering her anything and everything. He did not do on-his-own. So Alice had opened her heart and her front door. They'd got married, had an enviable lifestyle and finally he'd provided her, by way of the Petri dish, with the children she had so wanted. But that was all sperm under the bed. Now Ben was in his sixties and Alice wasn't.

'We all need boundaries,' she said, 'otherwise it ends in tears.'

But Sally wasn't really listening to her friend, she was too busy wondering what she was going to wear in Venice.

The rain had fallen all day, rain without a plan, rain with nowhere else to be but Manhattan. A late Spring shower it was not, more like the tail end of an early summer hurricane, Peter thought, as he ducked out of the subway, turned his collar to the cold and damp and headed for the bar. This was probably not a good idea, he'd already decided that, but Karen had been very insistent, she wanted to talk and if she needed closure he could do that. He certainly wasn't looking to start anything up again, even if things didn't work out with Sally.

He checked his phone, Karen was on her way. He ordered a beer, he wanted to keep a clear head, this was just an early evening drink; a drink with a friend. As long as she didn't start cross-questioning him, asking him about his 'wife' or his 'marriage' or why he wouldn't get a 'divorce'. He'd done the honourable thing, he'd made it very clear, he always did. Why did they always want the whole deal? Didn't they get it? And so what if he wasn't actually still married? This way there could be no misunderstanding, he was not the marrying kind.

Despite her best efforts, the pile of clothes on Sally's bed was not getting any smaller. She carefully laid out her favourite, Vivienne Westwood, best-bargain-ever, midnight-blue dress, bought in a warehouse sale and which instantly sculpted five pounds off anybody, at one end of the bed and then went back to the heap at the other end. She fished out a much loved, caramel-coloured, Zadig and Voltaire cardi, the tiny skull-shaped buttons an edgy twist on a classic, much like herself she thought; a pair of straight, black trousers she knew would look great with anything, well great as long as she ate nothing solid between now and Thursday, her new, really dark jeans, that she believed shrunk her bottom, a sage and plum, flowery pencil skirt, the shoes that looked like Prada but were in fact Office, a pair of Converse and a boat-neck, cashmere sweater in case it got chilly. Excellent, she thought, her wardrobe was coming together. She swept the remaining clothes onto the old armchair she was one day planning to reupholster, so as to better assess her choices. Why, she wondered, did it look less like a capsule collection and more like a charity shop collection?

'Darling.'
Peter was waiting when Sally arrived at Marco Polo Airport. She smiled, abandoned her mantel of cool and calm, and instead ran towards him waving, accompanied by the rolling clack of her wheelie suitcase. She was still feeling a little anxious but she needn't have been nervous.

'Come on,' he said, wrapping his arms around her and holding her close, 'the water taxi's waiting.'
Heading down the Grand Canal, Sally was quite awestruck by the brilliance of the city. And the amount of water.

'I don't know what I was thinking,' she said, surveying the canal, 'it's so big.'

'Grand,' said Peter, 'I guess it's all in the name.'
He smiled, put his arms around her and kissed her.

The hotel was beautiful; a 14th century palazzo once the private home of a rich Venetian, hung with Murano glass chandeliers reflected in tall, antique mirrors. Doors led out from their suite to a wonderful private roof terrace, perfect for alfresco dinners on warm nights, overlooking the Canal on one side and a secluded courtyard on the other. Sally was in shock, she had never stayed, never seen, such a place. She wanted to live there forever. And ever.

'Nearly didn't make it,' said Peter, as he took his wash things into the marbled bathroom, 'thought we were going to be grounded, storms on the east coast have kicked off early this year.'

But Sally was barely listening as she lay back on the bed trying to take it all in.

'Do you want to eat here?' he said, 'Or shall we go out? If you like fettuccine…'

It was almost too much. No, it was too much.

'I know this place…'

Supposing she fucked it up? She didn't want to fuck it up, she didn't want to give this up, she didn't want Peter to give up on her.

'Or do you want a drink?'

'You think I need a drink?' said Sally, perimenopausal confusion occupying the space where she'd once kept her personality.

'No, I just thought…' he said, 'I don't think you need… I thought we might both like…'

He came over and sat on the side of the bed.

'You don't think I'm just some mad, old middle-aged woman who can't hold her drink?'

Oh god. Mad? Old? Middle-aged? What was she saying? Shut the fuck up.

'No darling,' he laughed, 'you transcend the genre.'

'I do?'

She must not speak, she thought, no more words. She put her arms around his neck and snogged him instead.

'Or we don't have to go out,' he said, holding her close and kissing her back, 'we can stay right here.'

Later that evening they left their room and as they twisted and turned around the labyrinth of narrow streets, heading for fettuccine, Peter held her hand. Sally turned to him and smiled; she may be a Venice virgin but right now she was Julie Christie.

After a late breakfast taken on their terrace, Peter had suggested they go to St. Mark's Square. Sally had revelled in exploring the city with him and when she'd found a copy of a cookbook by Sophia Loren, *Eat With Me*, in a second-hand bookshop, signed by Sophia herself, she was ecstatic.

'But it's Sophia Loren,' said Sally, 'she's brilliant.'

'It's in Italian.' said Peter.

He gave her a quizzical look.

'Do you speak Italian?'

'No, that's not the point,' she said, flicking through the technicolour pages, 'look at these amazing pictures.'

Peter looked but he still didn't get it, he bought the book for her anyway and she was over the moon.

'I look forward to trying some of her recipes,' he said, 'just as soon as you've mastered the language.'

He smiled at her as she delighted in her gift.

'I can cook,' she said, 'I love cooking.'

'You don't say?'

'I do say, come for supper,' she said, imagining herself in a cocktail dress and a pinny, a la Ms. Loren, 'when we get back to London. I'll cook for you.'

Peter looked at her and paused for a moment. His phone started ringing and he pulled it out of his pocket, checked the caller and silenced it.

'Sounds like a marvellous idea,' he said, frowning, 'I'll hold you to that.'

She looked back at her book, what, she wondered had possessed her to issue such an invitation? Were they ready for domestic bliss? Would he ever be ready to meet her children?

Sally bought a feathered mask of gold and pink for Poppy and a mobile phone made out of chocolate for Max, instead of the ashtray shaped like a gondola she'd first toyed with, because she didn't want to send mixed messages about his smoking, of which officially she disapproved. And Peter took her to one of his favourite places, a tiny, family run restaurant near the Rialto Bridge.

'But,' said Sally, as they sat enjoying a delicious lunch of crispy sardines, lemon squeezed and salty, plump artichokes and carpaccio of beef, 'it's so beautiful and so sad, and at the end…'

'That's just Mahler's Fifth,' said Peter, leaning forward with serious intent, 'you didn't find it all too… camp?'
They'd been having such a lovely time until Peter started laying into *Death in Venice*.

'No, I don't.' said Sally, getting quite worked up.

'Too overblown?' he said, refilling their glasses, 'Bogarde's performance… too mannered?'

'No.'

'Honestly,' he said, raising his glass, 'it's a dire adaptation of Mann's masterpiece.'

'You've read it?' said Sally, somewhat surprised and rather perplexed, who the hell read *Death in Venice*?

'No,' said Peter, breaking into a broad smile, 'I read that while you were in the bathroom.'
He gestured to her *Time Out Guide*.

'Shut up.' she said, lobbing a piece of bread at him.

'It's not me. It's what it says in there.' he laughed, 'You should see your face.'

'Don't,' said Sally, 'I hate you.'

'Haven't seen the movie either.' he said, still laughing, 'But, I'm going to make sure I do.'
He pulled her towards him.

'Give me a kiss.'

'No.' she said, and pulled a face, 'You're taking the piss.'

'I never would.' he said, as he lent forward, 'You're too damn delightful.'
She relented and kissed him.

'I like it when you let me in.' he said, and kissed her again. Sally held him close, was he making fun or did he really get her, she wondered? It felt like he understood everything about…

'Come on,' he said, as his phone bleeped into action again. 'I want to show you something.'
Ignoring the text, he grabbed her hand.

At the Accademia, Peter and Sally wandered from the Byzantine to the Gothic, marvelled at Bellini and Tintoretto, and then tried to find their hotel in a Canaletto. Sally loved the way he got so caught up in a painting or a piece of sculpture, his enthusiasm was childlike but he was never childish.

'Look at this,' he said, his arm around her waist pulling her close, as he pointed out the hidden secrets, the stories behind the paintings of love and sex, God and money, 'you see here? The artist has captured the decisive moment.'
Sally leant in and looked.

'It all comes to a halt,' he said, his eyes searching the picture of the young couple embracing, 'the whole world stops when two people fall in love.'
He turned to Sally and held her gaze, and something in him seemed to shift. Or was it something in her?

They walked over the Accademia Bridge, the bright day turning to dusk, and stopped to watch the gondolas pass beneath. In the chill of the early evening air Peter felt Sally shiver, he was so glad he'd asked her to come, he thought, as he wrapped her inside his jacket and held her tight. She leant back into his embrace, she felt so comfortable with him, as long as she could keep it in perspective, she thought, enjoy the moment and not think too much about the future. She may not have figured out how to turn fifty yet, but she was definitely getting warmer.

In the late afternoon, on their last day, they drank ice cold Prosecco sitting at a round table by the open window in a little café they'd discovered together near the Squero di San Trovaso, in the Dorsoduro, where they'd earlier watched the craftsmen building the gondolas. Outside, in the dappled sunshine, an elderly woman, her hair coiffured, lips rouged, a large pair of glasses perched upon a hooked beak, was sitting silently next to an old man in a dark jacket, his well-worn shoes highly polished, his full head of waxy, white hair in stark contrast to his black sunglasses. They sat in silence, watching the tiny birds hopping about their table until the proprietor arrived carrying a tray with two large glasses of liverish yellow, viscous liquid and a small plate upon which were several twirls of almond biscuit. He greeted them with familiarity and respect, placing the glasses on the table and the plate in front of her, offerings before a deity. She dunked a biscuit into her drink and took a small bite, crumbling the remainder onto the table, waiting for the little birds to hop back and continue their feast.

'Look at that,' said Peter, smiling, 'perfect contentment.'

'They probably come every day,' said Sally, 'for their half pint of Grappa.'

'Not a bad life.' said Peter.

The woman continued to feed the birds while the old man watched as a barge laden with fruit and vegetables, a floating greengrocer, manoeuvred into view and set up shop. Silently, he took the woman's hand and held it in his.

'No,' Sally agreed, 'not bad.'

Peter smiled, leant over and took her hand.

'What d'you think Sally?' he said, 'Would you like to live in Venice?'

'Sounds wonderful.' said Sally.

'See out our old age sitting beside a canal, watching the birds?'

'Well we'll never end up an old married couple like them,' she laughed, 'if you don't get divorced.'

What the fuck? Why had she said that?

'I mean…'

She looked at Peter, perhaps he hadn't heard? His expression suggested otherwise, contorted with concentration as if he were sucking out something stubborn that had got stuck behind a molar.

'I didn't mean…'

Sally reached for her glass but it was empty.

'They probably aren't even married,' she wanted to shut up but she couldn't stop, 'they're probably having an affair.'

She laughed a shrill, loud laugh. Peter looked at her, had she actually said marriage? They were having such a good time, she seemed so cool with everything, she seemed to totally get him so what… his phone started ringing, it hadn't stopped all day. He swept it up as Sally glanced down at the screen and silenced it. It was Karen. Again. He felt suddenly rather hot; that had been a huge mistake, he should never have gone for that drink in the first place. He should definitely not have had that second martini. He was sweating now; he would sort it all out just as soon as he got back to New York, not here, not while he was with Sally. His chest felt tight, he needed to get outside, get some air, he couldn't breathe.

'Shall we make a move?' he said, standing up.

'Sure.' said Sally, desperate to get as far away as possible from what she'd just said, 'Let's go.'

Top tip: after too many late nights out drinking, when tired skin is in need of rejuvenation and a rich, moisturising mask, massage the face with Baby Bottom Butter from Waitrose, and leave on overnight.

CHAPTER 7

Standing in her kitchen, artfully arranging the discounted bunch of Pinks she'd bought at the market in an enamelled jug, Sally was feeling anxious. The flat was a mess, she still didn't know what she was going to wear and guess who was coming to dinner?

'There's no food.' said Max, lurching into the kitchen, the rounded face of a boy perched on top of the broad shoulders of a man.

'There's lots of food.' said Sally, distractedly checking the list she'd forgotten to take with her for any important items she might have missed, 'I've just been shopping.'

The trip to Venice had been brilliant, yes. Sally truly had loved every minute of it, absolutely. There had been much hugging and kissing and see-you-sooning at the airport before she'd flown back to London and Peter had headed off to Milan. It had all felt so right while she was there but now she was back home Sally was feeling a lot less confident. What if Peter hated her huddled messes? What if he hated her cooking?

Bare-foot in the kitchen, Max held the fridge door wide, twenty-one years of unfulfilled promise sandwiched between the end of school and the beginning of life without either the means nor motivation to take a leap out of the bedroom that

Sally had hoped would, by now, be rented out and paying her mortgage, and into the unknown.

'Where?' he said.

'There.'

Sally gestured wildly about the room with one hand while holding her dressing-gown together with the other.

'Open a cupboard.'

Max opened the cupboard and pulled out a pan as if he'd discovered a rare relic.

'That's a saucepan,' said Sally, heading for her bedroom, 'it's what people cook food in.'

'Can I cook this?' he shouted from inside the fridge packed with raw produce.

He started rooting about in the vegetable drawer, amongst the green beans, onions and rocket.

'I thought you were going out.' called back Sally, from her bedroom, now bent double and erratically blowing her wet hair dry, 'You said you were going out. I just wanted to look nice and these bloody jeans have shrunk or something and I just need to get ready.'

She was running very late and moving into full-blown panic mode; she hadn't even started dinner and Peter could arrive at any moment. Why, she wondered, had she so casually extended an invitation to cook dinner? Why hadn't she kept her mouth shut?

'Are you talking to me?' shouted Max, from the kitchen, 'because I can't hear a word you're saying.'

The smell of burnt onion hung heavy in the air and the sting of excessive chili use stung her eyes as Sally came into the kitchen, her hair now dry but still only wearing her bra and jeans. Max stood with his back to her, engrossed in some kind of alchemy. The peelings and choppings of numerous onions, garlic, red and green peppers, lay strewn across two work surfaces and the table top, along with a bag of rice, a packet of spaghetti, a loaf of bread, several cans of tomatoes, chickpeas and a jar of anchovies.

'What are you doing?'

'Cooking.' said Max, stirring violently with a metal spoon at something dark and sticky in her non-stick pan.

'Don't use metal in that,' said Sally, lunging towards her

son, 'you're cooking the chicken! Why are you cooking the chicken?'

'Don't freak. You said I could cook anything.' said Max.

'I did not.'

Max turned to see his half-dressed, fully demented mother, waving a plastic spatula at him.

'Aaagh. Why don't you put some clothes on? God mum, you can't just do that.'

'You said you were going out.' said Sally, yanking the metal spoon out of her son's hand and replacing it with plastic, 'And turn it down.'

The flames were now licking dangerously high around the sides of the pan.

'Well now I'm not. Go away.' said Max.

'But you said you were.'

'You can't just walk in here like that. That's abuse. I'm going to spend the rest of my life in therapy.'

'Why are you here?' wailed Sally.

She was freaking out now as she realized she had nothing to cook.

'I don't walk around in my underwear.' said Max, turning away from his mother, 'Gross.'

'You shouldn't be here. Peter's coming.'

The ear-piercing wang of the smoke detector broke through her argument. She gave up and grabbed a tea towel to wave at the alarm.

'I'm making Fajitas.' said Max, proudly.

'I didn't know we had any tortillas?' said Sally.

'We don't,' said Max, 'but we've got bread so I'm making fajita sandwiches.'

He beamed as Sally pushed passed him to assess the collateral damage caused by his cooking. Why had she asked Peter to come to her home? It was too soon. Too soon to start dishing up domestic bliss. Too soon to introduce Peter to Max.

'What's that smell?' asked Poppy, appearing at the kitchen door, 'Oh God, what is that?'

And much too early for him to meet Poppy.

'Fuck you.' said Max, punching his sister in the arm.

Poppy tried to slap Max on the back of the head but he ducked and she caught her hand on the chair.

'Ow, fuck off.'

'For godsake you two,' said Sally, 'stop it.'

'Ha loser.' said Max, flipping Poppy the finger.

'Now!'

Sally checked the time, this was a disaster.

'And why are you here?' she said to her daughter.

'Thanks, nice to see you too mommy dearest. I just wanted to put a quick wash on.'

'No,' said Sally, 'not now. My… friend is coming. Leave it and go.'

Having jettisoned her daughter and finally finished dressing, Sally returned to the bathroom mirror to apply the second layer of make-up. She would just have to head Peter off at the door, tell him the cooker had broken and suggest they get a take-away. Get an Indian. Americans loved that, didn't they? Or maybe, she should call him right now and suggest they meet in a restaurant. That was a much better idea, she decided, as the wail of the smoke alarm filled the air again.

'Max,' she screamed, when there was no sign of the noise abating, 'Max.'

She couldn't decide whether to go for a lick of eyeliner and a full red pout or a smoky eye with a nude lip, so she ended up doing both.

'For fucksake…' she said, walking into the kitchen, 'what are… oh!'

Sitting at her kitchen table with Max was Peter, in front of a plate on which was perched a precariously stacked sandwich, it's ominously crisp filling spilling out on all sides.

'Darling.'

Peter beamed up at Sally.

'Max said you were still dressing, and I didn't want to… anyway, he kindly offered me… this.'

'Oh, but I was going to…'

Sally collapsed into the chair next to him.

'It's all gone wrong, he's used all the… this wasn't what it was supposed to be.'

Peter took a bite of his sandwich.

'I was going to do chicken and chorizo and… he said he was going out but he hasn't.' she said, pointing at her son to illustrate her point.

'Actually,' said Peter, raising an eyebrow as he wiped the corner of his mouth with the tea towel Max had provided by way of a napkin, 'this is not bad.'

'Cool,' said Max, nodding his approval at Peter with whom he had clearly bonded, 'it kind of works with the mayo.'

Sally smiled as her son proudly offered her a plate.

'Want some?'

Why was she freaking out, she wondered? Peter didn't mind. Peter was brilliant.

Leaping out of bed with a newfound energy, Sally was full of the joys; Peter had most definitely put a spring in her step. She smiled at people at work, even if she'd never seen them before, instead of just ignoring the endless stream of intern and ingénue that appeared and disappeared in the office kitchenette. She joined in Tricia's after-work, birthday drinks, just for one but it was one more than last year, and she didn't even get depressed after she'd pulled the last of her in-your-dreams sized, summer clothing from the hidden recesses of her wardrobe only to return them back there once more, still too tight.

'So,' said Alice, 'how was it for you?'

Sally and Jaz were sitting at Alice's zinc-topped kitchen table, drinking Prosecco and enjoying delicious Spaghetti all'Arrabbiata, as the last of the light from a beautiful early summer's day slid through the French windows, still open despite the late hour. Her friends were of course keen to hear everything Sally had to say about Venice.

'Fabulous,' said Sally, 'really fabulous.'

'Really?' said Jaz, refilling their glasses, 'No going tits up in the canal?'

Sally gave her friend a look.

'I was perfectly behaved,' she said, 'throughout. And Peter said he had a fabulous time and seeing the city with me was fabulous and I was… seriously fabulous.'

Sally beamed her fabulous smile.

'Wow,' said Alice, 'that's quite a glow job, where is he now?'

'Back in New York.'

Although Peter's time in London had been brief, Sally had felt they were making excellent progress, the relationship had definitely gone up a notch. Maybe two.

'And he asked me if I wanted to live with him,' she said, reaching for her Prosecco, 'when we were in Venice.'

'He said 'together', 'we' and 'live' in the same sentence?' asked Jaz.

'He did.'

'Wow,' said Alice, 'we weren't expecting that.'

'What do you think?' said Jaz, 'Does he mean it?'

'What?' said Sally, 'Move to Venice?'

'No, not Venice, live together. Does he actually want to live with you?'

'Well,' said Sally, 'he didn't actually say…'

'What did he actually say?'

'Shall we live in Venice?' said Sally, 'Sort of. Wouldn't living there be a nice thing to do. In our old age.'

'So,' said Alice, 'what he actually said, according to you, is wouldn't it be great to live in Venice? Generally?'

'Yeah, I suppose,' she said, she hadn't really thought of it like that, 'point taken.'

'Talk is cheap.' said Alice, as she emptied the bottle into Sally's glass, 'Anyone can throw a line out there. It's all about the follow through.'

'She's right.' said Jaz.

Had she herself not been lured down many a blind alley with less substantial lines than that, all eventually leading her into a cul-de-sac of doom and gloom based on her misguided belief that nothing meant something.

'But,' said Sally, still willing to analyse Peter's words one more time, 'he doesn't have to make hollow promises. He has already put his cards on the table. He has said he's married, this is the way things are and this is the way things are going to stay. He's not a game player, thank god.'

'And you've agreed,' continued Alice, 'but now, you may be beginning to grow weary of the arrangement, no?'

'Well,' said Sally, 'since Venice… I suppose it would be nice if…'

'Exactly,' said Alice, 'and he's not stupid, he knows you will eventually want more even though you've been told there isn't any more. This is it.'

'Right,' said Jaz, nodding her agreement.

'So he throws you a bone.' said Alice.

She picked up the bottle and put into the recycling bin before taking another from inside the door of her double-fronted fridge and popping the cork.

'A bone?' said Sally.

'Plants the seed of hope.' said Jaz, seeing where Alice was going with this.

'A seed that you think just needs a bit of nurturing.' said Alice.

'Exactly,' said Jaz, backing up Alice's argument.

'So you'll stick around,' said Alice, 'give him a bit more tender, loving care. He takes you on a lovely trip...'

'All expenses paid...' said Jaz.

'Wines you and dines you...' said Alice.

'Buys you gifts.' said Jaz.

'Yes.' said Sally, fingering the silver and amber necklace that he'd given her the night he'd come over for dinner, it's interlocking loops nestled in her décolletage.

'Peppers his conversation with a few comments he knows you could misconstrue, a suggestion of more to come.'

'Yes,' said Jaz, keen to confirm her friend's view, 'but if you call him on it, he can and will get out of it on a grammatical error, i.e. you misunderstood.'

'Exactly.' said Alice, 'At the end of the day relationships are all about semantics.'

'Clever,' said Sally, 'very clever.'

She reached for the bottle and refilled her glass as she reviewed Alice's new evidence.

'But,' she said, 'it's not like he has a real marriage.'

'You hope.' said Alice.

'They don't live together.'

'You think.' said Jaz.

'I know, I did say he could be lying but I don't think he is now,' said Sally, taking a large gulp of her wine, 'I really don't.'

'What does she look like?' asked Jaz, 'The wife.'

'No idea.' said Sally, 'How would I know, I've never seen her?'

'What, no pictures?' said Alice, 'when you Googled him?'

'I haven't Googled him.' said Sally, taking a sip of her wine.

'What never?' said Jaz.

'No.' said Sally, cutting herself a wedge of Gorgonzola Dolce

'You've never Googled him?' said Alice, shocked.

'Never ever?' said Jaz.

'No.'

'But there must be pictures,' said Alice, 'from before. He writes art books, gets awards.'

'Everybody Googles,' said Jaz, in disbelief, 'why haven't you Googled him?'

'You have to Google him.' said Alice, shaking her head and stabbing at her iPad, 'I'll Google him.'

'Who doesn't Google their boyfriend?' said Jaz, 'I can't believe you sometimes.'

'Oh my God.' said Alice, sitting upright and squaring her shoulders.

'What?' said Jaz, 'Is it her?'

'Is she gorgeous?' said Sally.

'Is she a dog?' said Jaz.

'Doesn't matter what she looks like.' said Alice. 'He's not married.'

She handed over her iPad.

'He's divorced, has been for years.'

Top tip: for a cheap and effective way to de-stress and relax, add a couple of handfuls of Epsom salt to your bath. Works as a great body scrub too.

CHAPTER 8

It was late but Sally couldn't sleep. She lay on her sofa, watching *Summertime*. Old movies were usually her happy place, what couldn't be put right by spending a couple of hours in the company of Katharine Hepburn and Rossano Brazzi? But this time it wasn't working. How could Brazzi lie like that to Hepburn? How could Peter have lied like that to her? How could she have been such a fool to trust him? Halfway through the second bottle of wine she was entering into another dark night of the soul and now sobbing openly. She ejected the DVD and reached for her wine and *Some Like It Hot,* maybe Marilyn could make it better. Why, she wondered, did this keep happening? She emptied the bottle into her glass, what had she done to deserve this? The tears rolled up and ran down her cheeks in a tsunami of grief and loss; almost 50 years of sadness had welled up. Sally cried. She cried about her crap ex, all her crap exes, about her hostile son and her ungrateful daughter, her missed opportunities and misadventures with inappropriate oafs with whom she had an unholy need to be aligned.

'I trusted him,' she said, lying back on the sofa, wiping her eyes, 'I trusted him and I loved him.'

And there it was, she loved him and he obviously didn't love her. She would never love anyone ever again. And then, through the salty, snotty, self-obsessed sea of self-loathing, she heard a voice, a voice she knew well:

'How many times have I told myself I'm through with love?' said Marilyn.

'I just don't' understand,' said Sally, wiping her nose with her sleeve, 'I loved him and he lied to me.'

'Oh don't get me started,' said Marilyn, handing Sally a small cotton handkerchief, 'another no-goodnik. How many times have I ended up with the fuzzy end of the lollipop?'

'I don't know.'
Sally dabbed at her eyes.

'Too many, that's how many. Just when you think you've met the biggest thing, your spine turns to jello, you go all goose-pimply and then the bubble bursts. All that's left behind is an old sock and a squeezed out tube of toothpaste.'

'What do I do?' said Sally, offering her handkerchief back.

'Oh you keep it honey,' Marilyn smiled, 'I'm not very bright I guess, but I'm learning. These guys with glasses, guys like Peter, they may look all sweet and helpless, but he doesn't look so helpless to me.'
She pulled a lipstick and powder compact from her handbag and reapplied a slick of scarlet.

'You don't want your heart to get put back in the ice-box do you?'

'No.' said Sally, 'I don't.'

'No, you deserve the sweet end of the lollipop for a change.'

'I do?' said Sally.

'Sure you do. Don't get sad, Sally.' she said, blotting her lips with a tissue, 'Get out there.'

'Out there?' said Sally.

'You got to think about the future.' said Marilyn, 'You tell him you're not standing for this anymore, d'you hear?'

'Ah ha.'

'It's over, you're through, finito, sayonara and good-bye.' she blew Sally a kiss, 'Then you get up and you put on your make-up, do your hair and you get right back out there.'

'I do?'

'You go find yourself a nice guy and take your mind off it.'

'D'you think?' said Sally, sniffing violently.

'Why sure I do.' said Marilyn, 'Now, do you have anywhere for my pony to sleep?'

A small horse wearing pink satin pyjamas trotted forward and Sally's primary school teacher, Miss Joseph, dressed in an over-sized yellow sowester, started knocking on the window as Sally drifted deeper into sleep and another fitful night on the sofa of broken dreams.

Through the bathroom window the cold light of dawn was breaking over Sally's hangover. She wiped her mouth, stood up and flushed the toilet. She'd thrown up twice and she still felt sick. How much had she drunk? She still could not believe Peter had lied to her. Peter was not married. Peter was divorced. Why had he lied to her? Was he getting married? To someone else? What if… stop, she thought, enough with the torture and self-doubt. Her dream swam back towards her through the sea of vomit, Marilyn's words circling her throbbing head: she may be down but she was not out.

Using all her might to squeeze the toothpaste out of the tube and onto her toothbrush, Sally steadied herself against the basin and peered into the mirror; she still felt upset, confused and betrayed but now she also felt angry. She'd agreed to see him on his terms. She'd agreed to see him even though he was still married. He'd made the rules and she'd played by them. And he'd lied. She would never see him again. Ever. That was it, it was all over, she would delete him from her life. And her phone. He shouldn't even think about calling her because she wouldn't answer. He should lose her number now because she would never speak to him again. Ever. And just as soon as she stopped throwing up, she would call him and tell him so.

'Oh my god,' said Will, putting the white linen napkin onto his lap, 'not married?'

'Yep,' said Sally, 'not married.'

'But that's a good thing, no?'

'No.' said Sally, 'That's a bad thing.'

Outside, summer sun burst shadows across the terrace. Inside, at a corner table, Sally and Will sipped their Bloody Marys surrounded by the relaxed sounds of happy Sundays:

the clink of glass and good cutlery, the laughter of a long lunch.

'But you're not the other woman now.' said Will, feeling a little confused.

'Exactly.' said Sally, her tone sharpened, 'He lied to me.'

'But why?' said Will, his brow now furrowed with thought, as he took a sip of his drink, 'Why would he say he's married if he's not married?'

'Fuck knows.'

'Are you sure he's not married?'

'I'm not sure of anything anymore,' said Sally, 'but Jaz Googled every possible permutation and it's all true. He was married. A long time ago. Now he's not.'

'So,' said Will, 'he tells you he's married when he isn't actually married because… he…'

'Doesn't want to marry me, I guess.' said Sally.

'Genius.' said Will.

'Genius?'

'Well…'

'Fucked up is what it is.' said Sally, slamming her hand down on the table and startling her companion.

'But if you think about it…'

'I have thought about it.' said Sally, jabbing her fork in a menacing fashion at Will, 'I've thought about nothing else.'

'But you're having a good time,' said Will, trying hard to calm his friend, 'he seems to really like you and…'

'Yes,' said Sally, 'but… he lied to me.'

'He lied, yes,' said Will, 'but it's not like it's a big lie, it's not…'

'Oh you're right, no, it's not like he's a convicted serial killer.'

'Exactly…'

'He might as well be.'

Sally gave her friend a look.

'Why don't you just confront him and see what he's got to say before you go……'

'No way, I'm never speaking to him again.'

'You've dumped him?'

'Yes,' said Sally, 'almost, I'm about to. I'm just working out exactly how I'm going to word it, you know, so I get everything in, don't leave anything out.'

'That sounds bad.'

'So he knows I know just what a heel he is, I know the truth…'

'A truth.' said Will.

'And I won't stand for it. I want to say something really mean so he'll lay awake at nights, feeling really bad and…'

'You think that's how men think?'

'Hopefully.' said Sally.

She sucked down the last of her Bloody Mary.

'He is not going to play this little game again.'

'Right,' said Will scanning the wine list, 'I see.'

'I'm doing this for womankind.'

'Good. Fancy a red?' said Will, trying to change the direction the conversation was going, 'Food looks great, we're coming here for your birthday?'

Sally groaned at the B-word. She was turning 50 and the thing about 50 was, it's half a hundred, and with all the other birthdays you could double it: 2x30=60, 2x40=80, 2x49=98, and imagine it. But who could imagine 100? She was on the home stretch, definitely in the second half. All the possibilities based on the fact that there's still more time. Well, now there wasn't. It was game over. The beginning of the end. 50 may be all fine and dandy if you've lived a full and happy life, had your relationship ups and downs, your career ups and downs, but you've sorted yourself out: the husband has come home to roost, the kids are spreading their wings, the nest is comfortable. Then great, bring it on, sit back and enjoy the encroachment of old age; downsize and make the most of the cash, travel where you will, prepare to bounce those grandchildren on your fit-for-life knees. Make jam and make love to the man you're growing old with. But what happens if it's not all hunky-dory? Sally had hoped, nay assumed, that by now she'd be sorted. By now, she'd have mastered the relationship, the family, the career. Or at the very least one of them. But no, she hadn't, and she certainly wasn't ready for that particular f-word, it was too soon. She was not feeling much like celebrating her half centenary because whatever 50 was, it was not the new 40. 50 was the old 50.

'Oh for goodness sake,' said Will, 'it's an achievement, it should be celebrated. Some people don't even make it this far, as well you know.'

Sally did know. Hadn't her friend, Mia, died when she was just 48, only two years after she'd been diagnosed with breast cancer?

She'd hated those visits when Mia was ill, walking back towards the tube, the lights of the cars blurring through her tears. Her friend had been dying and all she'd been able to do was cry. She'd hated the packets of pills piled so casually on the coffee table, the mugs of un-drunk herb tea. She'd hated the wig. She'd hated what the steroids had done to her friend. She'd hated the false hope and the new diets and the endless treatment. She'd hated it when Mia's kids argued with her, made petulant demands, arrangements Mia would find hard to keep or just fought with each other. She'd hated them doing all the things ordinary kids did. She'd wanted to scream:

'Shut the fuck up, your mother is dying don't you get it?' But she hadn't because they were only kids and they didn't get it, they hadn't known their mother was dying. But Sally had.

'I know,' said Sally, shamed but unbowed, 'maybe I should be more grateful, but I thought things would be different by the time I was… I thought Peter would be different… I didn't want it to be like this.'

'Then change it.' said Will.

The pretty, young waitress hovered expectantly. Will ordered the wine and surveyed the large dining space, once a handsome, Victorian music hall, now a gastro pub.

'It is a lovely room,' he said.

'You think I should,' said Sally, 'have my birthday dinner here?'

'Yes.'

'Not that other restaurant? The new one?'

'Well not unless you prefer it.'

'So you don't like this one?'

'No, I do like this one.' said Will, feeling the pressure.

'So I should come here?'

'Why not?'

'Because I came here with Andy, the memories…'

Sally plucked at a piece of the delicious, home baked bread that the smiley waitress had placed on the table to temp her.

'Reclaim it,' said Will, 'you reclaimed the oyster bar pretty quick after you and Ed split up.'

'That was different, that was years ago, I was younger, more resilient.'

'Not that young.'

'Suddenly it seems a whole lot younger.' said Sally.

The break-up of Sally's marriage to Ed had been a slow erosion. They had both taken their eye of the ball. And the penis. The kids, the mortgage, the bricks and mortar of their randomly constructed relationship, had ended up burying the love. And the passion. It was in many ways a relief and a release, the divorce was swift and fairly painless. And her disastrous relationship with Andy that followed was quite possibly in direct response to her need for adventure.

'Only you could fall for a coke-head.' said Will, who for all the obvious reasons had tried to warn his friend against her foolish ways, 'a fat coke-head too.'

'You can't help who you fall in love with.' said Sally.

'He was a toxic bachelor.'

'Yes, and so is Peter,' said Sally, returning to her topic du jour, 'as it turns out. And I thought he was different. Ha.'
She spat out the words as the waitress returned with the wine.

'Heartbreak is harder when you're older. It's like falling over,' said Sally, reaching for her glass, 'when you're a kid everyone falls over, you just get back up and rub your knees. If you fall over when you're old you need a hip replacement. I may need a heart replacement this time.'

'Oh my God.' said Will.

'What?'

'Just rub my nose in it why don't you.'
Sally turned to see two men in their thirties sitting opposite one another at an adjacent table, holding hands, smiling into one another's eyes.

'I've a good mind to go over there and tell them,' he said, 'I don't mind what you do in your own home but do you have to ram it down my throat? Yes I'm alone, totally alone, home alone yet again, thank you very much for reminding me.'
Will refilled their glasses with the rather good Italian wine he'd

ordered, and smiled up at the rather good Italian waiter, as he artfully slid the roast lamb in front of him.

'You'll find someone.' said Sally, tucking into her lunch, she needed to keep her strength up for the job of sacking Peter.

'Actually,' said Will, helping himself to mint sauce, 'there is a possibility on the horizon. I was coming back late from a work thing the other night and ended up on a night bus.'

'A night bus?'

'It was just there, you know, seemed so much cheaper than a cab so I hopped on.'

He reached for his wine.

'And?'

'And I fell asleep.'

'Will.'

'I was drunk. And exhausted. What can I say.'

He refilled their glasses.

'But anything could have happened.'

'It did.'

'No.'

'Yes,' he said, 'Goran, 6'7', former Yugoslavian, Buddhist, actor slash plumber.'

He beamed.

'Woke me up at the end of the line, no idea where I was, somewhere in Arnos Grove, he said come home.'

'No.'

'Nice to know I've still got it.'

Will took a large draft of his wine.

'Sounds more like you're still losing it.' said Sally, sternly, 'Imagine if…'

'But it didn't.' he said.

'But it could have.'

Outside, the storm clouds were gathering and in the distance the summer thunder rumbled. But inside, Sally was feeling restored by her roast lamb, she had a plan, she was going to verbally destroy Peter, and she was keen to get on with it. The wine was helping.

'So,' she said, 'I'll book this place for my birthday and then I'll go home and call Peter.'

'And you don't think you should give him a chance to…'

'I'm going to celebrate my birthday and get wasted and have a great time.' said Sally, 'And it's going to be great. Fifty will be… great. And I'm really glad he won't be there.'
There was a manic glint in her eye.

'Well good,' said Will, looking very worried, 'that's good.'

'D'you think?' she said, attacking her Bakewell Tart with gusto.

'Yes,' said Will, 'we'll all have a nice birthday dinner and move on.'

'Don't worry,' said Sally, draining her glass, 'I intend to. Like you said, I'm going to change the way I do things, starting with who I go out with. Time wasters need not apply.'

'Well, ultimately that's a good view to take,' said Will, reaching for the bottle but too late, Sally was refilling her glass again.

'That's what I thought,' she said, raising her glass, 'it's over, he's dead to me. Hasta luego baby.'

'Actually,' said Will, 'I think you mean hasta la vista.'

Top tip: feeling down but can't be bothered to do the laundry? Freshen up stale bed linen by running an iron over the pillowcases and pretend you've got clean sheets.

CHAPTER 9

Pouring the ginger and nutmeg, relaxing bath soak into the bath, Sally had decided she would call Peter later, she was feeling too fuzzy-headed from her long lunch. Being decisive, she thought as she pondered the extent of the wisdom she hoped might come her way with her next birthday, this was something she wanted in her new life, her new fifty-year-old life. And taking control, she wanted to do that too. She was just about to dip a chipped nail-polished toe into the steamy water when her phone rang. Perhaps it was Peter, she thought, perhaps she should just…

'He was a very strange little man…'
It was not Peter, it was Ellen, Sally's mother. She knew she had a choice: let it go to voicemail, for the second time that day, where it would hang over her like the sword of Damocles or bite the bullet and deal with it now.

'Kept following me around. Wouldn't take no.' Ellen: a thick-skinned woman, tall, elegant, her steel-grey hair pixie short, often found swathed in M&S Autograph cashmere in varying shades of charcoal or mushroom. Sally's father, John, had died of a heart attack when she was just nineteen. A man of his time, it was a classic case of 40 a-day and a diet rich in the wrong food. In her 20s Sally had acquired a stepfather, Neil: mild-mannered with a fondness for zip-up cardigans and crosswords. He was a divorcee, as Ellen liked to call him, making him sound like an exotic ingredient in the Cordon Bleu cookery course she attended at the time. Neil had two fully-grown sons, Justin, married and living in Australia and David, daringly gay and living in San Francisco. Which was handy as Sally already had a brother called David, albeit a straight one, the non-identical twin to James, but it could have become a bit confusing. And so, for a brief period, her family doubled in size and interest value until Neil died and the two stepbrothers became ex-stepbrothers although they still exchanged Christmas cards. After Neil came Mike, a small man in a sports jacket, dapper and annoying, part Lesley Phillips, part Jack Russell. Mike and Ellen had never actually married as Ellen, now embracing the freedom of the 1990s, along with her yoga class, her meditation class and her self-empowering, belly-dancing class, preferred to refer to him as her 'partner'; they retained their own homes and their own names, but spent every Christmas and all holidays together, often motoring through Europe, visiting vineyards or churches or both. Three years ago Mike had had a brain haemorrhage and that was that. Unbowed by bereavement, Ellen had soldiered on and now did much of her socializing with Jean, a woman five years younger than her who had never been married, never had children and bred chocolate Labradors. Sally refused to contemplate the nature of their relationship.

'The weather was marvellous, except the Friday,' Ellen had just returned from a tour of Tuscany with her church's singles group: *Eats, Prays, Loves to Travel*, 'when it did rain but only in the morning.'

'Right.' said Sally.

'I've put the pictures up on my wall.'

'What?'

'Oh you don't do the Facebook,' said her mother, 'I forgot. You should.'

'Why? Why would I want people I hardly know, knowing everything I do? I don't want people I know well knowing what I do.'

'You're being ridiculous.' Ellen had embraced the 21st century with far more gusto than her daughter, 'At least it wasn't too hot. And the food was good, but then you'd expect it to be. I wrote a marvellous description of the dinner we had on the last night, the Casa Dell'Arte,' she pronounced each word with the same relish with which she had enjoyed her pappardelle con la lepre, 'for the website. They love it when I do that.'

'Really.' said Sally.

'I met one woman whose husband ran off with another man. Fascinating. Poor woman. That's the sort of thing you should be writing about. Do you still do your creative writing? Why don't you join a singles writing group?'

'I haven't really got time right now.'

Just kill me, thought Sally.

'You have to make the time Sally,' said Ellen.

'I'm very busy.' said Sally.

'Well you need to do something, I don't know what's wrong with you.'

'For godsake, don't get at me, why are you shouting?'

'I'm not shouting. You used to have boyfriends.' Ellen continued unabated, 'Susan Barry's daughter just got married, she was only divorced two years ago. And she's older than you.'

'I have boyfriends.'

'Really, who?'

Who? Sally, wrapped in her towel, sitting in her kitchen, looked about her and wondered who her boyfriend might be. now it wasn't Peter

'Jack,' she said, 'Wills,' reading the label inside her son's hoody that hung from the back of the chair.

'Jack? You've never mentioned him.'

She had not mentioned Peter to her mother because she didn't want any relationship advice from the merry widow. Now she did want to mention him he was history.

'I don't have to tell you everything. Why do you have to know everything?'

'Are you still seeing him?' said Ellen excitedly.

'Don't shout at me.' said Sally.

How come every time she talked to her mother it ended like this, thought Sally, with her reverting to her former self: a sulky teenager laying on her bed beneath the pouting gaze of her Biba posters, dreaming of her escape to London. Why couldn't she have been born a Freud, she wondered? There were loads of them.

'I'm not shouting,' said Ellen, 'I'm just making adult conversation.'

'I need to relax. I don't have time to go out.' said Sally, 'I work hard and I've got Max and…'

'And what about Max?' said Ellen, 'What's he up to? Why doesn't he get a job?'

'I don't know mother,' said Sally, 'why don't you Facebook him?'

'Anyway, you must let me go,' Sally hated it when Ellen said that, especially as she'd called her, 'I've got a Zumba class, you should try it.'

'Don't let me hold you up.' said Sally.

'Oh and before I forget,' said Ellen, 'I've been reading a marvellous book, Mary Garrett from my book club, husband's got Parkinson's, recommended it. I've ordered you a copy. Amazon. You should get it any day.'

'What is it?' Sally winced.

'*Keep Your Hands Off My Orgasm,*' said Ellen, 'an American woman, somebody Katz. Everyone should read it.' Sally pulled the plug on her cold bath.

Standing in her kitchen, her mother's words still ringing in her ears, Sally stared out through the tear-stained window at the guttering rain, the faint sun, like a light bulb glimpsed through a shower curtain, all the colours muzzed to a smudge by the endless summer downpour. She checked the time in New York. She was ready. The relationship with Peter was over and she needed to get her phone call over. She really hoped it wouldn't go to voicemail, as she reached for her phone, she wanted to hear him hear what she had to say.

Peter had been surprised when he'd listened to the message. Surprised and a little concerned. He didn't see that much of his daughter, Carrie, even though she did only live in Williamsburg. But also delighted that she'd suggested they should meet for a coffee. The lack of communication was his own fault he knew that, he should have seen more of his girls when they were growing up but it had been hard. Hard to see their mother after she'd calmly poured him a whiskey one evening when he'd arrived home late from the city, their children asleep upstairs, and announced their marriage was over. And not because of his long hours and late nights, she understood he was building his business for the good of his family, but because she was in love with someone else, she was in love with Bill and she wanted a divorce as soon as possible because Bill wanted to marry her. Good old Bill, always there when Peter needed him. There for him through thick and thin. Wasn't that why he'd asked him to be his best man when he'd married Lee? Now Bill was Lee's best man.

Standing by the ferry terminal in Lower Manhattan, Peter leant against the railings, and waited for Carrie. For some reason quite beyond him, she had requested they meet there and take the short trip over to Staten Island and back, just as they'd done when she was a child on the weekends she and her sister had got to see him. It used to be their special ritual: a trip on the ferry then hot dogs from Gray's Papaya and a movie at the Waverly Theatre. Then they'd sleep over at his apartment on 9th Street and 6th Avenue, sharing his big bed while he'd slept on a pull-out in his study. Now considered a large apartment in an expensive area, it was all he could afford at the time, when the Village was a less salubrious neighbourhood.

'Daddy.'

He turned to see Carrie, waving at him from across the street, waiting for the lights to change. With her hair in two loose braids, wearing a long, flowery, summer dress and platform sandals, for a moment he thought he was looking at her mother back when they'd first dated.

'Sorry, got caught up with brunch,' she said, pushing her sunglasses up onto her head, 'don't be mad.' She hugged him and beamed. Prettier than her mother, he thought.

Standing together on the deck of the ferry, the breeze was a welcome relief to the city's heat. They watched the skyscrapers of Manhattan diminish as they glided past Ellis Island and The Statue of Liberty, Carrie talking with a heightened excitement as she told her father how her jewellery design business was doing, the revamped website, the new premises she'd found, the celebrity clientele she was building since two of her pieces had appeared in W Magazine. Peter listened and smiled and watched the sun bounce off the gleaming tip of the Chrysler Building and thought about Sally. She'd said it was her favourite building in the city and he wished she could be there now, with him, to see it. He wanted to share this with her. He missed her. Since their trip to Venice something had changed and he'd found himself thinking about her more and more. This was a new experience for him, it had been a long time since he'd thought this much about someone else.

'You must come over,' Carrie was saying, 'you hardly know Ted, I know you guys would really get on. You need to get to know him.'

'Is there any point?' Peter smiled, 'Your boyfriends come and go pretty swiftly.'

'Daddy,' Carrie pulled a face, 'that was before, I've been living with Ted for over two years.'

'You have?'

When did that happen, Peter wondered? Time seemed to be moving with alarming speed these days.

'Come to dinner.'

'Ok,' said Peter, 'I will, but we'll eat out unless you've learned to cook too?'

'Well,' said Carrie looking a little coy, 'I guess I'm going to have to learn now…'

Peter's phone started to buzz.

'Because the thing is…'

He pulled it out of his jacket pocket.

'Me and Ted, we're going to…'

He glanced down at the screen, it was Sally. He wanted to answer it, he wanted to talk to her, tell her he was looking up at the Chrysler Building and thinking of her, missing her. He hadn't told her enough.

'What?' he said, looking up, aware his daughter had said something important, 'Married?'

'Yes Daddy,' Carrie beamed, her smile was radiant, 'I'm pregnant and we're going to get married.'

She pressed a hand to her flat tummy.

'You're going to have to go on Facebook now so you can see my baby bump getting bigger.'

She laughed and looked back at her father.

'I am?' said Peter, suddenly short of breath.

'And see all the baby photos.'

'Married?' he repeated, his head was starting to spin.

'Nothing big, just a few friends, Mommy says we can use the old boathouse and the garden will look so pretty and people can stay over but you have to be there. You will come to the house won't you?'

Peter heard the words Carrie was saying but they sounded a long way away. He looked down at the phone in his hand, he'd missed Sally's call. His chest felt tight, he was feeling faint. He wanted to sit down but his feet wouldn't move. He put his other hand on the rail to steady himself and take it all in: his daughter was pregnant and getting married and now he would have to confront his wife, his ex-wife, and her husband, having successfully avoided doing so for all these years, missing birthdays and graduations and Christmas mornings. And he was going to be… a grandfather. He felt a sharp pain in his chest, he tried to breathe but his throat was tight.

'I know it's hard but if you really won't come then I guess we can do something else because you have to be there Daddy.' said Carrie, the same look in her eyes when as a child she would plead with him to come back home, 'say yes Daddy, please. You're going to be a Grandpoppi.'

Peter staggered, he couldn't catch his breath, the pain in his chest was acute. He was having a heart attack. He was going to die. He tried to get to the bench but the boat shuddered as it docked at Staten Island and he lost his balance, stumbling back against the rail, his phone slipping from his hand.

'Daddy…' Carrie screamed, as he fell, catching his head on the corner of the bench while his phone dropped into the New York Bay.

'Daddy, Daddy, oh my god.'

Carrie knelt on the deck by her father's unconscious body.

'Somebody help me.'

Top tip: to raise spirits and restore confidence, put on Courtney Love's, *Nobody's Daughter,* turn it up to eleven and dance. An excellent physical and mental workout.

CHAPTER 10

'I'm just going to cancel it.' said Sally.

'What?' said Martin, her straight-best-friend, 'The dinner or being 50?'

He'd arrived carrying an already unscrewed screw-top bottle of Argentinean Malbec.

'Sorry,' he said, 'I'd already opened it before you called but I didn't think it was worth, you know, buying another bottle as this one was virtually full.'

He put the opened bottle on the kitchen table.

'So this is what we're doing now,' said Sally, 'coming round with half empty bottles of wine?'

'Two thirds full,' Martin corrected her, 'maybe three quarters.'

He took two glasses from the cupboard.

'Ever get the feeling,' he said, 'that something's going on? Something you don't know about?'

'Like what?' said Sally, spooning nutmeg mash onto his plate with the herby roast chicken.

'That's what I don't know,' said Martin, pouring the wine into two tumblers, 'like how life works. How do other people do it?'

He handed Sally a glass. When Martin met Sally, she'd been travelling through Spain with Jaz, somewhere between Madrid and the rest of her life, a period which she could still recall with unnecessary ease while now not being able to remember what she'd watched on TV last night. How many hours had they spent making plans? What, she wondered, had happened to all those plans?

'I do know that I don't want to do anything on my birthday.'

Having tried and failed several times to get hold of Peter, Sally had finally left him a message to call her. Then she'd invited Martin to supper to cheer herself up and to help take her mind off him. However, she was still thinking about him.

'You can't just cancel turning fifty.'

'That's a bit rich coming from you, you just disappeared down your own rabbit hole.'

Martin was now fifty-two and still struggling to come to terms with his wasted youth. And middle years.

'I know,' he said, 'I didn't bother celebrating the day but I did mark my movement into maturity by taking up the ukulele.'

Sally pulled a face.

'I thought that was because Zac was learning guitar,' she said, 'and you thought you could form a band with him.'

Zac was Martin's 15 year-old son, the child he'd had with Marie, the woman who'd turned from being the one he wanted to spend the rest of his life with into the one he wished he'd never met, with alarming speed. But it still pained him that they'd failed to make the family unit he'd so desired when he'd first met her. That he always desired with every woman he met.

'Partly.'

Martin pronged a piece of chicken.

'I don't want to celebrate,' she said, 'I'm cancelling my birthday this year.'

'It doesn't work like that.' Martin said, with authority, 'It is going to happen. You will be fifty.'

'But Poppy's gone to Rome with Habib and Max will be working on some bloody video with bloody Tamsin in bloody Sheffield.'

'He's working,' said Martin, used to his friend's negative outpourings, 'that's good isn't it?'

'But it's my birthday. Ed knew that when he got Max the

job.'

Sally drained her glass.

'And Peter won't even call me back so I can dump him and…'

'Peter?' Martin spat the word, 'You're not still on about him? Fuck him.'

'But…' she said, putting down her fork and picking up her phone just to check, her appetite all but gone, 'I did really like him, before I hated him. I thought we had a real… connection. I can't believe he hasn't called back. He just didn't seem…'

'Like an axe murderer?' said Martin, helpfully.

'Maybe he lost my number,' said Sally, 'dropped his phone… on the subway track…'

'And maybe,' said Martin, 'it got run over?'

'Yes.' said Sally, hopefully, 'His phone might have been destroyed by a train. And that's why he hasn't called.'

'Really?'

'Or… he's in hospital?' said Sally, 'A coma?'

'No.' said Martin, 'That never ever happens. When does that ever happen?'

'He might be dead?'

'We can only hope.' said Martin, reaching for his glass, 'Forget him.'

'I'm trying, the thing is,' she said, 'I thought he was being honest but he was lying. He wasn't bloody married.'

'Yeah,' said Martin, 'that's the bit I'm finding a little hard to get my head around: he told you he had a wife when he didn't, and you were ok with that, but then when you found out he didn't… you got really angry.'

'Yes, of course I did. I loved him and he lied to me.'

'Right,' Martin screwed up his face in concentration, 'so, do you love him now?'

'Of course not,' she said, 'but I still loved going out.'

'You're always going out,' said Martin, 'I ask you out all the time.'

'You don't count, you're just a friend.'

Martin refilled their glasses.

'Yes, but I ask you to things: movies, dinner. Sometimes I even pay for the wine.'

'You do Martin, thank you,' Sally raised her glass, 'I should not under value the male friend against the boyfriend. Cheers.' They clinked their glasses.

'I had nothing for my birthday.' said Martin, now feeling more miffed at the memory than he actually had at the time, 'Not even a cake.'

'I know.' said Sally, who had thought this a bit of an oversight considering he was going out with a woman who baked cakes for a living.

'Katy didn't even give me a present.' Martin said, glumly recalling the non-event.

'I did.' said Sally.

'What?'

'The hi-vis vest.'

'That was not a birthday present,' said Martin, 'that was something you got free from Boris's ride-a-bike-to-work-week.'

'But I gave it to you.'

'Because you don't have a bike,' said Martin, 'and I do. It doesn't count.'

'You said you didn't want anything.' said Sally, reaching for the bottle.

'Anyway,' said Martin, 'I think me and Katy are done, I don't want to… lead her on.'

He tucked into his second helping of chicken with renewed gusto at the prospect of being single once more.

'That's fair enough, I suppose.' said Sally, trying to sound supportive.

'Exactly, I want to be honest. She always said we should be honest with each other.'

'Good,' said Sally, 'you should be. Honesty is important.'

'That's what you women always say you want isn't it?' Martin shook his head disapprovingly, 'The truth.'

'Yes, but…'

'She's so moody,' he said, firming his resolve, 'bites my head off all the time, everything I do is just wrong.'

'What do you do?'

'Nothing.'

'You do nothing?'

'Apparently,' he took another draft of his wine, 'and

84

apparently that's not allowed. She always wants to do something. Or know what I'm doing.'

'Well, when you're in a relationship it is nice to communicate,' said Sally, 'and it's nice to do things together.'

'Yeah,' he said, 'but I'm old and yet I'm denied the pleasure of inactivity, the freedom to adopt a fuck-it-and-don't-care attitude and let my middle age spread. She wants to know why I go to the pub on my own. Who do I talk to? I go to the pub on my own so I don't have to talk to anyone. So I can contemplate the crushing disappointment that is my life. It's bad enough being in your fifties without suffering the indignity of having your prostrate checked every five minutes, a teenage son who refuses to be your Facebook friend and aching knees. And then she's constantly asking me what I'm thinking about. And when I say nothing she says, I hate it when you say that. But it's true.'

He reached for his glass.

'So,' he said, 'I don't think I'll bring her to your birthday.'

'Well that's good because I'm not…'

'Yes you are and it will be great,' he drained his glass, 'and I'll be your date.'

'OK,' she said, and smiled, ' if you insist.'

Sally picked up her phone in case she'd missed a call.

'Give me that.' said Martin, snatching it from her hand, 'Delete him…'

'I wasn't…'

'You were.'

Martin started pressing buttons. Sally grabbed it back.

'Don't. I'm not delete-ready.' said Sally, 'Not yet. I have to tell him it's over.'

'Why not just never call him again,' said Martin, 'leave him hanging.'

He flicked his hand under his chin in the manner of some Mafioso.

'It's time to start celebrating.'

'Darling,' said Peter, taking off his glasses and putting his *New York Times* to one side, 'are you alright?'

'I'm fine Daddy.'

Carrie lent forward to kiss her father.

'How are you feeling? Can you go home yet?'
She sat down on the corner of the bed.

'I should think so, it's ridiculous I…'

'Excuse me.' said the nurse, bustling into the room.
She manoeuvred her sizable frame around the bed.

'Ah, nurse…'
Ignoring him, she rolled up his sleeve and went about her duty.

'I think I'm probably ready to…'
She stuck a thermometer into Peter's mouth before he could protest. He turned, petulantly to look out of the window of St. Vincent's Hospital, as the sky, blue and still, filled with a dart of birds.

'He's going nowhere,' she said turning to Carrie, 'while his blood pressure is this high.'
Carrie smiled at her father whose expression was that of a scolded child. The nurse looked at the thermometer and shook her head.

'Doctor will come and tell you when.' she said.

'There's nothing…'

'What's that?'
The nurse stopped in the doorway.

'It's not up to me, you just be patient.' she said, without cracking a smile.

'There's nothing wrong with me,' said Peter, turning back to his daughter, 'I'm fine, but I'm sorry if I scared you.'

'You are not fine.' said Carrie.

'It wasn't a heart attack.' said Peter.

'But it was a panic attack,' said Carrie, 'and you fell, you were unconscious.'

'I slipped that was all,' said Peter, 'when the boat docked.'

'Hi guys,' said the handsome young doctor, coming into the room and shaking Carrie's hand, 'nice to see you again, you came in with your father, no?'

'Yes,' Carrie beamed, she tucked an errant strand of hair behind her ear, 'that was me, I was in little bit of a state, I'm sorry.'

'No,' said the doctor, squeezing her arm and smiling flirtatiously, 'you'd had a terrible fright and…'

'She's getting married you know.' said Peter, from his bed.

'Congratulations,' said the doctor, turning his attention to his patient, 'and how are we feeling today, sir?'

'Better, thank you doctor,' said Peter, 'well enough to go home, I would say.'

'Good,' he said, looking at Peter's chart, 'all tests came back negative, heart's in good working order, but that is quite a nasty bump.'

He examined the ripening bruise on Peter's forehead.

'You don't say doctor.' said Peter, wincing.

'I do,' the young man smiled earnestly, 'and I want this blood pressure down before you go anywhere and…'

'Doctor, there is nothing wrong with me.' protested Peter.

'I know,' said the doctor, 'but I am the doctor…'

'Only just,' said Peter, 'how old are you?'

'Please excuse my father,' said Carrie, 'the fall must have affected his manners.'

The doctor smiled at Carrie.

'So we'll get you some meds and you can leave tomorrow…'

He turned back to Carrie.

'…I would imagine. Will you be coming to collect your father?'

'I think I can get myself home,' said Peter, 'thank you for your concern.'

'And our resident psychiatrist will be in to have a chat.' he said, as he was leaving.

'What?' said Peter, 'I'm fine. I haven't had a heart attack and…'

'Sure,' said the doctor, 'but stress gives you anxiety and it can also give you a heart attack. So let's try and not go there.'

'I do not need a shrink.'

'He's just going to have a chat,' said the doctor, ignoring Peter's protests, 'see what's causing those anxiety attacks.'

'Attack,' called Peter after him, 'I told you, it hasn't happened before.'

'And hopefully it won't again,' he said, over his shoulder, 'Dr. Julian Goodfellow, he's British, you'll love him.'

'That's the limit,' Peter said, turning to Carrie, 'between Dougie Howser and Nurse Ratched I'll never get out of here.'

'Daddy,' said Carrie, 'don't get all mad, they just want you to get better.'

Peter pulled a face, one thing he was pretty sure of, there was nothing wrong with his mind. But he was feeling exhausted and not a little unnerved by the event, a day of enforced bed rest wasn't the worst thing that could happen. He really had believed he was dying, just for that moment on the boat, and if his life hadn't actually flashed before him while he lay on the deck of the ferry, certain aspects of it had been brought into sharp relief while he lay in his hospital bed. What had he been doing all these years? Why hadn't he made more of an effort to see his children? He couldn't remember the last time he'd seen Ingrid. He hardly knew what was going on in their lives and they had left home years ago, there really was no excuse. That was something he was definitely going to change, starting right now. He wanted to make them a much bigger part of his life, if they would let him. And what about Sally? What was he so afraid of? Maybe this was a wake-up call, a shot across the bows. He was lucky to be alive. What if it had been a heart attack? What if he had died? He needed to get hold of Sally and tell her just how he felt, tell her he loved her. That's what he decided, laying there in his hospital bed. He should have told her in Venice, why hadn't he? He felt old. He certainly wasn't getting any younger and one thing he now knew, he didn't want to die any day soon. He wanted to see his daughter get married, he wanted to meet his grandchild and he wanted Sally. He would call her right now, they needed to talk.

'There's nothing wrong with me, I'm fine, all I need is a little rest, preferably at home.' he said, 'And a phone. Darling, do you have my phone I can't seem to find it.'

Top tip: to not feel like you're the oldest person in the room, forget the evening show, go to the matinee performance at the theatre and hangout with a more mature crowd.

CHAPTER 11

Sally still couldn't quite get her head around her impending birthday but she had agreed not to cancel it. She was going to be 50, be in her fifties; in her fifties and working in a place that increasingly looked like a sixth form college.

'Sally.'

And to add to the stress of this particularly stressful situation, work was not going well.

'Could you…'

Not well at all. Mike the MD, stuck his head out from behind the glass door of his glass walled office and beckoned.

'Quick word.'

He dropped a hand to his crotch and adjusted his balls, as if not realising the glass behind which he stood, was see through. He hoiked up his Diesel jeans which had slid beneath the gently rounding belly of a man who intended to go more frequently to the gym but the demands of his job and three kids… well it's tough. Sally didn't like Mike much; early 40s with a shaved head and highly polished, tan brogues, he was forever going forward, but seemingly getting nowhere. She left her coffee, steaming in its cup, and followed him through the glass door.

'No biggie,' he said, swivelling in his chair, 'just a quick catch up.'

The laptop on his desk sprung into life alerting him to a skype call. He grabbed his headset and gestured to Sally to sit.

'Mate,' he shouted at the screen, 'all good sir, and you?'
Sally sat down. Mike looked at her and smiled. It didn't help that Sally hated her job. It wasn't meant to be her job. It was only supposed to be something to tied her over until she'd found something better. Something she really wanted to do. But when the magazine had nearly folded she had panicked and then been grateful when it went online and she'd been kept on. Her stopgap had become her career. And now everyone said she was lucky to have a job, any job, at her age, and she believed them.

'Right, right, will do,' Mike was nodding violently, 'I'm right with you, we do need to pre-prepare, for sure.'
He laughed loudly at whatever his colleague in the Uxbridge office was saying.

'No worries mate,' he said, in a faux Australian accent, 'I'm all over it.'
Sally looked at his desk but there was nothing of interest to see there, so she looked past Mike, out of the window and into the office opposite where they appeared to be eating a Colin the Caterpillar birthday cake. Mike swivelled in his chair. Sally wished she had brought her coffee in with her.

'Will do, sir,' he said, nodding at her, 'will do. Leave it with me and I'll give it the full 360 degrees.'
Sally looked down at her hands and wondered what he was like in bed.

'Sorry about that,' he said, 'so, Sally, we've been doing a bit of number crunching, getting all our ducks in a row and…'
He clicked onto an excel spreadsheet and turned his laptop towards her, 'going forward…'

Peter sat in his hospital bed, doing his crossword and making plans. The problem was he now didn't have Sally's number because it was in his phone and his phone was at the bottom of the New York Bay, so he was stuck. He decided to call up Anna and David in London, the friends who'd thrown the party where they'd first met, just as soon as he got home, they would know who she was.

'B O U' he filled in the clue in his crossword, 'N D E R'
He smiled, excited by the plans he was making for Sally; he

would invite her to come over to New York for a vacation. Maybe they could go on a little road trip upstate. There were so many places he wanted to show her and he would take her to a ball game. Maybe she might want to move out there, her children were grown now, perhaps she…

'Hello there.'

A tall, handsome man in his late forties broke through his reverie. 'Dr. Goodfellow.' the man said, extending his hand to Peter.

'Now look here doctor,' Peter hoisted himself up on his pillows, 'I don't want to be rude but…'

'Just thought we could have a little chat, rule out any underlying…' Dr. Goodfellow, stood at the foot of the bed and ran his eye over Peter's chart.

'…psychiatric issues.'

'I don't have issues,' said Peter, 'psychiatric or otherwise.'

'Of course,' said the doctor, pulling the chair up to the bed, 'it's just routine. But you might want to think about starting some kind of therapy if you're suffering anxiety, maybe…'

'I don't think so doctor.'

'No? Perhaps there's other routes, meditation? Yoga?'

'Yoga?'

'To de-stress.'

'Really doctor…'

'Or perhaps self-help?' he said, 'There are a lot of good books about. I happen to have a copy here…'

He handed Peter a paperback on the front of which was a line drawing of a small figure apparently in the middle of a squiggly ocean, his arms held aloft. Peter read the title, slowly and with more than a whiff of disbelief:

'*I'm Not Waving…*'

'Exactly,' the doctor beamed with pride, 'I wrote it a couple of years ago, it's rather popular with…'

'You don't say.'

'Just finished the follow up, *I'm Not Drowning.*'

Peter put the book down.

'Take it home when you go,' said the doctor, 'you may find some useful…'

'A brown paper bag will probably suffice thank you doctor.'

'Ah, so you have had attacks before?'

'When I was a boy, once or twice, it's something my mother… look I'm fine.'

The doctor scribbled in a note pad.

'Shall we just get on with this?'

'Of course,' said Dr. Goodfellow, 'I had a word with your daughter yesterday…'

'What?'

'Says she's getting married.'

'I don't see what that's got to do with anything.'

'No,' said the doctor, 'but she was concerned the attack happened when she was telling you about her wedding plans. You're divorced?'

'Yes, over twenty years ago.'

'Right,' said Dr. Goodfellow, scribbling furiously, 'and since then?'

'What?'

'Any other marriages?'

'Are you mad?'

'Do you have a partner?'

'No.' said Peter.

'Have you had any other significant relationships?'

'No I have not.'

'None?' the doctor looked up, 'Not at all?'

'No, none to speak of.'

'But you have…'

'I have dated women over the last twenty years, yes doctor.' said Peter.

'And any problems with libido? Stamina? Erect…'

'Everything that needs to work is working just fine, thank you. Have I chosen to extend any of those short-term relationships into something more permanent? No.'

'And,' the doctor leant forward, 'you don't think there's anything unusual about that?'

Back in the comfort and familiarity of his West Village apartment, Peter instantly felt a whole lot better. He poured himself a large whiskey although it was only just gone six, opened the doors of the balcony wide, letting the early evening breeze ripple the drapes, and sat back in his favourite, winged reading chair. He would call Anna immediately, before it got too late in London, and if she couldn't find Sally's number, he'd decided, he would just get on a plane and surprise her, wasn't it her birthday this week?

Sitting at the zinc-topped kitchen table, the long light from a sunny day splashing through the French windows, open wide to the summer breeze, Alice was looking at colour charts for the potential repainting of the newly painted hall. She had got it down to three: Serenity White, Arcadia White or Phalaenopsis White.

'No, I know,' said Sally, flicking through the colour cards, 'thank god I found out about Peter before my birthday, now I can just draw a line.'

'Good.' said Alice, topping their coffees with foaming milk and studying her mug, 'Do you think they do a foaming milk white?'

She stared closely at her cup.

'I mean I'm fine with it, honestly, now I can just move on.' Sally said, spooning up the froth, 'The threat of losing my job has taken my mind off it.'

She laughed but actually Mike's chat had been more than a little disconcerting. Although not actually disconcerting enough to stop her thinking about Peter.

'Quite,' said Alice, 'that is something to think about. Do you need to worry?'

'Mummy.' screamed Olive, running across the kitchen waving a crayoned piece of paper, 'Mummy, mummy, mummy.'

'Great.' said Alice, lifting the child on to her lap, 'Lovely, Olive.'

She studied the drawing for developmental flaws in her daughter.

'Muuuummy, muuuummy' shouted Stan, from the other end of the open plan kitchen-diner, 'Muuummy, muuuummy.'

'Stan, come over here.' shouted Alice.

'Who knows,' said Sally, 'probably.'

'Don't think about it till after your birthday,' said Alice, 'we're all going to have a lovely evening on Friday.'

'Muuuummy.'

'Stanley.' said Alice, trying to silence her son from a

distance, 'Did he ever call back? Peter?'

'No.' said Sally, beginning to get a headache.

Stan ran over to his mother and sister and tried to climb up onto Alice's lap too but Olive kicked him away.

'Hasn't called at all?' asked Alice, trying to wrangle Olive's kicking legs, 'Do you think he got wind of being dumped? Was it your tone?'

'Don't know,' said Sally, 'maybe he was never that interested.'

'And you haven't called him again?'

'No.'

'Well done.' said Alice, trying to untangle her children, 'Don't.'

'I know but…'

'But nothing,' said Alice, 'you had some fun…'

'Yes…'

'Stayed in some nice places…'

'But…'

'Had sex… job done,' Alice grabbed Stan's flailing fists, 'and it had been awhile since Andy so think of Peter as your interim man, now you're back in the saddle, so to speak.'

'Come over here,' said Sally to Stan, trying to be helpful, 'sit on my lap.'

'No.' said Stan, hitting Sally hard on the leg to make sure she understood, 'I'm invisible.'

Alice's phone started beeping across the table.

'Bloody Ben.' she said, staring at the illuminated name.

She read the text and threw her phone down.

'Fuck off.' she said in the direction of her mobile.

Stan hit Sally again and then Olive, making her wail, and then flung himself on the floor, hit his head and started crying too.

'For goodness sake Stan, come here Olive, remind me again why I went through all that to get these. Basha,' she yelled, 'could you?'

The au pair slunk into the room.

'I ask him to do one thing, one bloody thing, they're his bloody friends and he's forgotten. I didn't invite them over. Well fuck him.' said Alice, scrolling through her text.

With the children now disappeared to the basement with the promise of carrot sticks and Cbeebies, quiet was restored.

Sally felt exhausted.

'He wants cheese tonight,' said Alice, 'he can fucking go and get fucking cheese. I want a divorce.'

Her phone sprung into life and she beamed as she answered it. Her voice became soft and girly. She bent forward and giggled. She threw her head back and laughed. And stepped out into the garden.

'Who was that?' asked Sally, when she returned, flushed.

'No one.' said Alice, busying herself with the dishwasher.

'No one? You were giggling like a lovesick teenager.'

'Just a dad.' said Alice, 'A single dad. Hot-and-sexy-single-dad. I met her at Bounce 'n' Sing ages ago, the only time I ever went, but we only ever see him now. She makes him have the kids most weekends. Punishment for philandering.'

'He's a philanderer?'

'Job is friends with Stan,' said Alice, ignoring the question, 'but they've got head lice.'

'Job?' said Sally, 'Seriously?'

'They've all got it.' continued Alice, 'So, no play-date for Stan. No fun flirting for me.'

'Be careful,' said Sally, 'you live by the sword…'

'I'm just flirting.' said Alice, 'We only had a coffee when the kids all went to the zoo.'

'You took all the kids to the zoo?'

'No, Basha took all the kids to the zoo. We went for a coffee.'

'It's a slippery slope.' said Sally, 'How would you feel if Ben was off having a coffee with… another woman?'

'Relieved.'

Sally looked astonished.

'Yeah, but you wouldn't actually do anything to jeopardize everything, would you?'

'It gets boring.' said Alice.

'What happened to boundaries?'

'It's nice to flirt.'

'Easily said from the comfort of your comfy marriage, but if Ben finds out…'

'There's nothing to find out.'

'Yet,' said Sally, 'nothing yet. But next time it could be drinks and then, who knows. And if Ben finds out and gets upset, well… there is always some girl in the office who is younger than you and she'll be a shoulder to cry on and the next thing you know he's moved in and she's pregnant and then he'll have a whole new family because even in his sixties he still can.'

Now Alice looked astonished.

'And you'll be home alone with your kids,' said Sally, 'old and unable to get a babysitter and then your flirtation won't look like so much fun.'

'Ben doesn't want any more kids,' she said, 'it won't happen.'

'It won't be up to Ben,' said Sally, 'he'll be with her.'

She looked at her friend, was she better off out of the messy world of relationships? All those ifs and buts and loose ends? One thing she did know, you can't out smart getting hurt.

The thing is, thought Sally, clasping her left ankle with her right hand, and twisting her body to look up, if Peter was so uninterested in her then she was glad it was all over.

'Look along your arm beyond your fingertips.' said Fenella, adjusting Sally's position.

Perhaps, she thought, it really was time to rethink her strategy.

'Relax the tongue.'

She had wanted to reclaim her life and have some fun.

'Release the eyeballs.'

Perhaps the whole conventional couple thing wasn't really for her.

'Are you breathing?'

'I don't know,' said Sally, after the class, 'I just think… it's all too complicated. It didn't seem this complicated when I was younger. Maybe I'm not cut out to be in a relationship anymore.'

She pulled on the dark green, men's cords that she'd recently bought because she'd seen a picture of Jane Birkin wearing a pair.

'Well dear,' said Rose, 'what you gonna do about it?'

'I'm going to be fifty…' said Sally, glancing over her shoulder at her reflected rear in the mirror, wondering if she was cut out to pull off the baggy, man's trouser look, or whether she just looked like she had a baggy, man's bum.

'Fifty!' laughed Rose, a woman in her eighties, 'You got a long way to go dear.'

'Keep your options open I always say.' said Joan, as she slipped her foot into her sequined flip-flop.

They may have been older but they certainly hadn't closed down their options, it was only society closing them down for them.

'There's nudity at the Almeida,' she continued, draping a brightly patterned scarf about her shoulders, 'Rose and I are going to a matinee. Come with us, might cheer you up. Put another perspective on things.'

They certainly hadn't lost their zest for life, Sally thought, as long as there was stuff to do they wanted to keep on doing it.

'I saw it last week as well, we get a senior discount you see,' said Rose, 'can't remember what it's called, but it's very good.' She grabbed Sally's arm with her bony hand.

'Fifty!' she said, shaking her head and laughing.

Joan joined in. Perhaps they were right, thought Sally, laughter ringing in her ears, perhaps she did need to change her perspective.

Top tip: eat yourself healthy. Turmeric is a powerful antioxidant, considered good for a variety of conditions including rheumatoid arthritis and Alzheimer's disease, use whenever possible

CHAPTER 12

Sitting at her kitchen table, Sally pondered the bag of baby spinach she was planning to cook. Why, she wondered, did she even want to be in a relationship? Her friends who were all seemed to do nothing but complain about the utter crapness of the people they were with, be it men or women. And she herself had not exactly fared well when involved with a significant other. All those wasted years with Ed when really they were done after three. What might her life have been like, she wondered, if they'd split up then? And what about Andy? If she'd acted differently, said something earlier, could she have stopped the train wreck of their relationship from occurring? Or would it just have postponed the inevitable? Andy was a troubled man who caused more trouble wherever he went. But even knowing everything she'd known, she'd always hoped the evidence would prove to be inconclusive, that once he'd known the love of a good woman, her love, they would work things out. That she could fix him. She was wrong. She had, much like Norman Mailer's final wife, bought a ticket to the circus and been surprised to see elephants. And now there was Peter. At least she hadn't wasted any time on him, lost any more precious years to a dead-end relationship. She wasn't going to make that mistake again.

'Hello darling.' she said, as Max lurched into the kitchen, 'Ready for Sheffield?'

'Yeah.' he said, by way of reply.

He opened the door of the fridge, peered in, pulled out a large block of cheddar and fumbled in the draw for a knife.

'Supper will be ready soon,' said Sally, ripping into the unsuspecting bag of spinach, 'how was the dentist?'

'Didn't go.' he said.

'What?' Sally's voice went up an octave, 'Why not?'

'Cos, I was busy,' said Max, 'it's only a check-up I don't even have to make an appointment or anything.'

'But, it's your teeth.' said Sally, thinking back over the many years of hard-fought dental care: the healthy snacks she'd administered, the tears and tantrums in supermarkets throughout the world as she'd ripped cans of coke and packets of crisps from those eager hands.

'Yeah, my teeth, and they're fine.' he said.

'Well they won't be if you don't go for check-ups.' said Sally, remembering the regular dental appointments she'd dragged him to, just to ensure he would grow up with a beautiful mouth, 'You'll be sorry when you get toothache.'

'Yeah, well you're giving me a headache.' he said, from deep inside the fridge.

'Did you have any lunch?' asked Sally, reaching for a pan.

'Er… no,' said Max, 'I mean why would I have lunch? It's not like I'm 21 or know how to feed myself in the middle of the day or anything.'

'I was just asking.' said Sally, dodging his terse response, her kitchen saw more flack than the Middle East.

'You're always asking me stuff.' he said.

'I'm not,' said Sally, 'I'm just making adult conversation. You say you're an adult, well this is what adults talk about.'

'Lunch?'

'Yes lunch. It's a normal thing to ask.'

'What? Like you ask your friends what they have for lunch?'

'Yes,' she said, 'I do. And they ask me.'

'Why do I have to tell you what I had for lunch? Why do you have to know everything about me?'

'I don't I was just making conversation.'

'Leave me alone. I don't want to tell you what I had for lunch.'

Max proceeded to hack off a sizable lump of cheese.

'Don't eat that.' said Sally.

'I'm hungry.' said Max.

'Supper's nearly ready.'

'I'm going out.' Max said, eating the cheese. 'Now.'

'But you said you were staying in.' said Sally, exasperation rising in her voice, 'you've got an early start. I asked you if you wanted supper, you said yes.'

'Well… now I'm saying no, you can eat it.' he said.

'I don't want to eat it.' said Sally, 'I wouldn't have cooked it at all if it's just for me.'

'Godsake.'

Max abandoned the cheese.

'But you need to eat something.' said Sally, 'Where are you going?'

'What does it matter where I'm going.' he said.

'It doesn't, I'm just making conversation.'

Sally called after the back of his disappearing head.

The front door slammed. Why couldn't they just have one day without slamming doors and shouting? And now she felt angry and sad and wished she hadn't shouted back, she hated it when he went out like that. She hated her life.

The bright morning light glowed through the insubstantial bedroom blind, as if an alien craft had landed outside, waking Sally early. She was fifty. She'd peered into the magnified bathroom mirror and what? Nothing. No more grey hairs, no new wrinkles, nothing had fallen off. Yet. But this was close encounters of an elderly kind. Now she sat, surrounded by her friends, at a long table in a busy restaurant. Everyone had arrived. Her presents had all been unwrapped. The wine had been poured. The food had been ordered. Her lipstick had worn off and still Peter had not called her back. She looked down at her mobile. Nothing. Yes, she was over him. No, she didn't want to be with him anymore. But she was still peeved that he hadn't called. How dare he deny her the opportunity to tell him she didn't want to see him.

'Wow.' said Alice as the waitress put a plate in front of her.

'Looks great.' said Ben as his food arrived too.

'Another bottle?' said Jaz.

'Definitely.' said Will.

'Put your phone away,' said Martin, 'forget him.'

They ate and drank and talked and drank some more.

'Another bottle?' asked the waiter, a handsome man in his 30s.

Sally looked down the table at the empty glasses.

'Yeah,' she said, 'why not?'

'You should stop looking at your phone and start looking at him,' said Will.

'Who?' asked Sally.

'That waiter. He's been flirting with you all evening.'

'Really?' said Sally, in disbelief, 'I'm too old for him.'

'Rubbish.' said Jaz. 'You don't even look 50.'

'And he's too old to be a waiter.' said Sally, dismissively.

'But he's gorgeous,' said Jaz. 'if you don't want him, I wouldn't say no, you don't want all those pelvic floor exercises going to waste.'

Jaz was listing dangerously to one side.

'Excuse me,' she waived at the waiter, 'can we get some waiter… I mean water. Please.'

'Sparkling?' he said, looking at Sally.

'Isn't she,' Jaz said, bursting into hysterical laughter and falling off her chair, 'it's her birthday.'

The waiter laughed.

'Oops, sorry,' she said, straightening up and composing herself, 'what's your name?'

'Guy.' said the waiter, smiling.

'Guy,' she leant forward to reveal a little more cleavage, 'just tap please.'

He nodded and headed for the kitchen.

'Yes,' said Jaz, as she watched him exit through the swing door, 'I'd do that.'

Alice told a funny story about Sally on holiday. Sally checked her phone again. Jaz told a funny story about Sally at college. Sally wondered if Peter remembered it was having a birthday. Martin told an hilarious a story about when she'd visited him in LA. Sally laughed and refilled her glass. A cake had been secretly hidden in the kitchen. Perhaps, Sally wondered, Peter was just going to turn up, surprise her and then she could…

'Happy birthday too you!' everybody sang, including Guy

the waiter.

There were candles and sparklers and it was great. It was fun. It was ok. Why hadn't he called her back, Sally wondered, trying to reapply her lipstick in the loo?

'Fuck him.' she said, to her reflection.

Outside the backdoor of the kitchen Guy was taking a breather. He was exhausted, his feet hurt and his back ached. He wasn't used to waiting tables but what could he do? His brother-in-law had been desperate: two waiters off sick, his sister about to give birth and a birthday booking, he could hardly say no. At least they'd been a good laugh, hadn't minded having to wait or him getting the orders confused and she was quite fanciable too. It maybe just for one night but he was glad it was over. And he could really do with a drink. He wanted to celebrate, it had been quite a week. Stressful, yes, but brilliant too; the biggest commission of his career as an architect specialising in carbon-neutral eco-architecture. That was definitely worth a drink.

'Right,' said Will, 'time to leave before Jaz tries to take her top off again. Let's get the bill and go to mine.'

'Where's that waiter?' said Jaz, 'I'm going to ask him back. He's so cute.'

The watery, late morning sunshine leached into her bedroom. Sally had always meant to get a blackout blind but somehow she'd never got around to it. This morning was definitely one of those mornings she regretted not having done so. She lay in the bleached glow praying for sleep to return. Or death. Whichever was quicker. Her ears throbbed with the ebb and flow of her blood as it pounded around her brain and her mouth was cotton-dry. She had woken with the headache she rightly deserved and she ached all over. She lay in her shipwrecked bed, a mass of tangled sheets and knotted duvet, doomed to spend the next fifty years alone, marooned with little hope of rescue. Around her lay the flotsam and jetsam of her carefully constructed party outfit. A tear welled up and ran down her cheek. She sniffed and wiped it away with a fist of sheet as the bedroom door swung wide and there he stood, his dark-hair dishevelled, one of her towels wrapped

103

low around his hips, a mug of her tea in each of his hands.

'Ah-ha,' he beamed, 'you're awake. Thought you might like a cuppa.'

Oh dear god. She realised, as the blur of the night-before was brought into sharp relief, she'd pulled.

Top tip: for an instant shot of youth serum, do something spontaneous without weighing up the pros and cons.

CHAPTER 13

Sitting in French Roast, on the corner of 11th Street and 6th Avenue, Peter ordered another espresso. He smiled as the pretty waitress asked him how he was; he was good, life was good. It was good to be alive, he thought as he spun his bacon filled fork through the egg yolk, alive and living in the city he loved. Good to have come to his senses too. Good to have realised halfway through his fruitless conversation with his friends in London, that he was never really dying. He was fine, in fact after a couple of days enforced rest he was more than fine. And maybe he'd been a little rash with ideas of love and road trips and Sally. He sat back, replete after his hearty breakfast and sipped his coffee. Maybe things were just fine the way they were, he was just fine the way he was. And now he'd lost his cell phone he couldn't call her anyway. David seemed to have no idea who she was although he did say he'd get Anna to ask around.

The enforced pause in his plan, and a few good night's sleep, had allowed Peter to take stock. Venice had been lovely, sure, but who couldn't fail to have a good time in Venice? But special? What's special? And love? Well… maybe he should let things cool down a little, take some timeout. He didn't want to give Sally the wrong impression, he'd already seen more of her than most of the women he dated and she didn't even live in the same country for chrissakes. And if he didn't have her number he couldn't call her, could he? And anyway, she hadn't tried to call him back since he'd missed her call that day on the Ferry. Not that they'd ever done all that calling and texting, god forbid, that wasn't Sally's style which was in Peter's opinion an attractive quality in any woman. She'd probably call him in a couple of days, he thought, and he'd explain why he hadn't been able to get back to her and then maybe they would hook up in London, when he went over for the Bacon Unzipped show at Tate Modern. But for the moment there was a lot going on right now, what with the wedding and the baby.

He pulled his new cell phone from his jacket pocket and read the text his daughter had just sent him. And now he'd have to deal with this dinner too, meet Carrie's prospective in-laws and her future husband. He suddenly felt very hot despite the fans gently humming overhead the humidity seemed to have increased. He waved for the check and drained his glass of water, he was beginning to feel faint. Not again, he thought. He couldn't wait for the waitress. Wedging the dollar bills under the glass he headed for the door. What he needed right now, he thought, was to get out of there.

After the sweetest phone conversation with Guy, the date was set. Sally couldn't quite believe what had happened, Peter was history and the universe had provided. Fifty might not be so bad after all. Guy was attending a meeting in Scotland with his big new clients, about which he was very excited. So she had a small window of opportunity before the big day; enough time to prepare but not enough time to lose half her body weight. She was trying to remain calm and not project all her hopes and desires onto the broad shoulders and wide smile of her potential new boyfriend. Which was hard because she was thinking about him quite a lot and she had been delighted when he'd texted his safe arrival in Edinburgh and an amusing description of the octogenarian who ran the B&B where he was billeted. Less so with the smiley face that she personally did not approve of when used by anyone over the age of eight. But no matter, Marilyn had been right, all she needed was a nice Guy to take her mind off Peter. Thinking about him made her happy. The only thing that was making her unhappy was the fact that her period was due. Or rather it was overdue.

In fact she couldn't remember when she'd last had her period.

'The thing is,' said Sally, 'I'm not sure when the last time was.'

'Really?' said Jaz, searching through a box of old black and white photographs in the back of a junk shop in Enfield, with a view to having them framed to sell at *Eat Me*.

'But it's probably nothing.'

'Well let's hope so.' said Jaz, 'Who might the father be?'

'Oh God,' said Sally, 'I didn't even…'

'Clearly.'

'It'll be nothing.' said Sally, 'Over excitement.'

'Over excitement? I didn't know we were using over excitement as birth control.'

'I can't be pregnant.'

'If you can get a period you can get pregnant.' said Jaz, knowledgably. 'And where were your condoms?'

'We did use condoms. They just ran out. With Guy.'

'No wonder you're over excited,' Jaz said, now rooting around in a box of old Christmas decorations, 'at least we know who the father is now.'

'I am not pregnant.'

'Do a test,' said Jaz, examining the delicate glass baubles, glitter coated and hand painted, 'but I agree, I very much doubt you're pregnant. Not at your age. But you never know.'

'I'm not.'

'One word… Cherie Blair.'

'That's two.'

Jaz gave her friend a look.

'Do a test.' she said, 'And buy more condoms.'

'I will.' said Sally, 'I wasn't fully prepared the first time. I was drunk.'

'Very drunk.' said Jaz, now studying a set of anatomically correct prints of the Bonobo.

'OK, very drunk.' said Sally.

Jaz discarded the chimps and turned her attention to some very large, old flowerpots. She examined them for cracks.

'The thing is,' said Sally, pulling out a box of fishing reels and assorted accessories, 'he was drunk too. Very drunk.'

'So?'

'So maybe he doesn't really remember.'

107

'What? That he was fucking you?'

'You wanna be careful with that.'

The elderly man who'd been sitting motionless behind a dusty desk in the corner of the shop, gestured to the tin that Sally was now holding.

'Hooks.' he said.

Sally carefully put the tin back. Jaz, picked up the box of decorations and the painting of the child with a tear in her eye, gestured to Sally to grab the enamelled water jug and headed towards the till.

'No, I mean… what should I do? This time. When we go out. I mean I don't even know if we're going to have sex again. I don't even know him.'

'What do you mean do?'

'Well, you know, usually I do my legs,' said Sally, 'I do my bikini line, in the summer, but Guy's younger, he may expect more. Or rather, less.'

'Ah.' said Jaz, piling her new found treasures onto the dusty desk for the proprietor to tot up, 'I get an extra high bikini wax, sort of Brazilian lite.'

'But…' said Sally, 'is that enough?'

'You have to be careful, you don't want to end up with a Hitler moustache.'

She rummaged in her bag for her purse.

'I have this brilliant woman, I'll give you her number. I draw the line at the Hollywood but the Brazilian is not to be sniffed at.'

She paid the proprietor and they left.

Sally used the aromatherapy-facial vouchers she'd been given for her birthday, to have an anti-aging, deep-cleansing, regenerative facial and observed both the attack phase of the Dukan Diet and the 2:5 fast diet with gusto. Along with her oat bran mixed with seeds high in omega-3, she'd started a whole new ritual breakfast-performance to promote health and wellbeing, involving green tea and berries and a glass of warm water with organic apple cider vinegar. She couldn't quite remember what that particular remedy promised, pretty much everything bar paying her mortgage. Obviously not improving her memory. She had no idea if any of it worked or did any good at all but was reluctant to stop in case she might suddenly age dramatically overnight and crumble to dust like an unwrapped mummy, ripped too soon from its tomb.

'So,' said Sally, lying on her back, her legs bent, 'do you think it's OK? Or a bit odd?'

'Odd?'

'A woman of my age having a Brazilian?'

She stared up at the ceiling and braced herself.

'Umm, I don't know, can you raise your knees higher?'

'Well, I was just wondering,' Sally continued, 'do you see many?'

'Many?'

'Brazilians? Hollywoods? At my age?'

'I'm a doctor.' said the doctor.

'I know,' said Sally, 'but I just thought, during the course of your work…'

'Now,' said the doctor, 'just relax.'

Sally had done the pregnancy test as Jaz had instructed, which proved to be negative. But there was still no period. So she'd done another test. Sill not pregnant and still no period. So she'd made an appointment with the doctor, she was supposed to get a smear test anyway. It was probably nothing. It wouldn't be cancer. She tried hard not to worry about just what it might be and really, really hoped she wasn't about to be diagnosed with a terminal illness just when she might have got herself a fatally attractive boyfriend.

'Well,' said the doctor, after taking her blood pressure, 'that's OK.'

'Great.' said Sally, unrolling her sleeve.

What, she wondered, were the symptoms of ovarian cancer?

'And everything else,' the doctor peered at Sally over her glasses, 'looks…'

'Yes?'

'OK.'

'Good.' said Sally.

'But…' she turned back to her computer screen.

'Yes?'

'We won't know for certain, not till I get all the tests back.

But…'

'But?'

'But,' the doctor pushed her glasses back up her nose, 'I would say it's just the menopause.'

Just the menopause!

'I'm only fifty. Surely the menopause doesn't happen till I'm… old? Older? The menopause?'

The hot flushes, cold anxiety, confusion and spots: the menopause. Not perri-menopausal. Proper menopausal.

'Yep.'

'But am I old enough?'

'Of course you are.' said the doctor in the matter-of-fact manner doctors do so well, 'Average age is fifty-one, but commonly happens anytime from mid-forties to mid-fifties.'

Sally left her doctor's surgery feeling a little older than when she'd arrived, clutching a fistful of leaflets, a free sample of Evening Primrose Oil capsules and a text from her toy-boy.

'I think I'm having an affair.' said Martin, audibly swigging from a can of Heineken on the other end of the phone.

'Think?' said Sally, from her prone position on her sofa in her sitting-room.

'Mmmm… I'm having one mentally.'

It was late, she had been enjoying 'All About Eve', one of her favourite movies, but she could tell by the tone in his voice, Martin was settling in for the long chat.

'Really,' she said, 'well I'm having the menopause.'

Sally reached for the remote, Martin was always worth pressing the pause button for.

'Right,' said Martin, 'does that mean you don't want to have sex?'

'It's the menopause,' said Sally, 'not a death sentence.'

This is what Sally had read in one of her menopause leaflets, not necessarily what she believed.

'Great isn't it. Just when your kids are growing up and moving out…'

'Max isn't.' said Martin, a little a confused.

'Well not in my case, obviously.' said Sally, taking a sip of her wine, 'But, for most women my age, your kids grow up and leave and then, just when you get time to think about

110

yourself, have a bit of guilt-free fun and re-ignite your marriage…'

'But…'

'I know, I'm not married so not me, other women… with husbands… then you get the menopause. You wither and wrinkle overnight, can't remember anyone's name, where you've been, what you're doing, you get high anxiety, low libido and an expanding waistband. And all your aging husband gets is a leather jacket, a fast car and a new girlfriend.'

'Good thing you haven't got a husband then.'

'Thanks.'

'But really, that's a gross generalisation Sally. Not all men are like that. Not all men are Ed. Or Andy.' said Martin, in defence of his sex. 'Some of us do care. Some of us have evolved beyond the club-'em-over-the-head-drag-'em-to-the-cave period and we do see beyond the shallow depths of youthful beauty. We do value real women. Proper women. Woman of any age.'

Thank god for Martin, thought Sally.

'So,' she adjusted the phone under her ear, 'your affair?'

'I went for a drink with another woman. A woman that was not Katy.' he said, taking a sip of his beer.

'Did you have sex?'

'No.'

'Kiss?'

'Yes. On the cheek.' Martin took another sip, 'I kissed her good-bye on the cheek.'

'That,' said Sally decisively, 'does not an affair make.'

'But I wanted to kiss her,' said Martin, 'I wanted to snog her. I thought about it. I wanted to have sex with her.'

'OK.'

'I thought about it all night. When I got home I…'

'I get it.'

Poor Martin, thought Sally, he really did just want to settle down and yet now it seemed that another relationship was about to bite the dust. Why couldn't he find the right one, she wondered?

'I hardly ever have sex with Katy. She says she's not into it now because she's menopausal. That's why I asked.' said Martin, 'But you do.'

111

'But not with you.'

'Well Sophie does.'

Martin took a big glug of his beer.

'Sophie, that's her name, lovely isn't it. Sophie.'

'So, what are you going to do,' said Sally, remonstrating with the remote as the TV sprung, loudly, back into life, 'about Katy?'

'The thing is…'

Martin had walked with his phone into his kitchen and was now trying to retrieve another beer from the back of the fridge. He cracked the can.

'I had sort of said something about going away. Sort of going away with Katy. Together.'

He took a long swig of the cold beer.

'On holiday.'

Martin took another swig.

'And she's booked the time off work, and…'

'You told her you wanted to go on holiday…'

'Camping.'

'Camping?'

'Yep. She likes camping.'

'Why did you suggest the holiday,' said Sally, 'if you didn't really want to go away with her?'

'Well, she wanted to go away and I thought it might be… nice.'

He took a gulp of his beer.

'Sometimes,' said Martin, 'it's just easier to say what they want to hear, you know.'

'Really?' said Sally, taking this information onboard and mentally filing it under 'Interesting', 'And that's what she wanted to hear?'

'Yep.'

'Maybe, she's just feeling anxious about the aging process.' said Sally.

'Yeah, the menopause.' said Martin, necking the last of the can, 'So maybe, I think we're done.'

Now waxed, polished, plucked and buffed, Sally was ready for her date with Guy. But in light of her conversation with Martin she couldn't sleep, anxiously wondering, why lovely young Guy would want to be with a menopausal old woman like her? How could she compete with the myriad of young women he must know? With their firm bodies and firmer grip on reality, their minds un-befuddled by the menopause. Whatever would they talk about? What could they talk about? She'd celebrated her 21st birthday before he'd hit puberty. It was ridiculous, the whole thing. She would call him and cancel. He'd probably only called her out of politeness. And now she thought about it, had he really asked her out or had she just assumed he was going to ask her out? Did she not actually suggest they go see a movie or something? First? Before he'd actually asked her anywhere? Did he just say 'great, love to', because it was easier to say what he thought Sally wanted to hear?

Top tip: there are few things that cannot be helped with cake… the addition of omega-3 seeds can help the menopausal.

Cherry And Mixed Omega-3 Seed Madeira Cake
(adapted from Lily Vanilli's, Cherry And Seed Madeira Cake)
180g unsalted butter
180g caster sugar
3 eggs
250g self-rising flour, sifted
3 tbsp milk
75g of Omega-3 mixed seeds: sesame, pumpkin, flax, sunflower and hemp
100g fresh pitted cherries, sliced but you can use tinned or substitute blueberries
120ml raspberry jam
150g double cream, whipped
150g icing sugar sifted
Juice of a lemon

Pre-heat the oven at 180C/Gas Mark 6. Cream the butter and sugar, add the eggs, one at a time, and beat together. Fold in the flour, add the milk a little at a time to ensure the mixture falls slowly from the spoon. Fold in the seeds and cherries or berries. Divide mixture between two prepared cake tins. Bake for 20-25 minutes, until a skewer stuck in the middle comes out clean. Remove from oven, allow to cool and turn out onto a rack. Spread one side with the jam and whipped cream and top with the other. Mix the icing sugar with enough lemon juice to make it a pouring consistency and pour over the top and allow to set. Utterly delicious.

CHAPTER 14

Sally discarded the black, cashmere cardi; too hot. She then pulled off the Jigsaw sparkly vest she'd artfully teamed it with and tossed it onto the bed where the rest of her wardrobe now lay. She burrowed beneath the mound and fished out the scarlet-flowered, silk chiffon shirt she'd just bought in a sale, and tried it on again: still an incredible bargain and still a size too small. Too cold for the green dress with the stripes. Too hot for the blue plaid. The asymmetric grey with the weird pattern? Too dressy. The Antoni and Alison flower-print, pencil skirt said too much. The black pleated one not enough. And the beautiful Armani jacket she'd paid a fortune for, even though it had been in a warehouse sale? It had never been worn because she'd never deemed an occasion special enough to wear it and now it had been mothed. She had nothing to wear. Gingerly picking over the pile, Sally began to hang things up, sliding them back into her closet: the stuff she actually wore at the front, the stuff she aspired to wear at the back. Jeans. That was all she'd come up with. Jeans and black leather, ankle boots. With studs. A little bit chunky, a little bit edgy. Not too dressy, not too… old? But she couldn't find anything, nothing, not a single thing, to go with them that wasn't too tight, too old, too big, too young.

Feeling fed up, Sally pulled on her favourite old Eurythmics T-shirt and retreated to the kitchen. She switched on the kettle and snapped a piece of Lindt dark chocolate with chili, from the emergency bar she kept in the cupboard, wedged behind the tins of tomatoes, chick peas and coconut milk, then poured the boiling water into her, Pursuit of Love Penguin mug, poking the Earl Grey tea-bag down with her finger, to steep. Why, she wondered, hadn't she embraced the ethos of regular exercise in her youth to create the body she knew she deserved? Or had the will power for anorexia?

Still pondering her outfit, she pulled out the damp clothes languishing in the washing machine, in case there might be something amongst them she'd forgotten about. It was then she eyed Poppy's bag of left laundry. Tipping it out onto the floor, Sally paused for a moment, it might be worth a rummage. And there it was: black with a scarlet and ivory, Celia Birtwell print: the perfect top for a night out with her young lover. Styled to look good on a small-medium (Poppy) as well as a large-medium (Sally), she examined the garment for unmentionable stains or indelible marks. Nothing. She rinsed it in warm water and washing-up liquid, wrapped it in a towel and stamped on it in her socked-feet. Barely damp, she laid it across the radiator and turned the heating on despite the warm weather. Result.

Her going-out outfit now laid out on her bed, Sally began phase two of the preparations. She toyed with the idea of a drink to steady her nerves. When did it get so hard to go out, she wondered? It hadn't been like this with Andy, had it? Perhaps it was just easier to go out with a middle-aged, out-of-shape bloke than it was to go out with a young, lean sex-machine. Either way, right now a shot of vodka seemed a very appealing idea.

Pulling herself into her jeans, she rearranged her breasts in her black, lacey, going-out bra and released her wet hair from its towel. She hung Poppy's top on a hanger, the left sleeve still just a tiny bit damp, and hung her head down to blow-dry her hair. Would Guy like it she wondered, as she examined her reflection in the smudgy mirror? The wail of the smoke alarm filled the air as she administered another squirt of perfume. In the hallway, Sally found Ed violently waving a tea towel at the alarm flashing on the ceiling.

'Hi Sal,' he said, flicking the tea towel over his shoulder, 'thought I'd just pop in. Say Hi. See how you're all doing.' He bobbed forward and kissed her on the cheek.

'You look nice,' he said, stepping back and taking in the full extent of Sally's glamour, 'going out?'

His voice wedged somewhere between appreciation and surprise.

'Yes.' she said, heading for the kitchen where Max was busy being creative.

'So,' said Ed, eyeing his son's activities, 'you didn't cook?'

'No.' said Sally, spotting the bottle of red Ed had brought round in the hope that he might have been able to parlay it up into one of Sally's suppers.

'But I did.' said Max.

He smiled at his father.

'Shall we have a drink?' said Sally, un-screwing the bottle and pouring herself a large glass.

'It's my new hobby,' said Max, 'join me dad, there's loads.'

'Thanks son.'

Ed sat down at the table, poured himself some wine and took a large sip. He looked down at the plate his son had handed him and up at Sally.

'Enjoy,' said Sally, looking up at Max and down at the plate: spaghetti curled around a pile of rigatoni topped with tomato ketchup studded with pieces of fish finger and liberally sprinkled with crumbled Stilton.

'I'm going out.'

'Two types of pasta?' said Ed, to his son.

'Couldn't decide,' said Max, a look satisfaction on his face as he set his plateful on the table and prepared to tuck in, 'I'm experimenting with a sweet/savoury thing.'

He dug his fork in and hoist up a mouthful.

'That's why I put the blueberries in,' he said, 'and the olives. You weren't saving them were you mum?'

'No,' said Sally, looking at Ed's face as he chewed on, 'you go right ahead.'

'You look nice, where are you going?' asked Poppy, appearing in the doorway.

'Thank you,' said Sally, beaming 'actually…'

'Is that mine?'

Poppy peered closely at her mother.

'Mum are you wearing my top?'

'I'm just borrowing…'

'Mum,' whined Poppy, 'you'll stretch it.'

'No I won't,' said Sally, 'you're always borrowing my stuff.'

'Yes but I don't ruin it.' said Poppy, flopping into a chair.

'Come on Poppy,' said Ed, 'Mum looks lovely. To be fair, it doesn't look that tight.'

'It's not tight.' said Sally.

'Alright, wear it.' said Poppy, poking about in the Sainsbury's Bag For Life in which she'd left her clothes, 'Why are you here anyway, dad?'

'Nice to see you too daughter,' said Ed, licking sauce from his fingers, 'I just popped in to say Hi…'

'Mum, is this my laundry?'
Poppy held up a pair of skinny jeans from the bag.

'Yes,' said Sally, 'I haven't had time…'

'I can't believe it, I told you…'

'I know,' said Sally, pulling on her jacket, 'but I haven't done it.'
She turned to the mirror to apply one final coat of lipstick.

'Do it now if you want.' she said over her shoulder, 'Max, Ed, enjoy your supper. I have to go.'
She pecked at their reflection in the glass, pulled her bag onto her shoulder and left.

Outside the tube station, Guy stood smoking a cigarette. He was looking forward to seeing Sally. He wasn't sure what it was that he liked about her so much; the being older thing was sexy and a million miles away from his previous girlfriends. A million miles away with the actors and performers he seemed to always end up with, dating Ophelia one minute and a Spanish acrobat the next. Thanks to his older brother, Simon, a theatre director, he'd seen a lot of pieces in spaces, and met a lot of needy actors in pubs. But being rather attracted to the drama of it all he had enjoyed the tempestuous ups and downs until the disastrous Melinda. That was one head-fuck too far. No more actors. Now he wanted to find someone who was more sorted, less needy, a proper grown-up. Someone like Sally?

As he saw her approach, he flicked his cigarette butt toward the gutter and blew out a blur of blue smoke. She smiled. He embraced her, pushed the hair back from her face and kissed her.

'You're late.' he said, taking her by the hand.

'Sorry, Max was cooking and Poppy…'

'Come on.'

He grinned and led her towards the bowling alley.

'Bowling?' said Sally, fear and loathing unhidden in her tone.

'Yeah,' said Guy, pulling out his wallet, 'my treat.'

'But I haven't been bowling since Max was about ten.'

'Well it's about time then,' he said, as he handed over Sally's black-leather ankle boots with studs, to the spotty boy behind the desk, his over-sized, American-retro shirt blobbed with ketchup. She took the flat, stripy, bowling shoes he'd replaced them with and started putting them on. They clashed horribly with Poppy's top.

'But I'm rubbish at bowling.' said Sally, looking down at her clown feet.

'Excellent,' said Guy, 'cos I'm brilliant. I'll teach you. Loser buys dinner.'

And he did. He chose the right ball for her to use. He carefully instructed her on how to hold it and how to aim. He laughed hysterically as time after time the ball spluttered into the gutter and she scored another zero. And when she got a strike and flung her arms into the air shouting 'yes', he flung his arms around her waist and lifted her up. And snogged her. In front of everyone.

'Trust me,' he said, when the second game was over, 'they do the best hot dogs.'

'OK.' said Sally, as she nervously squeezed onto the L-shaped, red leatherette banquette, squeaking as she inched round the table. She hated hot-dogs.

They drank malt milkshakes and ate shoestring fries and hot dogs with everything-on-it, and Gene Vincent sang Be-Bop-A-Lula and Sally thought she'd never tasted anything so delicious. Or had so much fun. Maybe the HRT was kicking in.

'Oh no,' said Guy, when the pretty waitress with the perky ponytail smiled, tipped her pretty head to one side and handed him the bill, 'my date's paying.'

He pushed the saucer towards Sally.

'You lost, you pay.' he said, kissing her full on the lips.

The girl looked at Sally without hiding her surprise at the nature of their relationship, in any way what so ever. And Sally was never happier to pick up the tab.

'Thanks for dinner,' Guy said, as they walked toward the tube arm-in-arm, 'fancy dessert at mine?'

He stopped and kissed her. The smell of grapefruit shower gel and rain, fried meat and rendered fat, filled her nose as they snogged against the damp wall, under the awning of the now closed kebab shop.

'But,' said Sally, 'I still feel full after…'

'Sally,' said Guy, 'I don't mean food.'

'Oh.' said Sally.

'But I do have some beers in the fridge.'

'Ah.'

They walked past the tube towards Guy's flat.

Top tip: to do wonders for bingo wings, saggy bums and wobbly thighs, try body brushing: a few minutes morning and night will stimulate your lymphatic system and help get rid of toxins.

CHAPTER 15

Listening to the wail of a siren heading down 5th Avenue, Peter sat in his study, a drink in hand, and smiled. It had been a great evening, his dinner with Carrie and Ted and his soon to be in-laws, what had he been so worried about? He shook his head at his own stupidity. Why had he allowed himself to become such an absent figure in his daughters' lives for so long? He should have dealt with this long ago, his-ex, his feelings, the wasted years.

But hindsight was a wonderful thing, as his father used to say. One of the few things Peter remembered the shadowy figure of his father ever saying. Aver Jacobs, had been a short man; short in stature, short tempered, short of money, short on words. The height had come from his mother, Molly Duggan. The courtship between Molly and Aver, a typical New York, Irish/Jewish love match, had been brief, but the marriage was long, until Molly died at just fifty-eight from breast cancer, which came as a surprise to her children who had always thought it would be the drink that got her. Molly was a quiet alcoholic. She'd worked at her job in admin at Bellevue hospital and raised her children to fear God and their father, with food in their bellies and homework done on time. It was only her nicotined fingers and the constant sucking of mints at the school gate that hinted at another side to the quiet woman in the dark blue overcoat she always wore. The late night shouting in the small apartment had taught Peter and his two older sisters, Mary and Ruth, to keep their heads down and their mouths shut. The girls were considerably older than their brother and so by the time he was 14 they had both left home, and moved far away from Greenwich Village, Mary to start a life as a teacher and Ruth already married before she'd turned twenty. Peter had sought solace in the Jefferson Market Library, only a short walk away from their apartment, and yet once there he was transported out of Greenwich Village and off around the world with his new friends: Melville and Dickens, Lawrence, Hemingway and Ford Maddox Ford, whose name he would repeat at night when his parents fought, over and over like a mantra until he fell asleep. He'd loved his mother but the alcohol had built a glass wall between her and the rest of the world, as clear as the ice-cubes that clinked in her drink, she could see out but nothing could get in.

'Hindsight,' he said, refilling his glass, 'I'll drink to that.'

Outside the moon, almost full, was dropping in the night sky. He was pleased he'd opted to stay on at the restaurant with Ted and Carrie, sharing desserts and another bottle, talking about the trips he'd made with the girls when they were little. Not that there had been very many but he was touched by how fondly Carrie had recalled them, regaling Ted with stories of when, while trying to fix the shower head in one hotel, her sister Ingrid had turned on the water and soaked him right through or the time they'd tricked him into believing Carrie had been bitten by a snake so he'd run all the red lights to get her to the ER.

He looked out across the street; a young couple were standing on the stoop, caught in the dancing light of a street lamp as the breeze rippled through the tree above. Locked in an embrace, they kissed as if their lives depended upon it. He thought about Sally and the way they'd kissed. Kissed like teenagers. And the way she'd listened in wonder, and asked so many questions, her enthusiasm as keen as his for so many of the things that excited him. Their trip to Venice had reignited his joy of travel. Being with Sally had made him see the beauty of a foreign city again. And he loved her smile, so beguiling, and the way she laughed: a lot and often, Sally could see the funny in most situations. She would laugh at him when he lost his glasses or his key-card or when he messed up trying to use some British expression. She thought that was hilarious. But she would laugh at herself too. And when she did, her hand to her face, unable to speak, it was quite magical. He felt an ache in his heart, he wanted to see her, she had made him feel more relaxed than he had felt in years. Relaxed and happy. Isn't that what the doctor had said he needed? Why had he avoided it for so long, what was he so scared of? Was he just being a fool, he wondered as he finished his drink.

'Sorry I'm late,' said Will, 'hell of a day, I lost my academic leg.'

As a doctor, Will was in charge of lots of people all over London. And he worked very hard. Very hard indeed.

'I've been working very hard,' he said, 'very hard indeed.'

'Don't worry,' said Sally, 'box set.'

She picked up the dishes of gnocchi and homemade pesto.

'Sofa supper,' she said, heading for the sitting-room, 'you bring the glasses.'

They settled themselves down for a double dose of Mad Men. Sally rearranged the cushions for maximum comfort and took a contemplative sip of her Rioja. The warm red filled her head with memories of balmy evenings in Barcelona on holiday with Ed, sat at a corner table in Plaça del Pi, when they were young and in love and there were no kids and no mortgage and no other things that mess with the unquestionable knowledge that this is truly the person you want to spend the rest of your life with. Right before you absolutely know that you don't.

'Don Draper makes me want to smoke,' she said, 'smoke and drink. God he's so bad.'

'But so gorgeous.' said Will.

After the shows were all over, emotionally spent but replete, Sally cleared their plates and returned with a bar of Lindt dark chocolate with a touch of sea salt.

'Why?' she said, helping herself to a couple of squares before lobbing it over to Will, 'Why would his wife want him back when he's such a bastard?'

'Because he's such a bastard?'

Will reached for the bar.

'But so gorgeous,' said Sally, raising her glass, 'a gorgeous bastard. He looked so sad, but he is so bad, what's that about, all the mad-for-the-bad-boy stuff?'

'You tell me, you're the woman, what do you really want?'

'Some more chocolate.' said Sally.

She leant over and reached for the Lindt.

'I don't want any more bad guys that's for sure,' she said, snapping another piece, 'why do I always meet bad guys?'

'Maybe you don't,' said Will, 'maybe you just don't see the good guys, maybe…'

'Maybe Guy is a good guy? she said, reaching for the bottle, 'I feel a bit nervous about the whole thing.'

'Keep an open mind,' said Will, holding out his glass, 'and an open heart.'

'He's so much younger, I've never done younger. Is it ridiculous?'

'Feel it, think it, don't react to it.' said Will.

'OK… and what does that mean?'

'You have doubts, sure, but give him a chance.'

Sally snapped the last two squares of chocolate in half and offered one to Will.

'So,' she said, 'how's it going with the Buddhist?'

'Way too needy, he's hard work.' he said, 'I mean he's a lovely person…'

'But?'

'But nothing. Well everything. I don't know. He was with someone before, they were married.'

'Wow,' Sally took a sip of her wine, 'even the gays are all married.'

'Yeah, a very uncivil partnership.'

Will nibbled the chocolate.

'But,' he continued, 'you just wonder, should it be this hard at the start of a relationship? Does it always have to be so complicated to be for real?'

'I thought you said he was a Buddhist?'

'He is.' said Will.

'Somehow,' said Sally, 'you'd have thought it would be easier, being with someone who's… enlightened?'

'Yeah, you'd think.' said Will, 'So, I had to let him go. I

124

could just tell, it's not going to work.'

'Om tiddely pom.' said Sally.

'What's the Dali Lama's favourite Pizza?' said Will, draining his glass.

'Dunno.'

'One with everything.'

The call from Peter had come late. Sally was lying in bed trying to sleep, trying not to think about Guy and the possible problems she may incur by dating a younger man. Trying not to think about Peter and what might have been if it hadn't gone horribly wrong. Trying to be positive about her future, whether it was with or without anyone else.

'Sally?'

She had run through all the emotions from A to Z as she'd reached for her glasses and seen his name light up on her phone. Although she'd believed that she was over him, she had certainly not even got close to deleting him from her mobile. Not yet. And in the nanosecond it took for her to grab for the phone and say:

'Hello.'

Sally had mentally conjured up several scenarios.

'Darling,' said Peter, 'there you are, you've led me quite a dance.'

'I have?' Sally could hear her heart beating in her ears and hoped he couldn't.

'Yes you have.'

Sitting at his desk in his apartment, he sipped what was not his first drink of the evening.

'But I called you,' she said, bleary eyed and confused, 'you never called me back.'

'But I wanted to.' he said.

'You did?'

'I did.'

She couldn't believe how good it was to hear his voice. She'd hardly spent any time with him but the thing was, what time they had spent together had felt so right, so easy.

'So why didn't you?' she said, she'd missed him.

'I had a heart attack.' he said.

Sally was now wide awake and sitting bolt upright as Peter

went on to explain it wasn't actually a heart attack but the damage was done. In her mind he had survived a near-death experience as he now told her how much he'd missed her and how worried he'd been when he couldn't get hold of her and how hard it had been to track her down through Anna after he'd lost his phone.

'She found a novelist and a photographer who answered your description,' he explained, 'and a woman who'd recently returned from Pakistan.'

'Ah.'

'Pakistan?'

'I didn't know anyone at the party. I was bored. I have done a photography course.'

'With David Attenborough?'

They laughed. She hadn't realized how much she'd missed him. Guy was lovely but…

'Well I'm glad I found you at last.' said Peter.

'You are?' said Sally.

What if he wanted children? Guy was young, he was bound to want to be a father. Would he want her to be one of those women that gives birth in her fifties and then goes on Woman's Hour? Oh no, she thought, sore nipples and nappies, night feeds and Jane Garvey. No, no, no absolutely not.

'Oh yes,' said Peter, 'very glad, I like you Sally.'

Top tip: improve your memory as you move into old age by memorizing the phone numbers of your family, friends, work colleagues and acquaintances… and write them in an address book, an old-fashioned concept but extremely useful when you lose your phone.

CHAPTER 16

'Like you?' said Alice, the light from the sun, still bright in the evening sky, lingering on the art books, piled high on the coffee table along with the remains of last Sunday's unread papers, stories of Wild Things, Charlie and Lola, Peppa Pig and Peter Rabbit, 'Is that what we're doing now, liking?'

'It's romantic.' said Sally, ignoring her friend.

'Is like this year's love?' said Alice, kicking off her shoes and swinging her legs onto the sofa, 'So you didn't say anything about his 'marriage'? You didn't dump him?'

'No.' said Sally, 'I was half asleep, he caught me off guard and…'

She took a sip of her wine.

'It was so nice to hear his voice, I'd forgotten how much… I've missed him, so that's what I said.'

'Mmm,' said Alice, reaching for her much needed post-kids-bath-'n'-bed drink, 'bet he liked that too.'

She scratched the back of her head.

'What now? You're going to dump Guy?'

'No.'

'So, you are going to dump Peter?'

'No, I've decided,' said Sally, draining her glass, 'to see them both.'

She smiled and reached for the bottle.

'Two-timing?' said Alice, 'Not like you, first you date a 'married' man, now you're cheating, what brought this on?'

She shook her head, scratched it and refilled their glasses.

'Maybe it's the HRT,' said Sally, 'blame it on my hormones, but why not? Men do it all the time. I'm a woman with womanly needs, I like them both so why not have it all? If I can't find what I want in one man then… Guy is young, and hot, and local, what's not to love? Sam Taylor Johnson, Demi Moore, Susan Sarandon… they're all at it, but he's not about to settle down any day soon and Peter obviously isn't but he is so charming and sophisticated and…'

'Rich?'

'I've decided it's my turn to have some fun,' said Sally ignoring her friend's remark, 'so I'm going to have two boyfriends and twice the fun.'

She refilled her glass and gestured to Alice.

'Or twice the drama.' said Alice, scratching behind her ear.

'Why do you keep scratching your head?' asked Sally.

'Lice.' said Alice.

'Lice?' said Sally, recoiling back into the sofa.

Alice leaned forward and emptied the bottle into her glass.

'Hot-sexy-single-dad had head lice.' she said.

'Explain yourself.' said Sally.

'No. Nothing. It was just a drink.'

'You had a date with hot-sexy-single-dad?'

Sally threw a rag Lola-doll that had been wedged behind her cushion in the direction of Alice.

'Not a date.' said Alice, batting the doll away.

'You went out?' said Sally, leaning forward.

'Yes.'

'Together? Without anyone else?'

'Yes.'

'In the evening? To a bar?'

'Yes.'

'That's a date.'

Sally sat back, triumphant.

'It's not, we're just friends. He's in marketing. We're looking to re-brand. I wanted to pick his brains. It's a work thing. It was loud in the bar, we had to sit quite close to make ourselves heard.'

'You snogged.'

'We kissed.'

'Oh my God, you snogged hot-sexy-single-dad.'

'We kissed good-bye, on the cheek, that's all. Then he sort of hugged me and kissed me again on the other cheek and I said I must go, got in a cab and that was that. That's all.'

'Really?'

'Really. That's all that happened. Except I can't stop thinking about him.'

'Oh my God.'

'I know,' said Alice, 'but the gods have spoken. I won't do it again.'

She scratched the back of her head.

'Now we've all got lice. I've deloused everything. Twice. The whole house. And I still itch. Only Ben escaped,' she said, aiming for the kitchen to fetch more wine, scratching her scalp, 'the joy of not having any hair I suppose.'

Rummaging through her top drawer for another pair of date-knickers, having already used up her best pair on Guy, Sally knew she was running late, she really needed to get cracking. And remind herself where the British Museum was. Peter was back in town and he'd arranged to meet her there.

'Hello.'

He was standing at the top of the steps, outside the entrance. Despite the coolness of the late afternoon his embrace was far from chilly

'Come with me,' he said, taking her hand in his, and leading her into the museum, 'just want to show you something before we go.'

In a back room, away from the public, Peter pointed out a tiny ice-age relic, some 30,000 years old, intricately marked.

'Look at this,' he said, 'isn't that something?'

Sally watched as the sophisticated Manhattanite spoke with the wide-eyed joy and excitement of a schoolboy while he explained the significance of the carefully carved object.

'You see, Sally,' he said, leaning forward and drawing her in, closer to him, 'art of this kind, this sophistication, it proves that all the cognitive faculties we value so highly today, they were all going on back then.'

Sally liked it when Peter said her name.

'They loved beautiful things.' he said.

He paused and turned to look at her.

'Just like we love beautiful things.'

He smiled and held her gaze. Sally smiled back and felt beautiful.

'Shall we go?' he said.

Sitting adjacent to one another on the L-shaped, soft leather banquette in the high ceilinged, Showroom, Peter talked of the art show he was helping to curate at the Brooklyn Museum. Outside the cold afternoon crept towards dusk as inside, the soft, gold light reflected in the vast mirrors made everything glow.

'They were using their imagination you see.' he said, his knee pressing hard against hers under the table.

And Sally did see: she saw her and Peter having Sunday lunches, Monday suppers, Saturday cocktails, she needed to stop using her imagination.

'They were experimenting even back then, with scale and movement, with perspective.'

Holidays in the Greek sun, thought Sally, Christmases in New York. She caught sight of her inane, grinning self in the mirrored pillar behind Peter's head, she needed to get a grip, stop projecting. She needed some of that perspective. Outside the day had turned from dull to dark. She ordered a Manhattan, in honour of her love of New York.

'And a martini,' said Peter, smiling at the handsome waiter with the green eyes, 'Ketel One vodka. With an olive.'

Two cocktails down, they were still deep in conversation.

'I don't really do films. Don't hate me for it.' he said, 'Maybe it's time I got back into going to the movies.'

He smiled, lent forward and kissed her on the lips. Sally definitely didn't hate him.

'You do have the most beguiling smile.' he said.

She really liked the way that he'd just kissed her as if it was the most natural thing in the world. And he made her laugh, just like she'd imagined Cary Grant might have made her laugh if they'd ever gone on a date.

'The worse thing was,' said Peter, as he explained how he'd been the un-coolest kid in his school, the geek who'd been sent away to stay with an uncle in Canada every summer, to chop down trees in the wilderness, instead of hanging out downtown, smoking pot. 'I actually enjoyed it, toyed with the idea of becoming a lumberjack.'

He drained his glass and looked wistfully out into the dark night.

'Only briefly,' he continued, 'till I moved in with an older woman who lived in a loft in Chelsea, then I fell out of love with trees and in love with Lou Reed instead.'

Sally laughed, she couldn't imagine anyone less like a woodsman than Peter, or a Lou Reed fan, but she loved that contradiction about him. And she liked his deadpan delivery, his self-deprecatory humour and the way he made her feel. She felt sexy and attractive and alive.

'Honestly,' said Peter, as he explained how his Aunt Celia had hoodwinked him into taking her to a ball game so she could surreptitiously scatter her dead husband's ashes, 'she said she'd always loved the Yankees, it was her 80th birthday, it was what she wanted and I'd believed her.'

'So what did you do?'

'I could hardly scoop him back up,' said Peter, 'he was everywhere.'

Sally held her hands to her face trying hard not to splutter dessert over him.

'Didn't you notice?' she said, regaining her composure, 'The urn?'

'She had him in a Cracker Jack box,' said Peter, 'she'd really thought it through.'

Sally spooned up the last of the crème brûlée that Peter had insisted she order after she'd declared it was her favourite. And so he could share because he loved it too. They had pudding in common at least, she thought, she could work on the movies.

'Do you like baseball?' he asked.

'I don't know,' said Sally, 'I've never seen a game.'

'Never?' said Peter, 'We'll have to put that right.'

Unsteadied by the wine they were now drinking, Sally held fast to the brass rail of the winding staircase as she headed to the loo. She smiled at her reflection in the mirror, a little hazy about the edges. This was shaping up to be a brilliant night, she thought. And so what if he did do this all the time? Shagged women all over Europe? All over the world? What did it really matter if he was an International playboy, only interested in her for sex? She was having fun wasn't she? She was a consenting adult wasn't she? She could shag whomever she wanted, couldn't she? Reapplying her lipstick, Sally grinned at herself once again, feeling emboldened and in charge. Wasn't this what all those spare ribs had burnt their bras for, the right for her to cop off with impunity?

Outside, the night was cold and damp but Sally didn't feel the chill, warmed by the wine and Peter's protective arm around her waist. She was dizzy with alcohol and expectation as they walked wordlessly, the short distance towards his hotel but as the lights loomed closer Peter stopped and turned to face her.

'Sally.' he said, his gloved hands on her waist turning her round to face him.

She could feel the soft cashmere of his mustard coloured scarf as he hugged her close.

'Yes?' she said, delighted she had reinstated him, it was an excellent idea.

'I really do like you,' he said, 'I like you an awful lot.'

And he leant forward to kiss her.

Top tip: to unwind after a difficult day and forget about those tricky issues, reintroduce the cocktail hour and see the world through a rose-tinted Martini.

Rose Vodka for a Rose Martini
I litre vodka
I tsp rose water
1 tsp caster sugar
100g Turkish Delight
Dissolve the sugar in the rose water. Pour some of the vodka out of the bottle (enjoy with tonic, ice and lemon later) add the sweetened rose water. Wash the icing sugar from the Turkish Delight, chop into small pieces and add to the bottle. Shake well and leave for a month. Strain and serve ice cold with a twist.

CHAPTER 17

Once Peter was safely back in New York, Sally started preparing herself for what Guy had referred to as a 'surprise' weekend in the country. Things were working out rather well, she thought, in fact better than she could have imagined. However, she was very surprised when Guy's 'surprise' turned out to be the Sun Ray Festival. Having done Glastonbury a long time ago, back when it was a couple of stages and a few blokes on stilts; three days of beanburgers and magic mushrooms and sex with an Australian called Josh while Ed was watching some naked men dancing with balloons in the comedy tent, she'd assumed her days of sex-in-a-field were behind her now.

'Cool.' said Martin.

'I don't know if I can cope with it.'

'It'll be full of middle-aged-middle-class-camper-vanners,' said Alice, authoritatively, 'you can buy flowery, festival tents in Tesco now, you won't have to get wasted.'

'So what should I take?'

'Paracetamol,' said Jaz, 'shorts and a pair of Wellingtons. It's all Kate Moss takes.'

'Oh god.' said Sally.

'He's got a car hasn't he?' said Alice, 'take it all.'

'Won't it be freezing at night?'

'Not if you take enough drugs.' said Martin.

'Oh god.' said Sally.

'It'll be great, you'll have fun.' said Jaz.

'But I get tired, what if he wants me to be up all night?'

'That's what the drugs are for.' said Martin.

'You are joking,' said Will, 'a festival? In a field? I can't think of anything worse. As a doctor I forbid it. Don't go.'

He sub-divided first the lemon polenta cake and then the chocolate brownie, as he and Sally sat in Jaz's cafe.

'Guy's younger he's into different things,' said Sally, 'so I'm going to do things differently. It'll be great.' She poured Earl Grey tea from the blue and white stripy teapot into the mismatched teacups.

'Mind the age gap.' said Will, digging into his cake.

'I feel like Joan Collins.' she smiled.

Sally took a sip of her tea.

'No need to start behaving like her…'

'His brother is a theatre director, he's doing a piece in the Space Tent, or he's got a space in the Peace tent….whatever, Guy is going to help,' said Sally, ignoring her friend's negativity, 'and we get to stay in the backstage area so proper toilet facilities. Elbow headlined last year. Sammy and Ems went, said it was fantastic, they spray paint the livestock different colours.'

'Why?'

'Like doing acid-lite, all the fun of the hallucinations with none of the fall-out. There's a cocktail bar in the wood. And a burlesque tent. They were off their tits for three days, saw Tom Jones play at midnight in the Tree House. Well they think they saw him, who knows what they saw after three days on class As. And we're staying in a yurt.'

'A what?'

'He says we've got a yurt,' said Sally, as she watched the sun through the rain-spattered windows bob behind the cloud, 'and it's got a chandelier.'

'A paramedic sounds more useful.' said Will.

He topped up their teacups.

'It'll be great.' said Sally, trying to convince herself as much as him.

'If it's so great why not just see Guy, forget Peter' said Will, stealing a bit of Sally's brownie having finished his own, 'I don't agree with all this messing around; deception, falsehoods and trickery, it's no good. Focus on Guy, save your energy for him. Quite literally at your age. What if he finds out?'

'He won't.' said Sally.

She was definitely enjoying herself and having a lot of fun with Guy. Good, uncomplicated, fun. No need to go down the 'what if' road to 'but maybe' land.

'How about you?' she said, changing the subject, 'Have you thought about trying online dating? You did say …..'

'Oh god.' said Will, leaning forward and pulling a face, 'Eugene, you know, Eugene the gay nurse at work? Always had a thing for me but he knows it is never going to happen, he put me on Gaydar.'

'No.'

'Yes.'

'You're joking?'

'Nope. He said I needed to get out more.' said Will, 'I needed to meet people in the gay community.'

'He put you on it without you knowing?' said Sally, 'That's awful.'

'Terrible.' said Will, 'But he meant well. I think. 237 hits in 48 hours.'

'Oh no, have you taken yourself off it?'

'Well I haven't got through them all yet.' he said, 'Actually they're quite good looking in some of the pictures…'

'But…'

'Yeah, I know,' he finished her brownie, 'some of them are just penises.'

With two piles of un-packed clothes still strewn across the bed, Sally emptied out the hold-all and began to re-asses its contents. Again. How could she pack-lite for three days in a field in England? Biker style boots? Wellington boots? Converse high-tops? Strappy sandals? Flip-flops chunky? Flip-flops regular? That was one bag alone. And what about all the toiletries she now needed?

By lunchtime on the Friday, Guy still hadn't arrived. Sally looked at her over-stuffed bags, neatly assembled in the hallway, checked she'd put her camera in her shoulder bag, with the extra loo roll, two more in the hold-all; double checked she had her sunscreen, factor 15 and factor 25, just in case. She peered out of the window at the ominously greying sky and wondered if Guy had had a change of heart? Thought better of it? Gone without her? Then she heard her phone bleep.

Running late
 bit of a night
  see you in 20 or 40! xxxxx

And two smiley faces. Sally took off her sunglasses and put on the kettle. What 'bit of a night' she wondered, had Guy had? Hadn't he said he was getting an early night in, on the phone, when they'd talked last night? Not that it was any of her business. He could do what he liked. So, where had he gone? Thoughts of Andy flooded her mind, the endless all-nighters, the excuses, all those lies. Guy didn't seem to be that kind of… guy. But if she could deceive him then maybe… It began to rain softly, the kind of rain you can't see unless you look really hard, unless you're looking for something bad.

'Do you think I'll need this?' said Sally, waving her woolly, sequined-beanie.
Two cups of tea, three texts and half a packet of Waitrose maple syrup and pecan cookies, essential for any road trip, later, Guy had finally arrived.
'As well as this?' he said, holding up her floppy, straw, hippie hat and laughing.
Sally felt stupid. She didn't want to go. What was she doing? A middle-aged woman, a middle-aged menopausal woman, going to a festival? In a field? Camping? And why was he so late?
'This is ridiculous,' said Sally, flinging her bag onto the floor, 'I'm too old to go mad in a field.'
Where had Guy been half the night? Who was he with? Paranoia was eating away at her.
'But you can go mad in your hall?' he said.
'I don't want to go.'
'You haven't been to a festival for a while have you?' he said, putting the hold-all and the bag of footwear he'd just

picked up, down, 'They're full of old people.'

Sally pulled a face, he was not making her feel better.

'Ah ha,' he said, nodding, 'it's all mums and dads and wrinkly, grey-haired old musos.'

An ill-suppressed smile spread across his face.

'And that's just the main stage.'

Guy doubled up, laughing at his own joke. He grabbed Sally by the hand as she turned away, pulling her back towards him and kissing her hard on the lips.

'We are going to have a brilliant time,' he said, and kissed her again, 'in the rain, the sun, whatever. Honestly. I promise.'

Sally kissed him back but she still felt stupid. She must stop talking out loud, she thought.

'Sorry I was so late.'

He pressed himself against her in her hallway, kissing her. He'd seized his moment so Sally seized hers.

'Where were you,' she asked, as casually as she could, 'last night?'

'Ah gross.' said Max, pushing his way through the front door.

'Oh.' said Sally, springing back, 'Hi Darling.'

Guy slid his arm around her waist so she couldn't escape.

'Y'right mate?' he said, and smiled at Max.

'Thought you said you were going early.' said Max, stumbling over the scattered bags.

'We were,' said Sally, wriggling free and following him into the kitchen.

He pulled open the fridge door and peered in.

'I got some things.' said Sally, 'so you won't starve.'

'Cool,' said Max, taking in the stack of pizzas and packets of tortellini wedged onto the shelf. He snapped free a chocolate mousse from a four-pack and closed the door.

'So,' he said, 'when are you going?'

Sally sat in the passenger seat, the map book open across her knees, Guy singing along to Alt-J. They were still on the motorway. Outside the drizzly day was turning from dull to dark. Inside the air was thick with stale coffee and biscuit crumbs.

'Are you positive?' said Guy.

137

'Ah ha.' said Sally, rooting through the debris in the M&S carrier of provisions they'd bought at a service station some 80 miles earlier, pulling out empty crisp packets and sandwich wrappers.

'I was sure I'd picked up a bag of Wobbly Worms.'

'Nope,' she said, 'just Percy Pigs and Colin Caterpillars.'

'Fuck. Caterpillars it will have to be then.' he said, 'Please.' He opened his mouth wide like an expectant baby bird and Sally fed him a sour fruit caterpillar. Like a mother bird.

'Cool.' said Guy, peering up at another signpost.
Sally popped in another worm.

'Thanks, can you just check that turn-off again, I can't believe we're still on the motorway.'

Guy took it well when Sally realized they had in fact missed the turn-off. He didn't really do anger or angst, freaking out wasn't his style even though they were now well-off course, and schedule, and it was beginning to pour. Sally liked that about him.

'Never mind,' he said, flicking through the tracks on his phone with one hand, the other holding the wheel, 'it's not like we've got to put the tent up or anything.'
And he laughed, leaned over and squeezed Sally's knee.

'Looking forward to yurt sex?'
Sally smiled, he was lovely. Lovely and uncomplicated. Lovely and uncomplicated and… the thing was, the thing that was on her mind right now, was…

'It's my fault,' he said, 'should have just picked you up earlier, like I said.'
That was the thing. Sally hadn't mentioned it in the car but she did still want to know. Where had he been last night to make him so late today?

'Doesn't matter.' she said, hoping he would just tell her without her having to interrogate him, 'Gave me more time to sort stuff out.'
She didn't want to come over all Third Reich, appear uptight or worse, insecure.

'Yeah… and Si was OK about it, says he's got loads of help, amazing what people will do for a freebie to a festival. You'll like him, he's really cool, we didn't get on when I was a teenager but…'

'So where were you last night?' asked Sally, unable to contain herself but trying hard not to sound like a Nazi.

'Oh god,' said Guy, 'is this it? Can you just keep an eye out because we're coming at it from the opposite direction.'

Fuck it, Sally thought as they turned off the motorway, again, and she read out aloud the instructions in reverse until they were back on the road she hoped they should be on. A 'B' road in the dark.

'Do you think this is the right direction?' asked Guy, 'Because I fucking hope so, I really need to pee.'

'Um… yeah… so vare did you go?' she said, in a strange German accent.

What was she doing? She must shut up, now.

'Damn.' he said, peering over the steering wheel and into the darkness, 'Sometimes I really hate the countryside.'

'Last night? Did you go out?' Sally pressed on, unable to let it go now; she'd started, she had to finish, she couldn't stop herself, 'Get…. wasted?'

She laughed a shrill, high pitched laugh.

'No.' he said.

Fuck, fuck, fuck. She must stop speaking. Guy started to indicate, looking for the turning.

'My sister was in a bit of a state about the baby, you know new mums.'

'Oh.' said Sally, wishing she'd never mentioned it.

'Dave was working in the pub, she was freaking out so I went round.'

Why had she mentioned it? So what if he had gone out with his mates? What business was it of hers? Why had she questioned him? Her own devious ways seemed to have created a culture of suspicion.

'Was he OK?' she said.

'Think so.' he said, peering up as they past another signpost.

'Good, poor thing,' she said, feigning as much interest as she could muster into the health and welfare of Guy's new nephew, baby Arthur, while hoping above hope that maybe he hadn't noticed he'd been questioned, 'what was it?'

'He was just crying a bit but I think it was because she was all in a state. I calmed her down, she calmed him down and they both went to sleep. Then Dave came back.'

Guy stopped at a fork in the road and turned to look at Sally.

'We had a couple of drinks,' he said, 'I crashed out on their sofa. Nothing sinister.'

Of course there was nothing sinister, nothing suspicious going on. He lent forward and kissed her on the lips. Damn, she thought, he had noticed.

'Which way?'

He sounded angry. Was he angry? Sally scanned the instructions.

'Right.' she said.

Guy turned the wheel.

'Bloody noisy things babies, glad I don't want kids.'

Sally shook her head and smiled. How could she have been so stupid? They drove on in silence. She had to say something. Change the subject. Change the atmosphere.

'Brilliant,' he said, turning the music up as The Cure filled the car. He banged the steering wheel with his right hand in time to the music.'

'We missed you hissed the… love cats… So wonderfully wonderfully wonderfully wonderfully pretty…'

Seizing her opportunity, Sally said:

'I saw them years ago, Glastonbury, amazing.'

'I've got to pee now,' said Guy, 'we need to find a petrol station. Or a pub.'

'And the Pogues…' continued Sally, pleased she could reel-off her festival credentials and delighted they seemed to have moved on.

'Wow, really.' said Guy, leaning forward, 'Is that a petrol station? Bingo.'

'The Cure were amazing…'

Guy began to indicate and slow down.

'Brilliant summer.' she beamed.

'Cool,' he said, switching off the engine, 'yeah, my mum used to really like The Cure.'

Silenced, Sally sat in the green glow of the petrol station.

'Want anything?' he said, getting out of the car.

Top tip: to get summer arms fit to be held aloft when dancing in a field, buy two 1.5 litre bottles of mineral water. Drink the mineral water, fill with tap water and voila, instant dumbbells. Even 30 reps done daily will improve strength and tone.

CHAPTER 18

Sally lifted the lid of the cast iron casserole, the aromatic spices from the slow cooked lamb made the kitchen smell like a Moroccan souk.

'So,' she said, 'how are you feeling?'

'Good,' said Martin, sucking on an olive stone, 'very good indeed.'

He smiled and reached for another olive, he appeared to be in much better shape than Sally had expected. Much better shape than she was after spending several days under canvas, even yurt canvas, in a corner of the countryside that will be forever damp.

'I've got plans.'

'Plans?' said Sally, closing the kitchen drawer and putting the knives and forks on the table.

She had invited Martin to supper because she thought he would be feeling down, or at least reflective, now that he had broken-up with Katy. But after an embarrassingly brief hiatus he had started seeing Sophie.

'Yeah,' he said, retrieving the olive stone and dropping it into a tiny pink and silver Moroccan bowl on the table, 'I think I might be in love.'

His face cracked into a broad smile.

'Love?'

'Yeah.'

'Again?'

'Yeah,' he said, looking wistfully into the middle distance, 'she is... death. We went to the Serpentine.'

He popped another olive into his mouth.

'What? Rowing?'

'No,' he said, 'not the lake, the gallery.'

Martin removed another olive stone.

'She's very into all that. Art, theatre... it's great.'

'Oh yeah, because you like all that.' said Sally.

'I like to look at art.' he said, helping himself to some of the lamb and couscous that had now been placed on the table in a large blue, Mexican dish Sally had found at the Rose Bowl Flea Market, many years ago when she'd visited Martin in LA.

'And we're going to a show at the Tate,' he continued, 'and it's free to her.'

'The Tate is free to everyone.' said Sally, handing him a tea-towel in lieu of a napkin.

'No,' he said, looking perplexed, 'she's a member. We get to go in a special bar.'

He beamed the full-beam of a man in the first flush of new love.

'The member's bar.' he said.

'Really.' said Sally, a tad dismissively as she poured the wine Martin had handed over upon his arrival.

'Yeah, I think she's pretty keen too, she tweeted 'miss you love you' this morning.'

'She's half your age.' said Sally, 'She's lived her whole life with a mobile phone...'

'So?'

'And wheelie suitcases.'

'Age doesn't come into it. She has a very mature mind.'

'And that's what you're interested in?' said Sally, 'You're just looking for a nurse.'

'Actually,' said Martin, 'she is a nurse.'

'Well,' said Sally, 'there you go.'

She reached for her wine.

'What about you?' said Martin, 'Guy is way younger than you.'

'But much older than Sophie.'

'How was the festival?' he said, forking up mouthful of couscous, 'Did you see Patti Smith?'

'Aaagh.' Sally groaned, and gave her friend a painful look, 'No, we missed her, got there too late. It didn't go quite to plan.'

Having got lost, again, somewhere outside Yeovil, she and Guy had finally arrived at Sun Ray very late. Very cold. Very tired. In the rain. Without network coverage. It took another hour to finally get through the Stasi-inspired, backstage security and find Guy's brother. Their two-man yurt turned out to be already occupied by two of Guy's old friends: Big Dave, known thus because he was 6' 6", and his boyfriend Seymour, a man of similar stature but fatter. Also expected in the yurt that weekend was Luz, a Spanish Marilyn Monroe look-a-like and cabaret performer, able to spin 7 hoops simultaneously on various parts of her body while doing a strip tease. It also turned out that Guy used to date Luz. No, the weekend had definitely not been a success.

'But did you see…?'

'Probably not.'

'Paolo Nutini?'

'Nope.'

'Jack White?'

'No.'

'Jack Whitehall?'

'No.'

'Jack Dee?'

'I didn't really see much of anything.' said Sally, refilling their glasses, 'It rained. A lot.'

'What about Prince? I read a great review in…'

'Yeah, no, that was the only time the yurt was empty and Guy wanted us to make full use of the opportunity.'

'What?' said Martin, 'He wanted to sleep instead of seeing Prince?'

'No, idiot, have sex.'

Sally took a sizable slurp of her wine.

'Prince is not really his era.'

She took another gulp. Martin drained his glass, trying to comprehend this calamity.

'I saw John Cooper Clarke in the bar.' she said, 'Buying a drink.'

'Ah.' said Martin, tucking into his lamb, 'You do look a bit rough.'

'Thanks, I'm in bits.' said Sally, moon-faced and glum, 'I can't do this… dating a youth, it hurts.'

'Great lamb.' said Martin, by way of consolation.

'With lemony fennel.' said Sally, quoting the recipe she'd ripped from a Sunday magazine.

'Interesting,' said Martin, 'didn't know I liked fennel.' He examined the vegetable on the end of his fork.

'It rained virtually none stop and it was cold,' she reached for her glass, 'there was this big fire pit in the backstage bar in a sort of open-plan, tee-pee affair so we just stayed there, trying to get warm. And dry. And drunk.'

'Doesn't sound too bad to me.' said Martin, raising his glass.

'Then Luz the hoop-twirling-ex turned up after her show, practically naked. I can't believe Guy went out with her.' she said.

'Was she fit?'

'She's 30,' said Sally, draining her glass, 'she has no children, only circus skills, what d'you think?'

'Right.' said Martin, painting himself a mental picture.

'So she's speaking Spanish, and Guy's speaking Spanish, and this Argentine fire-eater is there, speaking Spanish, and he had some MDFA…'

'MA.'

'What?'

'I think you mean MDMA unless he was planning to build shelves.'

'Whatever,' said Sally, 'anyway they were all doing it so I did it. Then we were all speaking Spanish.'

'I didn't know you spoke Spanish?' said Martin.

'Neither did I,' said Sally, 'I think I over did it, I drank way too much.'

'It's better if you don't drink alcohol when you're doing…'

'She's a fucking acrobat,' said Sally, 'what would you have done?'

'Well…' said Martin, 'you've got a point.'

Despite the journey and the rain and the yurt full of strangers, Sally had tried to embrace the event. And she'd thought she'd been doing quite well until the lithe Luz turned up in the bar.

Neither tall, nor short there was nothing average about Luz: her lean body was hard, her arms and legs cut with muscle, decorated in garlands of tattooed hearts and flowers. There was not a trace of spare flesh. Anywhere. Unfortunately, the drink hit Sally about the same time she realized Luz was the same 'Spanish girl' as the 'Spanish girl' Guy had gone out with 'for a bit'. The same 'Spanish girl' whose breasts were orbs of perfection, her skin a luminous gold, her eyes pools of green jade, her hair a tousled mess of dirty blonde curls. Sally was mortified, even though Luz hung from the arm of a handsome Argentine whose intense blue eyes rarely left hers. Sally had barely been able to concentrate when his craggy, tanned face broke into frequent smiles and frowns while he explained that although his mother was half Swedish and his father was from Libya, he was wholly Argentinean. Then Luz had proclaimed loudly to Sally:

'Ahhh, you don't speak Spanish? We must speak English. All speak English!'

She'd laughed and smiled and then said something in Spanish. Sally had been about to wimp out of the tee-pee and into the storm when a short, bald man in a red satin ringmaster's suit came in from the rain, wearing full drag make-up and sporting a red satin top hat.

'Darling,' he'd shouted at Luz, taking off his hat with a flourish, dropping to one knee and singing:

'You… light up my life.'

Luz had squealed with delight, shouted:

'Gerald!'

before cartwheeling across the bar and catapulting herself onto his shoulders. His face now buried in her sequined crotch, Luz had leaned back arms out-stretched, while Gerald stood and spun her around with the ease of a man who was not unaccustomed to performance. Luz had artfully dismounted as several more flamboyantly dressed men, their feathers dripping, entered the tee-pee and upon seeing her had launched into Florence and The Machine's: *No Light, No Light.*

'Here come the girls,' Guy had said, laughing as he'd looked over at Sally, 'they'll be at it all night now.'

Luz had joined in the singing. Sally had looked perplexed.

147

'Luz,' Guy had said, shaking his head with the hilarity of it all, 'it's Spanish for light.'

They were at it all night.

'Wow,' said Martin, unable to suppress a smile, 'sounds like fun.'

'I don't think I slept again which was fine because there was about a dozen of us in the yurt by the end.'

'I see.'

'We had to give his friends a lift back to London,' said Sally, as she toyed with her couscous, 'squashed in the back of the car: me, my hangover, his friends, it nearly killed me. Guy seemed to think it was hilarious.'

'Right.' said Martin, 'Very rock and roll.'

'No.' said Sally, 'It was humiliating. I threw up at Fleet service station, he should come with a warning.'

'Partying can seriously damage your health,' said Martin, knowingly, 'especially at our age.'

'Thanks,' said Sally, 'for reminding me I'm age impaired.'

Martin poured more wine.

'So maybe he's not the one for you.' he said, and raised his glass, 'To sex, forget the drugs and rock 'n' roll.'

'The worse thing is,' said Sally, 'I felt old and uncomfortable and stupid and I missed...'

'Yes?' said Martin, forking down the last of the fennel.

'It made me miss Peter.'

Summer had finally arrived, heralded by the trumpeting hum of police sirens and ice-cream vans, wailing through windows flung wide against the heat. As the warm evening air turned cool, Sally was reminded of the long sultry nights when as a child she was sent to bed while it was still light; her brothers fighting in their bunk beds in the room next door, the air heavy with the scent of cut grass as her father mowed the lawn outside. Her only problems then the nagging whine of a mosquito, forcing her under the bedclothes. She was still feeling out of sorts after the festival; with age the recovery period was forever being extended. To make matters worse, she'd had a complete meltdown in Sainsbury's when she couldn't find the rough oatcakes. She'd complained bitterly to the stunned, young man in an over-sized orange fleece, slumped at the till, about the un-necessary need for the store to keep moving things around. Then, when a mother wheeling her small child in a buggy who persistently blew tunelessly into a one-note-whistle, followed her down the road, Sally had wanted to turn around and shout at the woman. And at the child. She'd wanted to tell the child to stop and the mother that she shouldn't be allowed to… be a mother, if she couldn't control the delinquent in the buggy. But obviously she hadn't. Instead, she just thought about doing it, but she'd thought about it for way too long. And then she'd told the girl in the corner shop all about it. And now, she realised, it was official, she was not only menopausal and old but grumpy too.

Perhaps that was why she was finding Guy increasingly difficult. He looked gorgeous, yes. He was lovely, for sure. But, the last time she'd stayed the night at his flat he'd kept leaping across the bed to email his colleagues every time he'd had another grand idea for the new build in Scotland, which was about every four seconds. It was very annoying especially as she was trying to come to grips with the third series of Lost, because he'd assured her that she should have stayed with it because it was essential viewing, and prompting her to shout,
'Stop it.'
like she was scolding a small, hyperactive child. She wanted to feel like Guy's lover mot like his mother. She did not like that feeling at all. And now she was becoming obsessed about the book he had given her because he'd said she would love it. And she had. How lovely, she'd thought, that he'd been so perceptive, it was quite a bold move to give someone you barely knew a book. And when she'd laid in bed at night, she'd thought about him as she'd turned the pages, about them sharing the same story. And when she'd found the words:
my light will guide you home and ignite your bones and I will try to fix you
written in pencil on the inside cover she hadn't really thought about it. But since Sun Ray she had thought about little else. And she thought, no she knew, it must have been written by Luz and she must have given him the book.

Sally had tried to rationalize the irrational thoughts flying around her irrational head. And then she'd thought, no she knew, he must want to be with Luz. Was it the menopause that was making her feel like this, she wondered, or was a double-life making her paranoid?

Top tip: wake up a tired face with a quick massage. Use a facial oil or a little almond oil: cup your face and use the heels of your hands moving from the middle of the chin, along the jaw line towards the ear, 20-30 times, tap around the eye sockets along the bone, with the middle finger, half a dozen times. Pinch along the eyebrows with finger and thumb a few times then press the area between the eyes with the middle finger of each hand and draw out smoothly towards the temples, 20-30 times.

CHAPTER 19

'Darling.'

Peter was waiting for her when Sally arrived at Schiphol Airport. She smiled as she walked through the throng towards him, a calmer more sedate manoeuvre than her arrival in Venice. Still feeling undone by the festival, she was a little anxious about seeing him, would he suspect she was two-timing him? But she needn't have been nervous.

'Come on,' he said, wrapping his arms around her and holding her close, 'the car is outside.'

He took the handle of her case.

'One small bag?' he said, looking down at her luggage, 'I've never met a woman who travelled with so little.'

He laughed and she laughed but inside Sally panicked: what had she not packed? Why didn't she have more luggage? What other women? Sally followed as he led the way, trying hard to dismiss her insecure thoughts. It would all be fine, she thought, Amsterdam would be great. That was the brilliant thing about Peter, he made her feel like nothing bad could happen.

'You'll love Mae,' he said, handing her bag over to a suited man who popped the trunk of the black town car.

'Mae?' said Sally, getting in while the driver held the door.

'Yes, Mae, she owns the place.'

Sally looked blank. Who the hell was Mae?

'Where we're staying?' Peter said, 'Known her for years.'

'Oh.' said Sally, processing this new piece of information and wondering how such an important fact had slipped her by.

'Didn't I say?'

'No.' said Sally, staring out of the car window at the endless flat, remembering the first time she'd arrived in the city, 'I don't think you did.'

In her youth, Sally had spent quite a few lost weekends in Amsterdam, when she'd first fallen in love with the city while visiting Martin. He had been working as a roadie for Tax Evasion, the first of many bands he would work with, full of hope and promise rarely fulfilled, before he abandoned his proposed career in the music business.

'Oh, I didn't? I thought I did.' said Peter, 'We used to live together. Briefly.'

Oh no, thought Sally, they were going to stay in a hotel owned by Peter's ex-girlfriend? What fresh hell was this?

'And her third novel won a Pulitzer then…'

'She's a writer?' said Sally, snapping back into the conversation.

'Yes darling, that's what I was saying, and now she's moved back to Amsterdam. I've been meaning to come visit her new place but somehow we only ever seem to catch up when she comes to New York. Except one time in Paris.'

Paris, thought Sally? Who was this woman?

'That was all years ago,' said Peter, 'she prefers the quieter life these days. After she was briefly with Lou Reed…'

'Lou Reed?'

Peter's ex was Lou Reed's ex?

'She's a little older than me of course.' he said.

'Oh,' said Sally, brightening up, 'and she's Dutch?'

'Dutch, French, Italian and Chilean I believe, speaks a dozen languages. You're going to love her darling.'

Am I, wondered Sally?

The car stopped in a narrow, cobbled street and the driver got out to open her door before retrieving their bags from the boot. It was all very different from the day she'd stood on Prins Hendrikkade, her back to Central Station, studying the piece of paper on which she'd carefully written the instructions Martin had carefully explained to her. Just come, he'd said, after she'd told him she'd met a boy called Ed she really liked but he was going out with a girl she really didn't like. Just come, Amsterdam is brilliant, he'd said, it'll cheer you up, we're playing The Paradiso, get the bus. And Martin had been waiting for her, sitting at the bar of the sticky-floored, Dutchman, drinking a beer talking to Dan, an old friend from school now working there as a barman since he'd given up a promising career in graphic design and followed his heart, and Angelina-from-Glasgow. Angelina had worked in the peep-show and was saving up to get her teeth fixed by the apparently excellent Dutch dental system while Dan was mainly getting stoned and writing a comic book that involved a magic penis.

They'd eaten space-cake and drunk Chocomel in a wooden benched café full of glazed people and bad art, somewhere near the Zeedijk, and watched dark eyed boys smoking cigarettes chat up fresh faced girls in Dam Square. On Leidseplein, they'd met an English girl selling glittery scarves she'd brought back from India and Sally had bought one. The night Tax Evasion played the Paradiso she had worn her new scarf and Martin had said she was the coolest girl at the gig. Sally had known this was not really true but she had thought it was very sweet of him to say so and through the heady haze of yet another joint she'd kissed him. On the lips.

But later, back at the Dutchman, when Sally had sat at the bar dinking Jenever and waiting for Martin to finish his band meeting, she had been mesmerized by Dan and his comic intentions. And when Dan had lent over and kissed her before leading her behind the bar and up the stairs to his room, she'd followed. And Martin had barely spoken to her the next day.

On the roof terrace of The Merchant House, overlooking the canal, Sally and Peter sat in the early evening sun, doused in the warmth as the shadows lengthened. She had felt very happy as she'd unpacked her things, hung up her dress, ready for the following night, making plans with Peter. Happy and excited.

'Proost,' said Mae, smiling as she raised her own glass, 'at last you have come.'

Happy and excited until Mae had finally appeared, up on the

roof: a small woman with expensive hair, she appeared to have retained much of her youthful beauty. And her petite, cosmopolitan bottom.

'Now my friends,' she said, draining her glass and stubbing out her cigarette, 'I must go, I am meeting my Philippe for dinner. I will see you both tomorrow. But not too early.'
She waged a many-ringed finger at them. Age had certainly not diminished her.

'You never were a morning person.' laughed Peter.

'I shall take you for the best coffee at my favorite café,' she said, 'they make fresh Stroopwafel, very naughty.'
She patted her bony backside, laughed and rummaged in her large, red leather Birkin bag.

'I can never find a thing.' she said, pulling out a small black notebook, retrieving a card and handing it to Peter, 'This is a wonderful place to eat. Very romantic.'
She winked at Sally.

'Beautiful bag.' said Sally.

'I know,' said Mae, 'Jane is always so generous.'
 She pulled on her butter-soft, black leather jacket.

'But then she has so many.' she said, over her shoulder, 'Ciao darlings.'

'Jane?' said Sally, 'Jane Birkin?'
She had been somewhat taken aback by the vision that was Peter's-ex. Why couldn't she have been an orange-tanned, sun-dried, Euro-husk, thought Sally? Or fat? She began to develop an irrational hatred of continental women of a certain age.

'She actually knows Jane Birkin?'

'What's that?' said Peter, stabbing at his Blackberry, 'Yes I believe she was one of her bridesmaids. Look darling.'
He held up his phone with childlike delight so she could see the map he was looking at. Sally smiled thinly, she wanted to be Mae. He took off his glasses and leant over to kiss her, did he know she needed reassurance?

'I've found the restaurant.' he said.
 He smelt of wood and lemons and Sally felt better as she embraced his embrace. She needed to get a grip, get over it and not let it ruin what was supposed to be a fabulous weekend. Her phone started ringing, she knew it was Guy, she

should never have texted him to say she had arrived safely to see an, 'old friend'. What if Peter found out she was seeing someone else, she wondered? But what if he didn't care?

'Brilliant.' she said, with steely resolve, and kissed him right back.

'Shall we finish our drinks and go?' he said. 'Are you hungry?'

Sally nodded and smiled.

'Good,' said Peter, reaching for her hand, 'I'm so glad you came Sally, I think this was a really good idea.'

'Me too.' said Sally, really hoping it was.

She turned to look back across the red tile-topped roofs, such a different view from the nights of smoke and mirrors she'd spent with Martin all those years ago.

'I'll be just one minute,' said Sally, 'I need to pee.'

After a morning spent mooching around Amsterdam, and an afternoon in bed, 'catching up', as Peter had put it, they'd both fallen asleep. Now, they'd arrived late to the dinner to celebrate Antony Gormley's, Bridging the Dyke, part of the Brits Abroad art project, the reason for Peter's trip.

'No rush.' he said.

Still glowing from their recent afternoon activities, Sally was feeling much happier. A lot happier than she'd felt the night before in the restaurant when the raging imagines of Mae and Peter in their hay-day had been hard to dismiss. And when Guy had sent her two more texts she'd felt quite sick, making coherent conversation quite difficult to conduct. The deceit was proving harder to swallow than she'd imagined. But Peter was an easy talker, he never seemed to have nothing to say, and that, along with her mindful consumption of minimal alcohol had meant she'd kept her mouth shut. She'd been a bit quiet yes, but at least she hadn't cross-questioned him about his previous lover.

Waiting in the bar for Sally to come back, Peter pulled his phone from his inside pocket and checked the text he'd just received from Karen. Without responding to the message he pressed delete, that was definitely not going to happen. That, he'd decided, was a lucky escape and anyway, things with Sally were going even better than he'd hoped. Sometimes, he thought, she seemed to just glow with good energy. And their siesta had been seriously enjoyable, even if it had meant they'd now arrived late. She was so uncomplicated compared to the women he was used to, no strange dietary needs or crazy health regimes. She had a certain confidence about her too, didn't have to talk and talk, that was very sexy, Peter thought, Sally did silence very well. And being a little more mature than his usual dates meant for once he could have a conversation without having to explain every cultural reference, he could really open up to her, a new thing for him and he rather liked it.

'Darling,' he said, dropping his now bleating phone, still unanswered, back into his pocket as Sally walked towards him, 'you look seriously wonderful.'
He meant it, she really did, in her midnight-blue dress. Maybe, he thought, he might have missed a trick not dating women closer to his own age before.

'Thank you,' she said, as she kissed him, 'so do you.'
And he did she thought, now if she could only keep her paranoid thoughts in-check they would have a wonderful evening. A drink to calm her nerves is all she needed.

'Sally. Sally. Sally. SALLY.'
Slumped forward, sitting on the cold, stone steps, Sally was trying hard to open her eyes. She could hear the insistent booming of her name being repeated over and over from somewhere far away.

'Sally, come on, Sally. Sally. Sally.'
She felt chilly. Where was she? She needed to open her eyes and focus on something, anything, that wasn't moving. This, she believed, would stop her from feeling so sick. She swung her head up to seek out such an object and came face to face with the source of the noise. A man with a worried expression was shouting at her. Peter. It was Peter.

'Peter.'
She smiled up at him before flopping sideways onto the steps and passing out.

'Oh no you don't,' said Peter, 'come on Sally. Sally. Sally.'
But it was useless. Believing the walk would help, he had managed to get her most of the way back to the hotel, a

relatively short distance from the dinner, just along the canal. They were almost there but now she was out cold. There was only one thing for it. He braced himself, then hauled her forward and up over his shoulder in an inelegant fireman's lift. Staggering backward on the uneven cobbles, he almost lost his balance, before attempting the last few metres through the pain in his now throbbing right knee.

Once at their hotel, and with Sally now safely laying across the bottom step, Peter paused to regain his breath. This was not quite how he'd envisaged the evening would end. He searched through his pockets for the keys to the front door and having located them unlocked both the outer and inner doors before turning to find Sally had gone.

'Sally,' he shouted, 'Sally.'

He ran down the steps as Sally weaved her way across the cobbled road towards the canal.

'It's so beautiful,' she said.

He grabbed her arm and swung her round.

'All the lights.'

Indeed, the lights from the bridge did look beautiful, reflected in their twinkling glory in the inky canal below.

'Yes darling,' he said, 'shall we go inside?'

'We should go on the roof,' said Sally, flinging her arms around his neck, 'look at the stars and dance.'

She smiled up at him, Peter was so lovely. Amsterdam was so lovely.

'I'm hungry.' she said, 'Are you hungry?'

Lying beneath the crisp, white, Egyptian cotton duvet, Sally took a moment to work out where she was. She looked about the room, pale and muzzed in the white glow from the muslined windows. She could not remember getting undressed but there were her clothes: her dress, laid over the armchair in the corner, her bag on the floor next to her shoes, where presumably she had kicked them off last night, her earrings on the bedside table. Now she thought about it she couldn't actually remember leaving the dinner, or walking home. Beside her, the bed was empty but the sound of running water coming from the bathroom suggested that Peter must be in the shower. She smiled and reached for the glass on the bedside table where she assumed he had put it, how kind she thought, as she took a sip and reflected on the evening. What a brilliant time they'd had, hadn't they? She felt surprisingly well, considering she couldn't really recall much of what had happened after the dinner, which she could remember perfectly. And the speeches. And meeting Stephen Fry and talking about… what? What had they talked about?

Sally got out of bed and, in what she imagined was a cute move, picked up Peter's shirt from where he'd left it hanging on the back of an adjacent chair. She put it on, turned back the cuffs and poured herself a cup of coffee. Peering at her reflection in the large, pewter framed mirror she was not wholly disappointed with her morning-after look. Her hair was suitably bed-headed and now she had removed the sleep from her eyes and smudged the mascara a little more artfully with her finger, it may not quite be Bardot but it wasn't bad, especially if Peter didn't put on his glasses.

'So you're awake.'

She swung round to find him, robed in white towelling, wielding an electric razor in the doorway of the bathroom.

'Yes.' she said, smiling.

Glancing down, she noticed something on the front of her Vivienne Westwood.

'How are you feeling?' he said, a genuine note of concern in his voice.

'Fine.' she said, examining the dress, was that vomit? 'What… oh.'

'Oh.' said Peter.

Sally looked back at his stern expression, she felt hot and unsteady on her legs as a fuzzed memory began to take shape. Sitting down on the bed, she conjured the image of Peter looming towards her through the darkness of the night before, asking her if she was alright. And there were lights, lots of bright lights….

'Are you alright?'

And Stephen Fry, laughing…

'Are you alright?'

And flowers…

'Are you alright?'

And leaves…

158

'Sally.'

She looked up at Peter as he broke through her reverie.

'Are you alright?'

'Yes, no,' she looked over at the dress, 'what happened?'

'I thought you could tell me.'

Laying back against the pillows, Sally pulled the duvet about her. Clearly something had happened last night. Something bad. That was not supposed to happen. She pushed her hair away from her face and a small twig fell from the tangle.

'That'll be from the bush.' said Peter, removing the stem and raising an eyebrow, 'Well the ornamental foliage. On the terrace?'

Sally looked blank.

'You fell in.'

She felt sick.

'I don't remember that.' she said.

'Well I don't think the rest of the guests will ever forget it.' said Peter, raising the other eyebrow.

He turned away but he wasn't laughing.

'I remember the speeches and…' she sniffed, 'and everything and then we went to the bar and…'

'That's where I left you,' said Peter, pulling back the curtain to let in the morning light, 'you seemed fine then.'

'I was talking to Stephen…'

'You were drinking Old Fashioneds.'

'There was another man…'

'Jan, friend of Fry's, Dutch performance artist.'

'He wanted to go outside…'

'That's where I found you.'

'He had a joint…'

'Sitting in the bush,' said Peter, 'laughing.'

And then Sally did remember. She remembered another call from Guy and trying to silence her phone and then… Oh god, she'd smoked a joint and fallen in the ornamental foliage. In front of everyone. Peter turned and looked at her as her eyes filled with tears. He could not bear to see a woman cry. The silent sobs of his mother, her back to him in the tiny kitchen of their fourth floor, Greenwich Village walk-up, drawing heavily on her cigarette, oblivious to her young son's presence, were an abiding memory of his childhood.

159

'Sally.' he said.

Too late, big fat tears were rolling down her cheeks.

'But I didn't… I don't… I never… not for years…'

The rest was lost in snotty sobs. Peter sat on the bed and pulled her towards him.

'It's alright.' he said, smiling now as he hugged her.

'No it's not.' she said, from deep inside his towelling robe.

'No more tears.' he said, holding her tight.

'It's all ruined. I've ruined everything.'

'Darling,' he wiped her cheeks with his cuff, 'don't be silly, you just got a little high that's all.'

She sniffed violently.

'Well very high.' he said, 'Very, very high.'

'But it was only one…'

'They don't make pot like they used to,' he said, 'but you'll know for next time.'

He was laughing now.

'And you were very funny, sitting amongst the leaves and flowers. You really didn't want to come out.'

Sally groaned at the thought, she felt mortified.

'But it's awful,' she said, 'what did everyone… people will talk.'

'Darling, this is Amsterdam,' said Peter, 'no one really noticed. MOMA maybe. Or the Guggenheim…'

He furrowed his brow in mock horror at the thought and hugged her again. She struggled to free herself from his embrace, he was taking the piss now, laughing at her distress.

'Probably be looking at a law suit at the very least.'

He shook his head but couldn't keep a straight face.

'Don't,' she said, but she was smiling now, 'this is terrible.'

'That's better,' he said, 'I've made you smile and you do have such a beguiling smile.'

He kissed her again.

'I can't believe it.'

'Well,' he said, 'I was rather surprised. I blame Fry, leading you astray.'

'Are you limping?' said Sally, noticing his gait as he crossed the room.

'College football injury,' he said, 'plays up occasionally.' He didn't think it necessary to detail her undignified arrival at the hotel or Mae helping him get her into bed.

'And you're really not mad with me?' said Sally.

'No darling, as long as you don't make a habit of it,' Peter smiled, at her 'and thankfully Gormley's an old friend.'

Top tip: for a perfect pout and to ensure every day is an Angelina Jolie day, give your lips a quick brush with an electric toothbrush, sloughing off the dry bits and boosting circulation.

CHAPTER 20

'You threw up?' said Jaz, 'On Antony Gormley's shoes?'

'Well,' said Sally, 'technically only one shoe.'

'Sick.' Jaz shook her head, 'No Turner Prize for you.'

'I don't remember a thing. I was too out of it.'

'Maybe that's how to win the Turner, did you tell him it was art?'

They were sitting in the sun filled window of Home, a brand-new café, studying the menu; they were there to spy on the competition. It smelt of strong white flour,

...All bread baked on the premises...

jam,

...All preserves are made with fruit organically grown in the garden of our sister café in Southwold...

and turps

...the building has been lovingly renovated.

Done out in the manner of a post-war tearoom, it offered 20th century favourites such as Welsh Rarebit and Toad-in-the-Hole, all at 21st century prices. Polenta and pistachio cakes had been eschewed and instead there were scones and Chelsea buns, fondant fancies and a Victoria sponge on a crenulated, glass cake-stand. The waitresses wore different coloured, gingham pinnys and a bell jangled every time anyone came through the door.

'What do you think?' asked Jaz.

'I think I got greedy,' said Sally, 'I wanted my cake, and everyone else's cake, and I wanted to eat them all. I can't do this.'

'We'll have a piece of the Victoria sponge' said Jaz, to the waitress, pretty in pink and white check, 'and tea for two... and the lemon drizzle and the date and walnut slice.'

'And a little jam tart.' said Sally.

The waitress smiled, adjusted an errant curl from a mop of burnished-copper hair, held back with a matching pink scarf, and repeated their order for accuracy.

'Why did you get so out of it?' said Jaz, relinquishing her menu.

'I didn't plan to,' said Sally, 'I was freaked out. Guy kept calling and Peter was being so sweet and Jane-bloody-Birkin was...'

'Jane Birkin was there?'

'Just her bag but it was bad enough, it was all too much.' she said, sniffing back a wave of tears as her shameful behaviour was brought into sharp relief, it was a sobering thought.

'I'm going to stop the whole thing,' she poured the tea, 'right now. I've tried and failed to be a philanderer. I was wrong, it's not fun.'

'So what now?'

'Not sure, I'm still figuring it out. Anyway,' she stabbed at the sponge, 'did you go?'

'The doctor or Dorset?'

'Both.' said Sally, who'd been so appalled at her friend's lack of smear tests and breast checks, especially as she'd said she was getting more periods not less, that she'd badgered and bored her into making an appointment.

'Doctor said breasts are spectacular but,' she wrinkled her nose, 'might have something, doctor says probably nothing, but I have to have a colposcopy or whatever, sounds horrid.'

'It's not,' said Sally, 'well it is but it's nothing. It will be nothing.'

'You hope.'

Sally did hope. It must be nothing. She did not want to lose another friend. When Mia had first been diagnosed with breast cancer she'd talked about dying and Sally had told her friend to dismiss the very idea of such a thing, convinced in this time of modern medicine that cancer was about as bad as the common cold. The worse that would happen, she'd said, was that they'd be condemned to a life of running through the streets at night, wearing pink bras on their heads. It would all be all right. And if things didn't work out for the best, not that there was any chance of that, then they would have the death conversation. The one you see in the movies, movies that she and Mia had watched together when they were teenagers, where beautiful people died beautifully, leaving memory tapes and journals for their beautiful kids. Except it wasn't a movie and it wasn't beautiful.

'Make sure you go.' she said.

'It's not like I was party central,' said Jaz, 'blokes get away with it, drinking, smoking, shagging. I have a couple of extra sexual partners and tick the no-kids box and now what? I get penalised?'

She took a quick drag on her fake fag.

'It'll be nothing,' said Sally, 'you'll be fine.'

Mia's death had been slow and painful and ugly. And they never had had that conversation. Instead, Sally had talked enthusiastically each time a new procedure was suggested or another drug introduced and Amazoned her books about women who'd survived half a dozen cancers. Until, finally, the disease had taken Mia's mind and then her life.

'Don't not go.' said Sally.

'We're screwed from every direction,' said Jaz, 'single women out having fun are slags, single woman who aren't are pitied whereas the bachelor lifestyle is craved.'

'Don't just leave it.'

'It's not fair.' said Jaz.

'None of it is fair.' said Sally.

She missed Mia and she did not want to hear another friend say she'd wished she'd gone to the doctor sooner.

'Don't worry, I'll go,' said Jaz, 'it couldn't be worse than your nagging.'

She reached for the strainer and poured more tea.

'And Dorset?' said Sally, 'Tell me everything.'

Jaz had spent the weekend with the man she had lusted after for over two whole years of her life: 19 through 21. Now, thanks to the power of Facebook, after so many, many years of separation, they had been re-united.

'Moustache.' said Jaz.

'No.' said Sally, trying to stifle a laugh and failing.

Matt Boorman had been a god when Jaz had first laid eyes on him, while she was studying English and Drama at University, back before it was Uni. It had been love at first sight for her. Not so for him. A wiry boy in skin-tight jeans, a luxuriant head of tousled, dirty blonde locks framing dreamy-blue eyes and a Rotten sneer.

'Yep. And fat.'

Sally was rocking backwards and forwards now, gnawing her arm.

'Well, heavy.' said Jaz, straight faced, 'A lot heavier than he was.'

'But he was gorgeous.'

'I know.'

'And skinny.' said Sally.

'I know.'

'Didn't you see a picture? Before? On his Face… wall… thing?'

'Nope. It's a fish. A trout I think,' said Jaz, 'he's really into fishing.'

'Right.'

'We thought we'd just talk on the phone, we wanted to… surprise each other.'

'Well that worked.' said Sally.

'Yep.'

'That's why I hate surprises.'

Matt had been in his third year, doing English and French, when Jaz had made it her mission to engage him. Finally, he'd noticed her, in a pub near college in Brighton. He was working behind the bar. It had been late, last orders, there had been talk of a party. There was always talk of a party. Jaz had spent the entire summer holidays sulking because she'd thought she'd lost him, despite the distractions of a trip to pick things in France, and a brief dalliance with a Swede amongst the grapes or the olives or whatever it was that stained her fingers and scratched her hands. And then she'd found him, behind the bar of the pub near college in Brighton. He'd been there all summer.

'The thing is,' said Jaz, 'we did have a real connection.'

'You hardly knew him.' said Sally, poking the lemon drizzle.

'Love is not measured in weeks, hours, minutes.' said Jaz, dissecting the date and walnut slice, 'It was intense.'

Fuelled by her undying love and quite a lot of beer, Jaz had finally caught his attention, outside the pub, her back pressed against the rough, red brickwork of the Victorian hostelry, her tongue in his mouth. His hand in her pants. They'd never made it to the party. But they had made it to his room in a flat he'd shared with his brother, and his brother's friend, in Kemp Town. On the way there they'd bought more cigarettes and a bottle of cheap white wine. Matt's bed had been a single mattress on the floor, his sheets grey and disheveled, ridged against the wall; the room hung in an orange glow from an Indian prayer scarf draped over the lamp that stood on a milk-bottle crate topped with an album cover. The ashtray had been full. The matchbox empty. A candle melted almost flat in a saucer. Jaz had stood and looked around the walls, postered with Bob Marley, David Bowie and a garishly coloured Shiva, her heart beating fast. Matt had made them a joint with the last of his red Leb. They'd laid on the bed smoking and kissing, listening to Elvis Costello. The sex had been energetic, short but plentiful. The next day Matt had phoned her in the house she shared with two other girls from college and a pale boy called Jonathan. He'd told her he really liked her and that he would write. And maybe they could meet up somewhere in India. Or Nepal. If he wasn't back next week with dysentery. He'd laughed and said he missed her already. On the following Tuesday he'd flown to Delhi. Over the ensuing months he'd sent her two aerograms. Jaz had sent him seven.

'Yes,' said Sally, forking up a wedge of the Victoria sponge, 'but everything was intense then. Watching The Young Ones was intense.'

'It just wasn't our time.' she said, 'Then.'

'But he's got a moustache.' said Sally, 'Now.'

'He took me to a gig at some new arts centre,' said Jaz, 'one of those super-bands, you know, made up of old people:

a spider from Mars, a Mott the Hoople, one of them played with Bob Dylan. Once.'

'God,' said Sally, pulling a face, 'ghastly.'

'Actually,' said Jaz, tucking into the Lemon Drizzle Loaf, 'it was quite good, I'll send you the Youtube link.'

She started pressing buttons on her phone. Sally was quite surprised by her friend's enthusiasm for Matt and a bunch of old rockers.

'He was really sweet and he makes me feel… good.' she said, smiling at the thought of him, 'It's lot easier to feel like Elle MacPherson and less like Elmer Fudd when you're with someone like Matt.'

'Right.' said Sally

Jaz had a point.

'I can't believe you're still not on Facebook,' she said, as she topped up their teacups, 'you never know who might get in touch, opens up a whole new world into the future.'

No it doesn't, thought Sally, it's the past. She didn't want to go on Facebook and she didn't want to drag her previous life into her present. The future had failed to deliver on its promise of silver suits and jet packs; tomorrow's world looked suspiciously like the 70s. The arrival of the home computer may not have furthered world peace and solved poverty but at least everyone everywhere could now Google their boyfriend or track down their exes. This wasn't communication, Sally thought, this was rampant egoism. Was a life not yet Youtubed now considered not worth living?

'Matt has changed,' Jaz continued, 'and so have I but it's great talking about college and Brighton, all that stuff, catching up, he's still really into his music.'

'Is he still in a band?'

'No,' said Jaz, trying the Victoria sponge, 'he's in IT.'

She passed the date and walnut to Sally.

'And the sex was quite good.'

'But that was so long ago.' said Sally.

'No,' said Jaz, shaking her head, her mouth full of cake, 'now.'

'You had sex?' said Sally, 'You had sex with fat Matt and his moustache? Now? When you just went to Dorset, now?'

'Ah ha, course I did,' said Jaz, 'it might be time to settle.'

'Settle?'

'Yeah, settle for what I've got, rather than hang-on for what I want.' she said.

Sally winced.

'Besides,' said Jaz, 'he's not really fat fat.'

She pronged another piece of sponge.

'And people can shave.'

She finished her cake.

'Plus, do you have any idea how much the train ticket costs to get down there?'

Was Jaz right, wondered Sally, should she eschew younger men and long-distance lovers and go on Facebook instead, look up the lost lovers from her youth?

Peter gestured to the barman for his check. A cool breeze from the open door to the smoking yard blew over him, bringing with it a sudden release from the sticky humidity of the thunderous night. He took a couple of long, deep breaths as the breeze swirled once more like the ghost of Elvira, and caught the faint scent of a perfume, a familiar smell he knew but could not place. It was time to go to the restaurant, he could put it off no longer but it was the last thing he wanted to deal with: dinner with Carrie and Ted, his ex-wife, Lee, and Bill. He did not feel good but he'd promised he'd go and he wasn't about to start breaking his word to his daughter. Not anymore.

He hadn't felt great since getting back, Amsterdam hadn't exactly panned out as he'd hoped. What had got into Sally? He'd never seen her so agitated or so drunk. Or so stoned. Maybe he'd been wrong about her, maybe she didn't get him the way he'd thought she did. Maybe it was time to call it a day. Or maybe she did? Maybe she sensed he was lying about his 'marriage', maybe that's why she got so out of it? Maybe he wasn't being fare to her? Turning, he saw a woman now standing nearby at the bar, attractive, early 40s, she looked nervous. Peter caught her eye and smiled. She looked surprised, as if trying to recognise him, then turned back to her phone now beeping its message. She smiled, her date was here and coming her way. The man introduced himself and her obvious disappointment was palpable. A blind date, thought Peter, shifting in his seat. Was that the world he wanted to get back into? Still out there, still the big dame hunter? But it had been a long time since he'd made a commitment to anyone. His chest felt tight and his head was beginning to ache, he took another breath and remembered where he knew that familiar scent from, it was the same perfume Sally wore.

'The check?' said the barman, smiling expectantly at Peter.

'No,' said Peter, as he sank back into his seat, 'can I get one more of these?'

He gestured at his empty glass.

Top tip: to improve your cognitive function learn something new like a musical instrument or another language, it's never too late.

CHAPTER 21

'And release,' commanded Fenella, 'are you breathing?'

Barely, thought Sally. She had fucked up in Amsterdam.

'Shoulders away from your ears… look up.'

But had she fucked up with Peter?

'Chin down, let your thoughts go.'

But did she even care?

'Keep your mind in the room.'

Did she want to see Peter? Did she want to see Guy?

'All fingers flat on the mat, push back and lift.'

Did she want to see anyone?

'Downward facing dog.' barked Fenella.

Perhaps she wasn't cut out for relationships, she thought, perhaps…

'I think,' said Joan, zipping up her brightly coloured fleece, after the class was over, 'you think too much.'

'Yes,' said Rose, her German accent still strong despite having arrived in England as a Jewish refugee in the Second World War, 'really dear, is it such a problem?'

'No, I suppose not,' said Sally, well not compared to surviving Nazi Germany, she thought, 'but…'

'But what you gonna do?' Rose pulled on her windcheater, 'You've just got to get on with it.'

She was right, thought Sally, they were all right. These women had lived for so long, seen so much, watched babies come and children grow and friends die. They laughed at her worries. Laughed at her menopausal madness. Growing old certainly hadn't dampened their lust for life. She would stop thinking about Peter and Guy, at least for now, she had better things to do today.

The sky had curdled to a milky heat haze by the time Sally reached the cafe. She found a table in the cool shade at the back, where the French windows opened out on to the crowded terrace, and waited for Poppy to arrive. It was a hot day, hot but lovely, and really lovely to have such a lovely daughter, Sally thought, who'd suggested doing something as lovely as having tea with her mother. Catching her slouching reflection in the mirror on the wall opposite, Sally sat up straight and squared her shoulders, reminded of her Grandmother who still had such good posture, even in her nineties, her strong jaw and the soft lines belying her age, and Sally hoped, really, really hoped, the genes would eventually prevail.

'I'm getting married.' said Poppy.

'What?' said Sally, now fully focussed on her daughter.

'Married.' said Poppy, louder.

The marriage gene was still going strong in the family, if the bone structure was not.

'Are you mad?' said Sally, 'Are you pregnant? Oh god, I can't be a grandmother.'

They had ordered a pot of tea, and were sharing a slice of dark, rich ginger cake and an apricot and almond tart.

'A grandmother? Oh my god,' said Poppy, cleaving the tart in two, 'I knew you'd be like this. It's always about you. No I am not pregnant.'

'Then why are you getting married?' said Sally, reaching for her tea.

'This is so typical of you.' said Poppy, 'Why do I have to be pregnant? Why can't I just be in love and want to get married. Me and Habib love each other, actually, and we're getting married.'

She divided the ginger cake in half.

'But,' said Sally, stirring a teaspoon of sugar into her tea to combat the shock, 'why? Why can't you just live together like

172

normal people? Why do you want to get married? And why now?'

'Because that's what we want to do.' said Poppy, taking a bite of her cake, 'Some mothers might actually be pleased their child was in a proper, committed relationship…'

'I am,' said Sally, 'of course I…'

'And want to get married and buy a house and have a family,' continued Poppy, 'happy that their daughter has found the one.'

'But how do you know he's the one?' said Sally, wondering if she might be able to glean some insight from her daughter, 'You're so young.'

'How does anyone know?' said Poppy, smiling wisely, 'How did you know?'

That was something Sally was still trying to figure out of course.

'Have you told your father?' she asked, pouring more tea.

'No,' said Poppy, 'not yet.'

'Well, good luck with that.'

Sally dug into the tart.

'You were with dad at my age.'

'I wasn't married at your age.'

'But you ended up marrying him.' said Poppy, triumphantly.

'And look how well that turned out.' said Sally.

'Oh my god,' said Poppy, 'are you saying I am the product of a loveless marriage?'

'No,' said Sally, taking another sip of her tea, why were her kids so crap? 'not exactly.'

'Habib has his degree now,' said Poppy, taking another sip of her tea, 'and he's got a really good job. And when I've finished my furniture design…'

'I thought you were doing knitwear?' said Sally.

'I just feel that I'm better suited to furniture.' said Poppy, 'Anyway, that doesn't matter, it's all part of the creative process.'

'Right,' said Sally, resigning herself to the situation, 'congratulations.'

She wished the café was licensed.

'Thanks,' said Poppy, beaming, 'I knew you'd be pleased.'

Sally forked up a piece of cake, pleased might not be the first word that sprung to mind.

'And,' said Poppy, 'we're going to America.'

'What?' said Sally, mid-mouthful.

'Yeah, Habs has got it all sorted, he's got a job and a sponsor,' she said, 'and it's too good an opportunity to miss so I'm going to defer for a year and…

'Can you do that?'

Sally tried to take on board the enormity of her daughter's revelation.

'Mother,' said Poppy, rolling her eyes and prodding the tart, 'loads of people do it. Anyway, that's why we've decided to get married now.'

'OK.' said Sally, trying to convince herself it was OK. Maybe it wouldn't be so bad. Perhaps Poppy had a point, wasn't it a good thing she'd found the one? At least someone had found the one.

'But we would have got married anyway,' continued Poppy, 'because we're in love.'

Sally refilled her cup. She badly needed a proper drink.

Peter couldn't sleep. It had been a long evening and he'd felt quite exhausted when he'd finally left the restaurant, kissed his daughter good-night and hailed a cab, but now he was in bed the evening unwound, replayed in an endless loop. He got up and padded through to the kitchen, the amber glow from the street lights casting familiar shadows across the room. He poured himself a glass of water but decided better of it, a proper drink was what he really needed.

It had been a very different evening to the one he'd been expecting that was for sure, seeing Lee and Bill for the first time in however many years it was. Bill had looked so old. He guessed since they'd last seen each other, he must have changed some too, and Bill's failed knee operation had obviously taken its toll, he certainly talked about it enough. Boring was something else Bill never used to be. And Lee? He'd somehow imagined she would have retained her youthful bloom, or at least her sense of humour, yet she was so, what? Still an attractive woman but so… pinched. They had appeared to be more uncomfortable than him. And all that fussing over the food, what they could and couldn't eat, Lee watching every glass of wine Bill drank. All two of them. For years Peter had imagined their wonderful life, her living her dream with Bill. His dream. But if that mean life was her dream he was glad he was no part of it.

What, he wondered, had he been so worried about for all these years? If he'd only dealt with it at the time how differently might his life have turned out? He'd have seen a lot more of his daughters, he thought, as he noticed, lying on his desk where he'd thrown it when he'd first got back from the hospital, the book Dr. Goodfellow had forced on him.

'I've been a fool.' he said, picking it up and flicking through the pages.

'Really? Am I drowning?'

Top tip: to feel instantly youthful and supple, find an exercise class with a predominance of older people.

CHAPTER 22

Sitting on the bar stool adjacent to Sally, his right knee jiggling against her left knee, Guy talked animatedly about his eco-project while determinedly picking out all the cashews from the blue glass bowl of mixed nuts the barman had placed between them.

'The thing is,' he said, plucking out another nut, 'this is the future, it's got to be and…'

He threw the cashew into the air and caught it in his open mouth.

'I want to help create it.'

'Of course,' said Sally, taking a sip of her Peroni and wishing he would stop throwing nuts into the air as another one bounced into her lap, 'will there be jet packs?'

'What?'

The music was almost prohibitively loud in Guy's current favourite bar.

'You know,' shouted Sally, 'in the future, like Thunderbirds?'

'Who?'

She reached for her beer, she still hadn't heard anything from Peter since she'd called to thank him, again, for taking her to Amsterdam. And to apologise, again, for her behaviour. And although she knew there was every chance that he no longer wanted to see her, she had come to a decision.

'It's definitely the right… and when…' he shouted, before popping another cashew, '… I get the next project… I hope I get to… because they're the only ones that are so far ahead and…'

He raised the bottle to his lips and took a swig.

'Great.' said Sally, smiling as she desperately tried to follow his energetic but inaudible conversation.

The two-timing would have to stop. She did not have the stomach for it.

'It's a fantastic… it's my future.' Guy said, prodding the contents of the bowl, ferreting out another cashew from the bottom.

Or the energy. And on balance, Guy was proving far too demanding.

'It's everyone's future.' he shouted.

Stop it, is what Sally wanted to say as another nut hit the deck.

'Absolutely.' is what she did say.

She was trying really hard, but she couldn't help it, he was really annoying her. He just never sat still. He had been going over the plans for the sustainable eco-community he was helping to design, in great detail for about… one hour and forty-two minutes.

'Anyway,' he said, 'I'll shut up or I'll bore you to death.'

'No,' said Sally, trying hard not to sound bored to death already, 'honestly it's great. Fascinating.'

He smiled and ran his salty, cashew fingers through her hair, pulling her head forward to kiss him but as Sally turned to the right, her seat twisted to the left. Unable to unhook her heeled foot from the hooped footrest of the repurposed bar stool, she plunged forward and thrusting an arm out to save herself, she whacked Guy in the face.

'Owe.' he said.

'I am so sorry.' said Sally, regaining her balance and her beer.

'Yeah,' he said, 'then make it better.'

Sally lent forward and kissed the bridge of his nose.

'That is not an I'm-so-sorry kiss.' he said, drumming along to Public Enemy's *Get Up Stand Up*, now blaring from the speakers.

'It isn't?' said Sally.

'No,' he said, 'but you can make it up to me by getting those *Kill Bill* tickets.'

He beamed his boyish smile and continued to lip-sync to Public Enemy. Sally looked blankly.

'Remember? Double bill? 1 and 2? Tarantino retrospective? I told you?'

He bent forward and gave her a long, salty snog.

'Oh yeah.' she said.

Sally did not want to see *Kill Bill,* 1 or 2.

'Double espresso?'

The girl behind the counter broke through Peter's thoughts.

'Double espresso?' she smiled, and handed him the small, lidded paper cup of hot coffee.

He walked down 6th Avenue and across to Washington Square Park. In the early morning dappled shade, sipping his espresso as he sat on his favourite bench in his favourite park, Peter thought about Sally. He was excited by what he'd read in Dr. Goodfellow's little book of insights, excited by the plans he was now making for his new life, and he wanted to discuss it with her. He imagined them sitting next to one another. He wanted to take her to his favourite coffee shop and his favourite bar, so many things he wanted to do with her in his favourite city. Watching a couple of old guys play an early morning game of chess, he wondered at how much the neighbourhood had changed since he'd grown up there as a boy, and how much had stayed the same. He remembered his father and his cronies sitting at the chess tables for hours. Peter never felt he really got to know his father as an adult but the word he might best have used to describe him was unfulfilled. Although Aver had loved Peter's mother, Molly, in the early years of their marriage, he could never unravel the cause of her pain, despite trying. In the end he gave up, worked longer hours, found more to occupy him outside the home. He'd imparted his love of books and literature to all his children and had often taken the young Peter to play chess in the park or to a ball game, filling his head with all the ideas and plans he himself had never seen through. And Peter had loved it when his father told the apocryphal tale of how he'd once drunk with Dylan Thomas in The White Horse, before launching into a stirring rendition of *Do Not Go Gentle Into That Good Night*, a poem that had remained one of his favourites and that he could still recite. As a boy, it was to his father he would turn when things went wrong but when he'd died in a road accident in his sixties, Peter had barely missed his presence and it was that which had made him saddest.

Now, as he sat watching the old guys arguing over their game of chess, Peter did miss his father.

Rage, rage against the dying of the light.

He heard his father's voice in his head and felt the sadness in his heart of a life unlived and of a love unfulfilled. He would not, could not, let that happen to him too. He'd made a decision, he wanted to start living his new life with Sally. And he wanted it now.

'If I was having doubts before,' said Sally, helping herself to one of the white chocolate chip cookies she'd brought as a gift, 'then it's definitely over now.'

'Why?' said Alice, handing Sally a mug of tea to go with the cookie, 'I thought you were having double the fun?'

They were sitting in Alice's kitchen in the warm fug of a damp afternoon while outside the summer rain poured down.

'I was wrong, it doesn't make me feel good anymore,' said Sally, 'I'm not having any fun.'

'Maybe,' said Alice, 'it's your hormonal imbalance. Try upping your HRT'

'Guy's too young,' said Sally, 'his friends are too young.'

'You're not dating his friends.' said Alice, 'Try lowering your HRT.'

'No,' said Sally, her mind now made up, 'we're done, it's for the best, I'll call him, he's in Scotland.'

She reached for her tea.

'I guess we've learnt one thing,' said Alice, 'the menopause doesn't necessarily mean you don't want to have sex.'

'It's the menopause,' chanted Sally, 'not a death sentence. All the single women of a certain age I know are gagging for it, I think married women, women who've been in a relationship for tears, just use the menopause as a get-out-of-bed-free card.'

'Maybe,' said Alice, 'but who wants to have sex with
180

someone you've been sharing your life with for years and years and years; high days, holidays, sick days, fuck-off-and-die-why-don't-you days... very sexy. It doesn't get easier. It gets boring. All my married friends are having affairs.'

'All of them?' said Sally.

'No, but they all want to. I'd have an affair, I just don't have the time to have an affair. If I had the time, I'd have one. Men don't want it more it's just easier for them, all they do is go to work. Go to work and then go for a 'work related drink' after work, just a quick one, a couldn't-say-no one, a didn't-want-to-stay-but drink; they've got all the time in the world to have affairs and the opportunity.'

She paused to drain her mug of tea before continuing her rant.

'It's harder for women.' she said, 'We go to work and then come home and deal with the au pair and the kids and the violin lessons and the squabbles and the guilt of not being there to pick them up every day and bake cookies and go to the bloody museums. And we still have to be brilliant and sexy and awake when he comes home.'

'But you've got history, you've been through so much together, you and Ben are so close and...'

'Don't confuse intimacy with falling into a rut,' said Alice. Sally looked over at her friend as she refilled the kettle, she looked drawn.

'But you look fabulous.' she said, by way of consolation.

'I have to,' said Alice, 'but he doesn't. I wouldn't be too quick to give up your long-distance lassiez-faire love life just yet.'

But Sally had made her decision, she was going to stop seeing Guy and just see Peter, assuming he still wanted to see her.

'I've realized,' said Sally, 'being with Guy makes me miss being with Peter.'

One man now and then, she'd decided, was more than enough.

'But I haven't heard from him,' she said, reaching for another cookie, 'so that's probably over too.'

'I saw Anna and David the other night,' Alice took a sip of her tea, 'said something about him coming over for an art show.'

'When?'

Sally sat up.

'I forget, they were saying his daughter's getting married.'

'Really?'

'And how sad it was he'd never re-married, too fucked-up after the wife went off with his best friend.'

'No.'

'Yes,' said Alice, 'Anna's never seen him with a regular girlfriend. I didn't say anything about you.'

'So, his wife left him?' said Sally, taking in this new information.

'Apparently so.'

Sally took a sip of her tea.

'Maybe I was too quick to judge, too harsh… maybe I should call him, talk to him about it, maybe…'

She took another sip of her tea.

'At least you're having sex,' said Alice, 'don't over think it, just use it as a stress buster.'

'Daddy has a stress.' said Olive, looking up from her drawing she was now busy colouring-in, sprawled on the rug, where Alice had forgotten she was.

'Olive,' she said, 'come here darling, let me see.'

Olive jumped up and dutifully brought her piece of paper to the kitchen table to show her mother.

'Here,' she said, waving it at Sally, 'you can have my picture. It's a dog with sex.'

'Thank you.' said Sally, looking at Alice and smiling at the child.

'What's sex?' Olive asked her mother.

'Look,' said Alice, waving a small bag of organic, carob-coated, mini-rice cakes at her daughter, 'do you want to watch Jungle Book until Stan and Basha get back from violin?'

'Yes.' said the child, running to her mother, arms outstretched for her treat.

'OK,' said Alice, emptying half the bag into an orange plastic bowl and using it to lead her daughter toward the TV at the far end of the room, as if luring a kitten with a saucer of milk.

She put the bowl on the floor while the child arranged herself on the patchwork beanbag beside the bowl.

'I've really got to have sex with my husband,' she said, glancing over at Olive, mesmerised in front of her cartoon hero, 'it's been ages, he hasn't said anything but he must be desperate. Maybe this weekend.'

She picked up her mobile and stamped in a reminder to herself.

'Think yourself lucky,' she said, 'don't throw the toy-boy out with the bath water.'

'What's happened to hot-and-sexy-single-dad?' said Sally, changing the subject.

'Still hot, still sexy, sadly no longer single.' said Alice.

'Oh dear.'

'It's for the best, I suppose.' she said, wistfully, 'the fantasy was fine while it lasted. Actually, it worked in Ben's favour.'

'It did?' said Sally, 'How so?'

'Every time I saw hot-and-sexy-single-dad or got a text from him' whispered Alice, 'it would get me in the mood, and then I'd have sex with Ben, so he got the benefit.'

'Win, win.' said Sally.

'Win, win.' said Alice.

Sally finished her tea.

'The bare necessities of life,' shouted Olive, from the other end of the room, 'will come to you.'

Work had become a pressing issue and in light of Mike's predictions regarding her job, Sally had not accepted Guy's invitation to go to Scotland, using the excuse that it would be silly to let go the opportunity of covering for everyone else who was going away on holiday. That and the fact that she had decided the phone was the best way to end their relationship. Plus, according to his text with the un-smiling smiley face, it was raining up there whereas in London they were still enjoying a mini-heat wave.

Having been side swiped by a long emotional conversation with Poppy, regarding the problems Habib was having with their visa and sponsorship for America, Sally was feeling drained. Despite her attempts to come up with all sorts of ideas, Poppy had remained unconvinced and said nothing could be done, her life, and indeed Habib's, was over. Forever. Sally could not help them. Her disappointment and distress had upset Sally, and although, in truth there was nothing she could think of that was of any practical use, her suggestions had only made things worse, according to her daughter. So, to distract herself from her inadequacies, she reread Guy's text. Was Alice right? Should she keep going with her dual dating, just man-up and see both men, she wondered? She liked having a boyfriend: a boyfriend to go for a walk on the Heath with and perhaps for a cold beer outside an old pub with. A boyfriend to drive to the seaside with and walk by the water's edge and eat crab and potted shrimps sitting outside a clapboard shack with. Except that that wouldn't be Guy because he was allergic to shellfish. And Peter lived in another country.

Despite laying on the sofa with a mid-afternoon glass of rose, watching All About Eve; indoors even though the sun was shining outside, still Sally's favourite act of wanton rebellion, she felt restless. Now, in the half-light of the early evening, the sky smudged with smoke from so many BBQs, the scent of paraffin infused briquettes and burnt chicken wafting high over the rooftops of London, she wondered if it was a good time to call Guy. Call him and get it over with, tell him they were done. Doing it over the phone, she'd reasoned would be much better than face to face. She didn't like confrontation and the phone was perfectly acceptable if it was verbal. It wasn't like she would do it in a text. The phone ending was standard procedure. And so she'd been practicing her 'it's not you…' speech. Or should she call Peter first, she wondered, find out if he still wanted to see her?

'Hello? Sally?'

Guy's voice sounded a long way away.

'Hi.' she said, 'You sound a long way away.'

'What?' said Guy.

'What?' said Sally, walking around her sitting room as if it might improve the signal that was clearly being obscured by the highlands, 'I can hardly hear you.'

The phone went dead. Sally stared at it. It rang again.

'Hello?'

'Hi.'

The phone went dead again.

'Hello?'

'Hi, can you hear me now?'

Guy's voice was faint but audible. This was impossible, thought Sally, flopping back onto the sofa.

'Yes,' she shouted, 'just.'

The phone went dead again. It rang again.

'You should have come up,' he said, 'it's amazing, you'd love it.'

Sally wasn't loving the bad connection, she couldn't bear the thought of shouting, '…not you', half a dozen times down a dead line.

'I miss you.' she shouted, instead.

'What?'

'I miss you.'

'Yeah, loads of midges.'

'No, I…'

The phone went dead again. Sally waited. She tried calling back but now the line was busy as Guy tried to call her back. She called again; it was busy again. She left a message saying she was trying to call. Then she listened to the message he'd left her, clicking over when she saw he was trying to call her again. This, she thought, was ridiculous, communication was breaking down.

'Phone tag.' she shouted.

'What?'

'Phone… nothing, I just … '

He disappeared. Sally pressed redial feverishly. Ridiculous and very, very annoying.

'Hi?'

'The thing is,' said Guy, now sounding like he was calling from inside a diving bell beneath the North Sea, 'I think I'm planning to… '

'Yes?'

Sally strained to hear what Guy was saying.

'Sorry?'

'Sally?' he shouted, from inside his diving bell.

'Yes.'

'…love… place… think… want…'

She could only get every other word now.

'move… fulltime… do… think… spectacular.'

'Yeah,' said Sally, 'sounds great.'

185

'We…talk… yeah?'

The phone went dead again. She stared at it. It didn't ring again. She wouldn't do it on the phone, she decided, she couldn't. She'd do it when he got back, a much better idea. She'd cook dinner then she'd tell him.

'Sorry,' said Ashley, from the back of a cab, 'running a little late, order me a Martini.'

'Sure,' said Peter, draining the one he was drinking and gesturing to the bartender, 'see you soon.'

Sitting at the bar of the Tribeca restaurant, Peter was looking forward to seeing Ashley, it felt like ages since they'd had dinner together. She'd been his literary agent for the art books he wrote for years, his friend for longer, and she was always entertaining; like Sally, she knew how to have a good time. He smiled as he thought about Sally, she had such a great energy, one of the many qualities he liked about her. Loved about her.

'Bring her over,' said Ashley, when she finally arrived and they were sitting at their table, 'from what you've been saying she sounds fantastic. When can I meet her?'

'Well,' Peter said, unfolding his napkin, 'it's complicated.'

'Complicated how?' Ashley asked, putting her menu to one side, 'You like her, sounds like she likes you.'

'The thing is…'

'Invite her to come stay. What are you so scared of? You said she's divorced.'

'She is.'

'Her kids are all grown.'

'They are.'

'Try explaining to your kids you're dating another woman. That's complicated.' Ashley said, filling their water glasses from the blue bottle on the table.

'Yes, I know but I…'

'You're divorced. Your kids are all grown. So what's the…'

'I told her I was married.'

'What?'

'Married.'

His brow furrowed as he said the word out loud.

'Now. Still. And I can't get a divorce.'

Ashley sat back and looked at her friend opposite, his dark suit immaculate as ever, sitting in one of their favourite restaurants a few blocks from her office. How many times had they had lunch together? Dinner? Cocktails? How many times had they sat in this very restaurant? She'd seen him pull some smart moves over the many years they'd known each other, but this one she couldn't figure out.

'And you did that because why?'

'Because,' he said, 'it's what I do.'

'It is?'

'In my experience,' said Peter, nodding to the waiter to pour the wine, 'when a woman thinks you are single and available for marriage, she gets very keen on marrying you. And as I've said to you before, since my divorce I've decided I'm not the marrying kind.'

Peter paused to take a sip of his wine while the waiter hovered expectantly.

'However, when I explain to a woman that although I may enjoy her company and I want to spend time with her, but that I have no intention of marrying her, or anyone else, ever again, she may say she's all fine with that and it's not a problem, but invariably it is. Sooner or later.'

'So you say you're married?'

'Yes, I say I'm married so as not to give false hope.'

Another waiter appeared to take their order, while Ashley digested this information.

'I hear what you're saying,' she said, 'and I guess you're right, but it sounds so wrong.'

'Do you think?'

Ashley ignored her friend, deciding if she had to explain it he'd never get it.

'So, now what?' she said.

'Well… now… I think I may have changed my mind.'

'Oh.'

'Yes, I've definitely changed my mind.'

He took another sip of his wine to fortify his resolve.

'You see I read this book and…'

'A book?'

187

'Yes, Dr. Goodfellow, very illuminating… but that's not important, what is important is I want to change the way I've been doing things.'

'Things?' said Ashley.

'Relationships. I'm going to do relationships differently.' He smiled, having read Dr. Goodflellow's slim, but surprisingly interesting, book he was keen to start over.

'OK.' said Ashley.

'Starting with Sally,' he said, leaning forward, 'I do want you to meet her. I want her to be a part of my life. A proper part.'

'Well that's great.'

Ashley was surprised by how animated her friend had become as he talked about this woman.

'And she loves to cook you know,' he beamed at Ashley's astonished face, 'I want her to cook for me.'

'Cook for you? Are you saying you want to marry her?'

'No. Yes. I don't know. Maybe. I just think…'

Peter picked up his glass and drained it in one.

'I think I may have fallen in love.'

'You've fallen in love,' Ashley lent forward now, the better to understand her friend, 'with Sally?'

'Yes, I believe I have and I was not expecting that.'

Ashley sat back and whistled.

'Wow.' she said.

It was a long time since she had seen Peter so enchanted by anything, certainly anyone. He seemed suddenly younger.

'Yes,' he said, cutting through his own reverie, 'you see before, I just thought she was funny and charming and …'

'And you weren't prepared to commit. That story's so old they should put music to it…'

'Well maybe, but I thought it would be very nice to see her when I was in London and as long as she knew it couldn't get any more serious than that…'

'Then no one would get hurt?'

'Quite.'

'OK, I can see where you're coming from, kinda.'

Ashley gave him the disapproving look she usually reserved for her ex-husband.

'So what's the problem? Just get a 'divorce'.'

She'd waggled her inverted coma fingers at him as the waiter returned with their food. While they ate, Peter explained how he'd told Sally why he couldn't just get a 'divorce'.

'That's the problem,' Peter said, lowering his voice, 'if I tell her the truth now she'll never trust me again. No, I need something else. I thought I might just kill my 'wife', you know, have her meet with a fatal accident.'

'No good,' Ashley had said, leaning in conspiratorially, 'there would have to be a period of morning, she might feel guilty about it, you know, be sorry for your loss, that sort of thing.'

'So what do I do?'

'Tell her,' Ashley said, 'your wife has fallen madly in love, what a surprise, now she wants a divorce.'

'Do you think she'll buy it?'

'If she feels the same way about you, she won't question it.'

Peter was delighted with Ashley's idea.

'If I'm going to change my life,' he said, 'I might as well make it a big change.'

'That's great,' said Ashley, pleased that this woman made her friend so energised, so happy, she was obviously good for him.

'And I think you're right.' he said.

'About what?'

'I am going to ask her to marry me.' said Peter, smiling broadly and raising his glass to Sally, 'I'm going over next week, I'll turn up out the blue, surprise her.'

'Really,' said Ashley, reaching for her wine, 'you think that's wise? No one likes a surprise.'

'Sally does,' he said, 'she loves them.'

Top tip: when you're feeling down, or even if you're not, start your day with a poem; read something clever, funny, insightful, witty, wry or beautiful and make yourself feel instantly clever, funny, insightful, witty, wry and beautiful. And better.

CHAPTER 23

Sally had cleaned the house, well cleared up the kitchen, and planned her menu: Spanish chicken with chorizo and potatoes, courtesy of Nigella, a delicious and hopefully easy dinner. She'd texted Guy to confirm what time he was coming and he'd texted back a series of smiley faces, one glum because he couldn't wait to see her and two smiling at the joy of seeing her very soon. They would have dinner, she would explain the situation and that would be that. And then she thought, she would call Peter. If he didn't want to see to her, then so be it, but if he did want to see to her, and she really hoped he still did, then she wanted to know when. Perhaps she could visit him? A trip to New York really would be an affair to remember.

'Leave me alone.' said Max, filling a bowl of Weetabix with the last of the milk.

'But don't you want a nice girlfriend?' said Sally, as she set about getting creative with her chicken thighs and a red onion.

'What?'

'A girlfriend?' she said, 'Wouldn't it be nice to have a nice girlfriend?'

'Godsake.'

Max turned away from his mother, his head hung low.

'I think it would make a big difference, you know, if you had… a girlfriend.'

'I'm not having this conversation.'

Max poured sugar onto his cereal.

'Don't you like girls?'

'Yes I do like girls.'

He pulled open the drawer and fumbled for a spoon.

'Because if you don't it doesn't matter…'

'Shut up, I do have girlfriends. I don't want a girlfriend. Not that it's anything to do with you what I do.'

He slammed the drawer shut.

'Leave me alone. I can't believe you're even saying this. It's got nothing to do this with you. I have friends who are girls if I need to spend time with a girl.'

'Oh right, what girls with benefits?'

'Oh God, just stop talking will you. I'm not discussing my private life with you. I'm not discussing anything with you.'

'I'm just saying…'

Max picked up his pre-dinner snack and lolloped out of the kitchen.

'Don't forget about tonight,' called Sally, to the back of his head, 'I'm not cooking.'

Max stopped and turned and surveyed the raw ingredients his mother had littered about the kitchen.

'Yes you are.' he said.

'Yes, but not for you.' said Sally, panic rising in her voice, 'Remember? I said I needed you out of the kitchen tonight. Out of the house?'

Max looked blankly at his mother.

'You said you were going out anyway?'

'Did I?'

Max leant against the worktop and took another large, mouthful of cereal.

'Don't remember.'

'You said you would stay at Jack's?' said Sally, 'I'm not cooking for you and you need to be out of the house. Guy is coming for supper and I need…'

'Whatever,' Max was already exiting the kitchen, 'I'll go out. Please, stop talking.'

Now sitting in his hotel bar, Peter was feeling jet lagged. Jet lagged and anxious, it was not a good combination. He'd come to surprise Sally and tell her everything; almost everything. Sitting in his study looking out on 9th Street, the hum of cross-town traffic a distant mummer, it had felt like the right decision. Now he was here in London, he was not so sure. What if it was the wrong decision? They hadn't seen each other since Amsterdam. Maybe she'd changed her mind about him? Maybe this was a mistake.

'What email?' he said, disappointed it hadn't been Sally on the phone.

'Peter.' Ashley was losing her patience.

'You send me so many emails,' he said, taking another sip of his Martini, 'I'll check.'

'Do that.'

Peter appreciated Ashley was just trying to do her job but he only had one thing on his mind right now.

'Can this wait,' he said, 'till I'm back?'

'Really?' Ashley was aware of her friend's emotional state but she still had a business to run, 'Peter, I've got a lot on right now with that new client in Vancouver to take care of.'

'Vancouver?'

Peter checked his watch.

'I told you. The woman we signed last year? The blogger?'

'The what?'

Peter scanned the bar.

'The woman who walked away from twenty-five years of marriage? For the lesbian doctor? Went with her to Darfur for Medicine Sans Frontiers? Remember?'

'Sure.' he didn't, 'How's that going?'

'Movie deal.'

'No.'

'Yes.'

Peter finished his martini.

'They're talking Aniston and Sarandon.' said Ashley, 'It's going to be huge.'

'No kidding?'

'So I am pretty busy.'

'Of course.' said Peter.

'Are you listening to any of this?' said Ashley, knowing he wasn't, 'Have you talked to Sally yet?'

'No.' he said, suddenly feeling rather warm.

He looked about for the bartender, he needed to get the check if he was going to go see her.

'I guess,' he said, fingering the stem of his glass, 'it does make sense to…'

'Damn right it makes sense. For heaven's sake,' said Ashley, crackling down the line from New York, 'just get over yourself and go see her.'

'I don't think it's such a good idea,' he said, finding it hard to breathe, 'I really don't.'
He scanned the bar again, nodding in the direction of the busy barman.

'Oh really? Well I don't think telling a woman you're married when you're not is such a good idea.' said Ashley, 'I think it stinks.'

'OK,' said Peter, 'yes, I made a mistake.'

'You're damn right you did.' said Ashley, 'Maybe, if she'd thought you were a little more serious about her…'

'Alright.' said Peter, sitting back down, 'I get it.'
He gestured to the barman for another drink.

With the chicken and chorizo now safely in the oven, Sally had decided it would be a good idea to serve up gin & tonics when Guy arrived. Take the edge off things. She had read an article in a Sunday magazine about long, cool cocktails on sultry, summer evenings and was keen to try the G&T with cucumber and black pepper, preferably right now. Despite the bruising of the sky and the promise of stormy weather to come, she grabbed her bag and headed for Sainsbury's Local to purchase the necessary ingredients, having first secured Max's assurance that he was definitely going out and would be gone by the time she got back. So it was with some surprise, that when she returned from her errand, she could hear him talking animatedly in the kitchen. It was with utter shock, laced with what-the-fuck, that she found him seated at the table with Peter.

'Darling.' said Peter, leaping to his feet and stepping forward to embrace her.
Sally dropped her bags of booze onto the table and wordlessly allowed herself to be hugged and kissed. Why was Peter in her home? Sally could hear her heart beating, what was

happening? Had she stepped through some portal into another dimension?

'Peter?'

He beamed at her. Emboldened by his second Martini and a fistful of macadamias, he had decided to seize the day after all, hailed a cab and found the flat. And boy was he pleased he had, the moment Max had welcomed him in he'd felt right at home, this was undoubtedly the right decision.

'I've just been talking to Max, he's been explaining about…'

'Good thing I was in.' said Max.

'Why?' Sally turned on her startled son, 'Why are you here? You said you were going out. Go out.'

'I am,' said Max, sloping out of the kitchen, 'jeeze, I thought you'd be pleased I let him in, you're cooking him dinner.'

Dinner? Sally looked at her son in horror, what was he talking about?

'Why,' she said, turning her attention back to Peter, 'are you here?'

'Darling,' he smiled, 'I've been trying…'

'You never called,' she said, 'you didn't…'

'I wanted to.' he said.

'So why didn't you?'

Sally's voice was reed thin as she tried to take it all in. Peter was back in her kitchen like he'd never been away.

'It's been too long.' he said, smiling again, that easy comfortable, smile as he bent forward and kissed her on the lips.

'I told you Sally,' he said, 'I like you.'

He laughed, his beautiful face cracking into a broad grin and Sally looked into his dark eyes, she liked him too.

'Here.' he said, handing her a bottle of wine and a paper bag containing a loaf of the sourdough bread he knew was her favourite and which he'd stopped especially to pick up from the deli near his hotel, 'You look lovely, darling.'

Peter moved closer to kiss her again. But Sally turned her face causing his kiss to land on her cheek instead. She snapped open the screw top.

'Drink?' she said.

'Er,' Peter noticed a look of concern had streaked her face, 'sure, thank you darling.'

She poured the wine.

'Are you alright Sally?' he asked, taking the glass, 'you seem a little... out of sorts.'

'No,' said Sally, 'I'm fine. Just fine.'

What she needed was a drink.

'Well then, cheers,' said Peter, raising his glass, 'If things were different...'

'Yeah, but they're not.' said Sally, taking a large gulp of her wine.

'I want to talk to you about that,' he said, 'and it can't wait.'

'Really?' said Sally, she took another gulp of her wine.

'Yes,' said Peter, noting the distant tone in her voice but deciding to press on, 'I know we haven't been together very long but... well... some things... you can't measure love in weeks and months... and... I mean sometimes you just know something...'

'And?'

'Yes, and well the thing is...'

'What?'

'My wife wants a divorce.'

Peter sat back and smiled. He'd done it. He'd got Sally's attention now.

'What?'

'Yes,' he continued, 'she's started seeing someone and... she's in love and she wants a divorce and...'

Peter took a gulp of his wine, he'd rehearsed the first part but now he was working without a script. He'd thought Sally might have jumped in at this point, jumped up, jumped for joy. But she was just staring at him and it was somewhat unsettling.

'I thought we might start to see more of each other and...'

Sally sat open mouthed, what was he saying? What was she hearing? He looked so vulnerable, stumbling over his words.

'And,' he leant forward and took her hand, 'I thought you could come to New York.'

'New York?'

She had definitely entered a parallel universe.

'Yes,' Peter was on a roll now, 'come and visit. Come and stay. Move…'

'To New York?'

'Yes.' Peter said, surprised at how right the words felt.

'To live with you?'

'Yes Darling,' he said, 'to live with me.'

Sally gave him a quizzical look, she felt a pain rising up inside her and clutched at her stomach.

'Darling?' he said, 'Are you sure you're OK?'

He couldn't tell if she was pleased or angry, happy or hungry. He searched her face for clues.

'Um…'

Sally couldn't breathe, she took a sip of her wine but it turned to bile in her throat, she thought she might choke.

'You're getting a divorce and you want me to move to New York to live with you?'

Peter paused for a moment just to check that that was what he wanted.

'That's exactly what I want.' he said, and pulled a ring box from his pocket and put it on the table.

Sally seemed to be having some kind of out of body experience now, perched high above her fridge, watching these curious events unfurl down below in her kitchen: what had Peter just done? The timer on the cooker buzzed loudly and brought her crashing back to earth. Fuck, dinner. Dinner with Guy, who would be arriving at any moment. Peter would have to go, immediately, she couldn't deal with this now. One plan at a time, she would focus on ditching Guy.

'You've got to go,' she said, staring at him, 'now.'

Peter looked at her, confusion written across his forehead, frustration on his mind. He loved her and he'd imagined she would be overjoyed at such a declaration of his love. However, Sally didn't seem to care. In fact she seemed to be quite annoyed.

'What?'

'Yep, sorry,' she said, standing up, grabbing the ring box and thrusting it back at him, taking his arm and guiding him towards the door, 'it's just that… the things is…'

'Yes?'

'The thing is…'

'What Darling? What's happened?'

'Poppy.' stammered Sally.

'Your daughter?'

'Er… yes, my daughter,' said Sally, flailing through her imagination, 'my daughter is coming and you have to go.' Sally felt pleased with herself, her daughter was a good excuse, good enough to get Peter to leave. He had to get out of her home immediately. Before Guy arrived imminently.

'But I'd love to meet Poppy. Max was just telling me about her plans and I think I…'

'Max is an idiot.'

'I told him I may be able to help her with…'

'No,' said Sally, shaking her head with violent enthusiasm, 'not now, she's very shy.'

'Oh.'

'Yeah,' said Sally, 'doesn't like strangers. And she's got a problem…'

'I know and I think might…'

'So you have to go,' Sally was on a roll now, 'she needs a bit of mum-time.'

Peter stood in the hallway. Sally turned away from him her hand on the latch.

'Sally.'

'Yeah?' she said, opening the door.

Peter took her by the shoulders and turned her towards him.

'What I said?'

Sally looked at her watch. Peter had been about to ask her to marry him, at least that's what she thought he was about to do. This was everything she'd ever wanted once but now, any minute now, the man she'd been sleeping with, a different man, was about to walk through the door. Her blood was whooshing loudly through her ears, she felt sick, her throat had closed up, she couldn't speak and breathing was becoming hard.

'Well?' said Peter.

'Sure.' croaked Sally, 'Let's talk.'

She pulled open the door and ushered Peter out, her hand on his back, giving him a gentle but firm nudge.

'Call me,' she said, 'tomorrow.'

He turned and looked at her.

'I love you.' he said.

'Yep.' said Sally.

She slammed the front door shut, turned and lent back against it, trying to breathe normally. Trying to breathe full stop. The doorbell buzzed. Fuck, what did he want now? She lifted the receiver of the intercom.

'Sally?'

Sweeping up Peter's glass of un-drunk wine, she downed it in one as Guy came into the kitchen. He stood behind her, lent forward to kiss the back of her neck and circled her waist with his arm.

'Whatcha.'

Sitting in the back of the taxi, the rain now gently drizzling, Peter was puzzled by Sally's reaction. He'd distinctly felt her hand on his lower back pushing him out of the door. He wasn't expecting that. What he'd been expecting was delight, perhaps a few tears but only of joy. He'd thought she might have flung her arms around his neck, when he'd imagined the scene, and kissed him. Passionately. They would have gone out to dinner and made plans for their future; gone home to bed and made love. That's the sort of thing he'd expected. What he had not expected was, *Yep*.

The lights of London's West End began to blur through the rain-striped windows as he headed back to his hotel. Perhaps he should have called first, he thought, perhaps surprising her had not been such a good idea. Had she thought he didn't want to see her anymore? That he wasn't interested in her anymore? Maybe that was it. Perhaps, he thought, his declaration of intent was too little too late. Had she needed more, sooner? He fingered the ring box in his jacket pocket, it hadn't really gone as he'd planned. He would call her as soon as he got back to the hotel and explain it all again, something wasn't right. There was a crack of thunder overhead and the flash of summer lightening lit up the black sky. Damn it, he'd left his phone on the table.

Guy was thoroughly enjoying the chicken and chorizo, it was his favourite, when the door buzzed.

'I'll get it.' he called out to Sally.

199

In the bathroom, Sally was bracing herself for the conversation she knew she was about to have with Guy. She wondered who could possibly be at the door at this time, but it was only as she went into the hall that the faintest flicker of a thought crossed her mind, could it possibly be Peter? Or perhaps it was the distant mummer of two male voices that might have subliminally suggested it could be him. No matter really how or why, because there he was, standing in her narrow hallway, a look of fury, shock and hurt, but mainly hurt, on his face. And there too was Guy, kind, sweet Guy, standing just behind him, his hand still on the door where he had closed it, a look of mild surprise on his unknowing face as the stranger strode into her kitchen.

'Sorry to interrupt your dinner,' said Peter, standing with his back to the sink surveying the intimate scene: the near empty plates, garlicky and oil smeared, the orangey juices from the chicken and chorizo waiting to be sopped up with the sourdough bread that Sally was so fond of and that Peter had brought with him earlier that evening, now sliced and crumbing in the shallow, blue ceramic dish in the middle of the table.

'Or should I say my dinner?'

He snatched up a piece of bread and took an angry bite.

'What?' said Guy, now standing next to Sally.

He slid a protective arm around her waist, the tone of the man's voice and the look on Sally's face was sufficient to alert him that all was not well. In fact, he could see something was very, very wrong.

'What the fuck?'

'Peter,' said Sally, stiffening at Guy's touch, 'it's not...'

'Not what?' he said.

'The thing is...'

'Sally,' said Guy, now looking worried, 'who is this?'

'Oh, so sorry,' said Peter, stepping forward and thrusting his hand out towards Guy, 'how rude of me, I'm Peter, Peter Jacobs.'

Guy, still confused, shook Peter's hand.

'You must be Poppy,' he continued, 'I'm Sally's fiancé.'

Guy stopped shaking his hand and turned to look at Sally.

'What?' he said.

'Well technically…' said Sally, looking from Guy to Peter, 'I can explain …'

'Oh good,' said Peter, 'I was hoping you would.'

He smiled and folded his arms.

'Do please continue.'

'Well…' said Sally.

'And I bought you the goddam bread.' shouted Peter.

'Hi Sal.' said Ed, opening her front door with his key and finding the hallway now filled with Peter, Sally and Guy, 'Ah, hello there.'

Ed pocketed the keys and dropped the overstuffed holdall he was carrying onto the floor.

'And who's he?' Peter shouted, as anger now became his number one emotion.

'I'm the husband.'

Ed smiled and extended his hand to Peter who was now pushing past him and his bag and opening the front door.

'Ex,' shouted Sally, from behind Ed, 'Ex-husband.'

But the door had slammed shut.

Top tip: an easy, one pan supper for sofa friends and family:

Spanish chicken and chorizo, courtesy of Nigella:
2x tablespoons of olive oil or rapeseed oil
12 chicken thighs
750g of chorizo sausages chopped into chunks approx. 4cm
1 kg new potatoes halved
2 red onions peeled and chopped roughly
2 teaspoons dried oregano
grated zest 1 orange
Preheat the oven to 220C/gas mark 7. Lay the chicken in the pan, skin up, and splash over the oil. Pack in the onion, potatoes and chorizo around the chicken pieces. Sprinkle the orange zest, salt and black pepper over the top. Bake for about 45mins-1 hr. but check after 1/2hr and baste with the orangey-spicy juices. Any leftover potatoes make an excellent salad and the chicken is delicious eaten cold from the fridge while wondering what to cook…

CHAPTER 24

Ed sat down at the kitchen table and filled a glass with wine from one of the two bottles he appeared to have brought with him.

'Why is that bag in the hall?' said Sally, still in shock after the evening's events, 'Why are you here?'
She wanted him gone. Peter had gone. Guy had gone. Why was he still there?

'Drink?' he said, offering Sally a glass.
On balance the need for a drink outweighed the need to evict Ed.

'Fuck it.' she said, raising her head from its prone position on the table and rubbing her eyes as she tried to comprehend what had just happened.

'It's Tamsin,' said Ed, taking a gulp of his wine, 'Tamsin and I… me and Tams… we really haven't been getting on and…'

'You get on fine.' said Sally, reaching for her glass and wishing Ed would just leave the bottle and go home, drowning her sorrows didn't come close to what she was planning, 'Why is there a bag in the hall, you going somewhere?'

'Not really, like you said before,' he took another swig of his wine, 'I've let her dictate to me for far too long.'
Ed went to the stove and spooned the remainder of the chicken and chorizo into a dish he'd found in the cupboard.

'Can I finish this Sal?'

'What I said…' said Sally, taking a large gulp of her wine and remembering how the last time he'd been there for supper she might have mentioned that he deserved to be given a little more consideration by Tamsin. But she'd only said that because he was looking so miserable, and complaining so much, and she had had such a lovely time in bed with Guy, watching Breaking Bad on Netflix, and she'd felt sorry for him, 'I said, yes you did… you do… deserve respect…'

'And consideration.'

'And consideration… and that if sometimes you feel …'

'I do feel,' Ed said, refilling their glasses, 'I feel I don't get any respect. In my own home. Like you said.'

He drained his glass in one.

'But,' said Sally, finishing hers too, 'what you also have to take into consideration Ed…'

'Yes?' said Ed.

'Is Tamsin.'

She refilled her glass.

'I do,' said Ed, tucking into his late supper, 'I do take her into consideration, that's all I do. This is delicious Sal, can you pass the bread?'

Agh, the bread. Sally looked at the bread. Peter had brought her the bread and she had given it to Guy. Now Ed was eating the bread. Peter's bread. Her eyes welled up as the numbing shock of evening begun to ware off and the realisation of what had happened began to kick in.

'And there's the kids,' said Ed, taking another slurp, 'I love those boys and I do everything with them.'

'Ed,' said Sally, tears welling up, 'I really don't think I can…'

'I do homework and take them to school and I do their bloody school trips,' Ed reached for the bottle, 'if the au pair is ill. And it's hard, you know?'

'I may have just made the biggest fuck up of my life Ed and…'

'So,' he said, finishing his wine with alarming speed, 'I think that's it, I'm out.'

He opened the second bottle.

'Ed, I've just…'

204

'I've made up my mind,' he said, pouring the wine, 'I've left her.'

Sally reached for her glass.

'So can I stay here for a while? On the sofa? Till I'm sorted? We've been getting on really well recently, you and me and… you look great by the way.'

'But… well… OK… but…'

'So, you've blown it with your boyfriend, or is that boyfriends?' said Ed, sitting back in his chair.

Sitting in the pink glow of the fairy lights, artfully hung about her kitchen, Sally stared at her ex-husband. How, she wondered, had she ended up here?

'Ed.' she said, raising her glass for moral support, this had to stop.

'What?'

And stop now.

'You have to go.' she said.

'Go? Now? But,' he took a draft of his wine, 'the thing is…'

'No thing Ed, go home.'

'Well, I suppose,' he took another sip of his wine, 'I may have over reacted.'

'Yes,' said Sally, 'you have. Go home to your home and sort it out.'

'And she does work really hard you know.'

He sopped up the last of the juices from his remarkably good supper, with a heel of Peter's bread.

'I know.' said Sally, resisting the urge to suggest that styling boy bands was not a proper job, 'She does.'

Ed pulled on his jacket and Sally ushered him towards the front door. She hadn't exactly told him never to come round again, but she hadn't offered him her sofa.

'Ed,' she said, 'can I have my keys back please?'

That was it she thought, no more turning up unexpectedly, he needed boundaries, she needed boundaries. Alice was right, it had all ended in tears and they were all hers.

'Keys?' said Ed, flustered, 'But…'

'You don't need them now,' she continued, 'it's not like when the kids were younger.'

'Right.'

Sally held out her hand as he ferreted in his pockets. He fisted over the keys, said goodbye and Sally shut the door behind him.

Subsisting mainly on Lindt dark chocolate with a touch of sea salt and red wine, Sally was on lockdown for the remainder of the bank holiday. Alice was in the country. Will was by the sea. Jaz was away with Matt. Martin was in Sophie. Sally was home alone. She called Peter but he didn't answer. Wouldn't answer. She hadn't expected him to answer but now, with hindsight, she realised her message suggesting that thcy really should talk probably wasn't helped by her little joke about there being no men in her life and then two coming along at the same time. She should not have finished that second bottle of wine after Ed had left. She tried immersing herself in her favourite choice of escape from the cruel world that she felt had conspired against her, but this time even her old movies had failed to compete with the misery she was now enjoying. If anything, the pain was getting worse: she couldn't stop crying into the pillow of her dishevelled bed, the sheets in need of a change, the unwashed laundry spilling from its basket and banking up by the door.

Wrapped in her sick-and-sorry cardi, Sally was morphing into Miss Havisham: plates of nibbled toast littered the kitchen, stained coffee mugs filled the sink, she was slipping into the abyss.

'It's been seven hours…'

Laying on the sofa she was going nowhere, listening to the saddest songs she knew, songs full of heartbreak, loss and self-loathing, wasn't helping. From Burt Bacharach through to Nick Cave by way of Martha Wainwright, it was now the turn of Sinead O'Connor.

'Nothing compares…'

Sally wailed along, tunelessly. Why was she on her own again, was she really such a bad person? And now her job was leaving her too.

'Don't know why…'

She would never feel all right again.

'Stormy weather…' she sniffed, duetting along with Lena Horne, 'and I ain't together…'

She could never feel all right, again. There was no cake left, no chocolate, no wine, she had lost her appetite for everything except her own pain.

'Hello darkness…' she sung, 'my old friend…'

By Tuesday morning little had changed. Sally had still heard nothing from Peter or from Guy, for whom she had left a much more apologetic message. Sitting at her desk, staring at her emails and nursing a colossal hangover, acutely aware she was the architect of her own misery, she really wished she'd called in sick.

'Sally.' Trica said, pointing earnestly and nodding, 'Mike wants you.'

Surprised by Tricia's face looming up so close to hers, Sally snapped back to reality and away from trying to figure out how to get herself out of the gutter and back on track. Behind her, Mike was poking his baldhead around his glass door, and waving.

'Oh, sorry,' said Sally, breezily as she swivelled round in her chair to face him, 'I was just trying to work out what we were going to do with the *Most Stimulating Cuppa* comp, now that the winning café has closed down.'

'Just a quick word.' said Mike.

Sally realized he was beckoning, not waving, and she knew she was drowning. How had it all got so complicated? One minute she was snogging Peter by the Grand Canal and the next she was waking up with Guy. She was out of control.

'So, Sally.'

Mike leant back in his chair and clasped his hands behind his bowling-ball head, his Diesel-jeaned legs sticking straight out in front of him crossed at his stripe-socked ankles.

'Just wanted to catch you.' he said.

'Right.' said Sally, trying to focus on Mike.

'As you know more than most,' he said, 'expansion means growth, right?'

Sally nodded, not knowing why she should know more than most, and crossed her legs.

'Survive and prosper.'

'Right.' she said.

What? She thought.

'And what I need, what we need, across every platform, is a hundred and fifty percent, you can understand that?'

'Absolutely.' said Sally.

'So, off the record, as you know I like the whole holistic cradle to grave approach and who wouldn't, isn't that what we all want?'

Sally nodded and uncrossed her legs.

'Good, we're on the same page then?'

'Of course.' she said.

'So, that said, we need to capturize this, and frame the conversation in context, we're not just going outside the box, the box isn't even in the room.'

'Sorry.' said Sally, what was Mike talking about? 'Could you just clarify…

'In order to grow,' said Mike, leaning forward, his elbows on the desk, his hands now cupping his face, 'obviously we need to cut back and we will need to let people go…'

Whoa, what?

'And we will also need to take people on.'

Ah, OK. Panic over.

'So instead of your column being every week it's going to be every month.'

'What?' said Sally, alarmed again, 'Once a month?'

'But you'll still have your other bits and pieces.'

Mike leant back and folded his arms across his chest.

'You'll spend fifty percent of your time here, fifty percent of your time working from home and…'

'Yes?'

'Fifty percent of your time in the field.'

He articulated the words carefully.

'That's a hundred and fifty percent.' said Sally.

'Well maybe.' said Mike.

Well definitely, thought Sally.

'And that's what I want,' he jabbed an index finger at Sally for emphasis, 'a hundred and fifty percent. On a freelance basis of course, starting now.'

'Oh.' said Sally, trying to work out the implications of this declaration.

'But I will still need your expertise in the office.' said Mike.

'Right.'

'I want you, Sally,' he lent forward and pointed at her again, lest she be in any doubt who she was, 'to write down everything you do, in detail, all the other stuff around here.'

'Why?'

'For the work placement kids we're bringing in.'

Mike lent back in his chair, crossed his arms and swivelled from side to side.

Top tip: to clean coffee or tea stained mugs, fill with hot water and add a tablespoon of lime or lemon juice, let stand overnight and hey presto!

CHAPTER 25

'That doesn't sound very good to me,' said Ellen, 'that sounds very bad.'

'It'll be fine.' said Sally, wondering why on earth she had said anything about her work. Was she insane? Why had she even answered the phone? She really didn't need to be lectured to by her mother.

'But freelance?' said Ellen, 'What does that mean exactly?'

'Well,' said Sally, 'it could mean it works out better because I can work from home.'

'And why is that better?' asked Ellen.

Because I can stay in my pyjamas all day, thought Sally.

'Because I can save money on travel and…'

'Spend more on electricity instead,' said Ellen, 'then there's the heating, the phone and…' 'I can claim it all on my tax…'

'And the food. You'll be eating all day, I know you. How was that diet I emailed you?'

'I didn't do it,' said Sally, 'it looked very unhealthy.'

'Really? Seemed very well balanced to me, I've lost six pounds.'

'Great, the thing is,' said Sally, exasperated, 'I'm running a bit late…'

'Now, I just wanted to tell you,' said Ellen, ignoring her daughter's plea, 'I've had a marvellous idea. I'm going to liquidate.'

'Liquidate what? Do you mean juicing? Juice fasting probably isn't wise at your age.'

'I'm talking about my assets.' said Ellen, 'I'm going to sell the house. I was reading an article in The FT and then I heard something on Radio 4 and it all makes perfect sense, we should all sell up and die broke.'

'Radio 4 told you to sell your house?' said Sally.

'No, but that was the gist, you can't take it with you, and you're going to find it very tough in this economic climate if you're not earning…'

'I am earning.'

'We should buy a house together…'

'What?'

'Pool our resources. Jenni Murray was talking to this very nice…'

'Mother,' said Sally, 'I am a bit busy.'

'What about Gammy's birthday?' said Ellen.

'What about it?'

'You will be there.'

'Of course.' said Sally, swapping ears as her mobile turned from red hot to white hot, while Ellen talked at her.

'Both your brothers are coming,' she said, 'and the children.'

'I said I'll be there,' said Sally, 'I told you, we're all coming.'

'I've booked The Calico Cat, the long room at the back.' she continued, 'Gammy loves it, it's near the home, we can get her in and out without too much fuss.'

'OK.'

'So, I need numbers,' she said, 'when you've decided if you're coming.'

Dorothy 'Gammy' Barton-Hay, Sally's 94-year old grandmother, was turning 95. She had seen out two husbands and several lovers and was still going strong. Considered quite a beauty in her youth, and something of a social butterfly, her dance card had always been full. She'd married young, too young as she would frequently say, to Brian Hamilton, a man of considerable means who was busy expanding his family's fortune in the world of foreign imports. The war had done nothing to dim her light and as a volunteer driving supply-trucks around the country she had never been short of nylons or lipstick.

'I've already discussed this,' said Sally, 'we're all coming and Habib, all four of us.'

'Don't forget her card,' continued Ellen, 'and a present.'

'I won't forget,' said Sally, 'when have I ever forgotten?' Having briefly stepped out of the limelight to produce Ellen, an heir and a spare sister, in quick succession, duty done, and nannies hired, Dorothy had rejoined the party scene with renewed vigour.

'Marriage is for money,' she would often say, when asked for romantic advice, 'position and security. Make sure you always marry well the first time.'

Sally may not have heeded her Grandmother's advice but had, as a young child, loved listening to Gammy's tales of champagne and roses, late suppers at The Stork Club in New York, long weekends in Paris and dinner at the Savoy. As a friend of Noel Coward's, Dorothy had often visited him in Jamaica where she'd been introduced to Ian Fleming and Errol Flynn. She had been a little scared of the former and had had an affair with the latter, 'a very special fellow', and one of Sally's favourite bedtime stories, much to Ellen's horror. Parties were always glittering affairs, and amongst the many boxes of curling black and white photographs of Dorothy behind the wheel of a fast motor car, or Dorothy posing in a swimsuit with a striped beach ball, were pictures of Dorothy in beautiful ball gowns of silk chiffon and duchess satin, standing on a curved staircase or beside a grand piano, surrounded by flowers, staring off at some lover or other just out of shot.

'I'm just reminding you,' said Ellen, 'and did you listen to Money Box, like I said?'

'No mother, I missed it.'

'Well don't worry, you can catch up,' she shouted, 'on the iPlayer.'

'Yes, I know I can,' said Sally, with no intention of doing so, 'the thing is…'

'Very good piece about the financial future of the over fifties,' she said, 'that's you.'

'Thank you I know,' said Sally, 'the thing is…'

Sally had no choice, she had to get off the phone.

'I've got to go, I'm going out,' she said, she would have to lie, 'with a man.'

'Oh a date?'

'Yes.'

'Well I've got to drive Margaret Mead to her IBS support group, *Bowels Under the Microscope*.' said Ellen, 'so I need to get on.'

'So do I,' said Sally, 'I need to get ready.'

'It's the middle of the afternoon, shouldn't take you that long,' said Ellen, 'nobody's looking at you.'

No, thought Sally, not anymore.

Despite never wanting to leave her sofa again, Jaz had assured Sally exercise was just what she needed now, to move on from her relationship whine-athon. Although she was unconvinced, she had agreed to go out.

'They've reduced my hours,' she said, as they power walked through the park.

'Great,' said Jaz, 'you hate your job.'

Sally had recently read in a magazine about the need for middle-aged women to maintain SAS levels of exercise if they were to have any chance at all of making it into old age on their own two legs, let alone their own hips.

'I know,' she said, 'but I don't hate the money. The way things are going, it's only a matter of time before I'm out altogether.'

There had been charts to chart progress, talk of gyms, personal trainers, increased stamina and squats. Sally had thought this was all rather unrealistic and felt quite exhausted just reading about it.

'So now you can do something else, something you'd like to do,' said Jaz, 'might be a blessing.'

'I'm fifty, what else am I going to do?'

'Don't let your age define you,' said Jaz, jogging circles around her friend.

The 15-minute a day exercise suggestions Sally had subsequently read about, in a free newspaper left on a tube seat, had seemed much more appealing by comparison. Apparently, it would increase her metabolic rate while helping to build and maintain that all important core muscle and bone density. Their power walk had, however, become more of power amble.

'I know,' she said, bending to re-tie her shoelace, 'I do need to tackle what I'm going to do with the rest of my life, to avoid moving into my mother's commune if nothing else. She pulled her phone out of her bag, no calls, from anyone.

'So, that's it,' said Jaz, 'Peter and Guy are both gone?'

'Looks like it,' said Sally, 'Guy has forgiven me, sort of, he's off to the Outer Hebrides but Peter won't speak to me. I was trying to have some fun but all I've done is fucked it up. I think it's time to hang up the date knickers.'

'What about Martin?' said Jaz. 'I always thought you two would end up together.'

'Martin is not my type.'

'And look where your type has got you.' said Jaz. Sally flung the phone back in her bag.

'Run away,' said Jaz, 'come to Greece with me.' Jaz had decided that maybe the one-that-got-away had got away for good reason. Maybe the past should stay in the past and she should go to a foreign country.

'I read about this place,' she said, unzipping her Stella McCartney hoody, 'a life altering journey of self-discovery to enhance my life skills.'

'Life skills?' said Sally, putting her sunglasses on as the sky began to brighten.

She was surprised by her friend's planned odyssey, Jaz was not known for her spiritual journeys into the unknown.

'And maximise my natural charisma…'

Sally's scepticism was growing under the warmth of the sun.

'Through the power of dance, yoga and improv.'

'Improv?

Jaz had found that once the rosy glow of wow and what-if had worn off, and she and Matt had caught up on the missing years, she'd been left wondering, is this it? Did she go to all those places, do all those things and meet all those people just to end up with the man who'd broken her heart when she was at college? Was it romantic?

'It's a healing experience.' she said.

Or was it just sad?

'You need to heal?' said Sally.

'Probably.' said Jaz, 'And so do you.'

They sat down on a bench by the pond, to enjoy the weak sunshine that had now fully broken free of the cloud. A skinny woman in her middle years jogged past, clinging on to a double buggy. Sally glanced in as the sleeping new-borns sped past.

'When I had kids,' she said, 'I spent the first six months in leggings and a stained sweatshirt, eating biscuits.'

'I remember the look.' said Jaz.

'Expectations were lower,' said Sally, 'thank god. That Victoria Beckham has a lot to answer for.'

She scanned the stream of bobbing women pounding the park's pathways with their dogs and buggies and bottles of water.

'This is less like a place of recreation and more like an Olympic training ground.'

They ambled off towards the park café.

'The whole Matt thing,' said Jaz, returning to the pressing issue of her own romantic life, 'the fishing, the countryside, M&S ready meals in front of the History Channel, it's not me.'

She tossed her newly highlighted hair back over her broad shoulders, the summer sun catching the streaks of chestnut, auburn and gold.

'It all feels a bit like the last chance saloon for the peri-menopausal. I'm not ready, not yet.'

'I thought you were getting on so well, skyping and texting.' said Sally.

'I know, we whine when we don't have a boyfriend, we whine when we do,' said Jaz, 'but Greece is booked and it's hot and sunny and somewhere else.'

The article she'd read had promised not only sun, sand and tzatziki, but also a sense of wellbeing hither to unknown. Set amongst the cobbled beauty of white-washed houses and peeling blue paintwork, dripping with bougainvillea and ripe with red geraniums, the holistic centre would give her the chance to explore her inner conflicts with expert psychotherapists, empower her true self with trained life coaches and enhance her creativity and communication skills while learning to wind-surf, sketch and write creatively.

216

Stepping over lemons in the September sunshine on her way to the beach, was all that Jaz was really after. But the thought of being in a 'nurturing environment to 'explore' her own needs had sounded very appealing.

'You're single now,' she said, 'why not come with? How bad can it be?'

The bee-buzzing, golden afternoons in the long-grass were drawing to a close and the house was once again unhealthy with cake and chocolate as Sally dispensed with exercise and tried to eat her way back to happiness instead. The arrival of the jumper season would cover up a lot of guilty pleasures, she'd reasoned, as she sat in her kitchen with a cup of coffee and finished off the last of Nigella's Everyday Brownies for breakfast; plus if she was going to spend the day with her family she would need to keep her strength up. There was something rather wonderful about the suggestion that there might be a brownie just for best, she thought, as she pondered what she could bake next. Reaching for the cookbook Peter had bought her in Venice, its jacket tattered by time but Sophia's face, still ageless and beautiful, beaming from the cover, she leafed through the gloriously technicoloured pages: Sophia, resplendent in 1970s glamour, her almond eyes lined and lashed, her hair lacquered, a beatific smile playing across her magnificent mouth while she stirred pasta, kneaded pizza and grated Parmesan. Sally thought about that day in Venice when Peter had bought her the book. He couldn't believe she'd wanted it so much, she couldn't believe he didn't want a book with a picture of Sophia Loren peering out from between a giant set of salad servers, as if she had two enormous wooden ears. She missed Peter. Or did she just miss the fun she'd had with him? He had lied about his marriage, who knew what else he had lied about. Had she let the wrong one in? Her phone bleated through her reverie: a text from her mother reminding her of the time and address of her grandmother's birthday lunch. She looked up at the clock but she already knew she was already running late.

'I'm parking,' said Sally, craning her neck to avoid the Audi Avant that was straddling two spaces, 'I'm in the car park right now. I can actually see you through the window.'

With both Poppy and Max, and Poppy's boyfriend Habib, all in the same car, the journey to Gammy's birthday lunch had been long and argumentative.

'Well, we're all here,' said Ellen, 'waiting.'

Sally flung her phone at her bag, squashed in the passenger footwell next to her son's legs, but she missed and it accidentally bounced off his shin causing him to swear.

'Sorry.' she said, turning off the ignition and taking a deep breath, 'Now, let's just have a nice lunch, no fighting, no swearing.'

She reached down to retrieve her bag.

'Fuck, where's the bloody present?'

The gift and card finally located in the boot, where Sally had put them in with the recycling by mistake, they eventually joined the party. Ellen was looking cool in a dove-grey wool dress and a charcoal silk and linen scarf, her grandmother by contrast was in full colour.

Always a gregarious woman, it hadn't taken her grandmother long to 'pull herself together' after her first husband had died of cirrhosis of the liver.

'What else was a gal to do,' she'd always said, 'I had children to support?'

Dorothy had married a divorce lawyer, Corin Barton-Hay who had reminded her of her darling Noel. As it turned out, she was bang on the money, because Corin was gay. He didn't come out until the late 80s when he'd discovered the joy of disco; the couple remained the greatest of friends and never divorced. Alzheimer's finally undid them and Dorothy ensured he'd had the very best of care until the end.

Sitting with her children, grandchildren and great-grandchildren, at the long table in the back room of *The Calico Cat,* Dorothy had enjoyed a delicious lunch and a glass of wine. The whole thing had gone very well, Sally felt, once her own children had been settled at opposite ends of the table, with sufficient family members between them. The presents were being unwrapped and Dorothy had finally come to the Dior silk scarf, printed with splodgy cerise and red roses. Sally had bought it in a flea market she and Peter had found in Amsterdam. She knew she would never, could never, wear it

218

again, so thought her Grandmother might like it. Plus, finances being what they were there was a limit to how much she could afford to invest in someone who may go at any minute.

'Lovely darling,' said Dorothy, 'rather similar to this one.' She fingered the splodgy peony, printed scarf tied about her neck.

It was now, while the kitchen was carefully preparing to light the candles on the large cake: chocolate with vanilla frosting, which Ellen had brought in especially for her mother's birthday, that Poppy had chosen to announce that she and Habib were getting married.

'Is she having a picaninny?' shouted Dorothy.

'Mother!' said Ellen.

'Gammy!' said Poppy.

'A pica-what?' said Max, laughing.

'A picaninny?' Dorothy shouted louder, turning to the elderly man sitting on her right, who looked a little startled. She may have survived the past decade without a marriage, but she was still dating: Richard, her toy-boy, seventy-something, widower. Apparently, men were a rare breed in her home, the trouble being women lived longer so if one came in you had to be quick. He'd only been there 48 hours when she'd had him moved, permanently, to her table in the dining-room.

'Mother, stop it.' said Ellen, 'You know we don't use that word anymore. You're doing it on purpose.'

'She doesn't understand.' said Sally, in her grandmother's defence, 'And Poppy isn't pregnant.'

'She's doing it on purpose.' said Ellen, turning to Habib.

'Poppy isn't pregnant Gammy.' Sally shouted, louder.

'Isn't she?' said Max.

'Max,' said Poppy, 'shut up.'

'She's not,' said Sally, 'are you?'

'Habs said she is.' said Max.

'He didn't.' said Poppy.

'Poppy?' said Sally.

'I'm not,' said Poppy, 'tell him mum.'

'I thought she was looking rather fat,' said Dorothy, 'that's why I asked if she was having a…'

'Mother.' said Ellen, 'She's doing it again.'

'She's not pregnant.' said Sally.

'I'm not pregnant Gammy.' said Poppy.

'She needs to sit up straighter,' said Dorothy, 'she'd be much better off in a girdle.'

'You're not pregnant?' said Sally, turning to scrutinise her daughter, 'Are you?'

'No,' said Poppy, 'I am not pregnant now. But I will want to be.'

'That's lovely darling,' said Ellen, 'lots to look forward to.'

'She's too young,' said Sally, 'she hasn't even finished college.'

'When I was her age,' said Ellen, 'I'd already had you.'

'Look how well that turned out.' said Sally.

'And I've seen a marvellous house on the Internet, big enough for all of us, Willows End, Swallows End, some kind of end, it's got an annexe,' said Ellen, ignoring her daughter, 'absolutely ideal. Poppy and Habib will be needing somewhere with the baby, we'll have to get our skates on.'

'There is no baby.' said Sally, disappointed there was no more wine.

'And being single,' Ellen continued, unabated, 'and not working you can help with the childcare.'

'I am working,' said Sally, trying to curb her Mother's enthusiasm, 'and I'm too young to be a grandmother.'
What was her mother talking about now?

'Not that young.' said Ellen, sternly.

'We will want to have children,' said Poppy, 'but not till after we're back from New York.'

'Of course,' said Ellen, 'that'll be marvellous.'

'New York?' said Sally.

'Now Habs has got his visa sorted and…'

'But I thought you said America had all fallen through.' said Sally, recalling her daughter's utter distress after Habib's sponsorship had not materialised as planned.

'No,' said Poppy, 'it's all good, Peter helped us.'

'Peter?' said Sally, confused, 'Peter who?'

'Your Peter,' said Poppy, 'that guy you were going out with.'

'Guy?'

'PETER,' said Poppy, slowly and loudly as if talking to someone with less than a full command of the English language, 'American? Peter? Dah.'

'What?'

'He's really nice, you shouldn't have let him get away.'

'Oh dear,' said Ellen, 'another failed…'

'What are you talking about?' said Sally, turning to her daughter, the room was getting very warm, she couldn't breathe; hot flush or a heart attack? 'What has Peter got to do with any of this?'

'Max told him,' said Poppy, rolling her eyes, 'when Habs couldn't sort out his visa. He was really helpful.'

'But I don't understand how…'

'He's got a friend who runs a design company…'

Sally looked blankly at her daughter.

'He introduced Habs so he's sorted.'

'What?'

'SPON… SOR… SHIP.'

Poppy was shouting at her mother now.

'We'll be in New York,' she smiled at Habib, 'way better than LA.'

'But how do you know Peter?'

'For godsake mother.'

Poppy widened her eyes, mirroring her mother's look of disbelief, the woman understood nothing.

'Facebook,' she said, 'he's Max's friend.'

'Facebook?' Sally spat the word, 'What Facebook?'

She could not take any of this in: her children had formed a virtual friendship with Peter and now he was helping Poppy and Habib move to New York.

'But he doesn't do Facebook.' she stammered.

'Does now,' said Max, 'he's got all these pictures of his daughter's wedding and stuff.'

'You never told me.' said Sally.

'Why do I have to tell you everything?' said Max, 'I don't have to tell you anything.'

'She's a jewellery designer, Carrie, and I'm going to meet her because I'm like a designer and she needs help,' said Poppy, 'because she is pregnant.'

'You don't want to leave it too late.' said Ellen.

221

Sally sat in shocked silence.

'Easier to shift the baby fat when you're younger.'

She beamed expectantly at Poppy.

'You never really did though, did you Sally?'

Peter was going to be a grandfather and Poppy was going to work with his daughter.

'Of course,' said Ellen, turning back to her granddaughter, 'I was back in my trouser suit six weeks after I had her. You're like me, you'll be fine.'

And now Sally's future was being mapped out in pampers and strollers; living with her mother and her children. And her grandchildren. In an annexe.

'He's on Facebook?' is all she managed.

'Yeah,' said Habib, picking up his cigarettes and gesturing to Max to join him outside for a smoke, 'he's pretty cool.'

Back in the safety of her own home, Sally tried to take in the enormity of the afternoon's revelation; lying on the sofa watching Brief Encounter, she thought about Peter. Having cross-questioned her son about their cyber-friendship for as long as he would allow, she had now discovered just how much he had done to help Poppy and Habib, and that he was currently back in London at his usual hotel. She reached for her mug but the tea had turned cold and bitter. Slowly, through the Rachmaninov, as the credits began to roll so did the tears. Why had she been so quick to judge him? Now it was all ruined and there was nothing she could do about it. Absolutely nothing.

Top tip: for dark circles and puffy eyes look no further than the apple. Put a couple of slices of Granny Smith over your eyes, relax for 20 minutes and let the tannic acid in the apple go to work.

CHAPTER 26

In the mirror-lined lift to the rooftop restaurant at Peter's hotel, Sally felt anxious, yes, but also excited as she checked her make-up in the reflection. Buoyed up by the large vodka she'd had in the pub next door, she really had, she believed, nothing to lose and everything to gain be confronting him. Peter must know how truly upset she was about what had happened. Upset and very sorry. And he must know it now. It was absolutely the right thing to do.

It had definitely felt like the right thing to do when she was lying on her sofa but as she stood before him at the table in the crowded, and alarmingly well-lit, dining-room, Sally felt less sure. For one thing, she had not factored in the surprised faces of his dinner companions: four dark-suited men and one woman wearing, Sally noted, a dress in a rather unforgiving shade of yellow. She had imagined him sitting alone, perhaps toying with an uneaten steak, when the young man at reception had said he was upstairs, in the restaurant.

'And so,' Sally could hear herself saying, 'I just wanted you to know that. How much I loved you. Before. And how sorry I was. Am. Still.'

The words were definitely coming out of her mouth. All the right words, but she wasn't sure they were in the right order. Peter didn't look very pleased to see her, of that she was sure.

'And I would never have done that, any of it, if I'd known. Before. About your wife. You don't have a wife.' she

223

continued, almost as if she had to keep reminding herself, 'Why did you say you were married?'

Everyone sitting at his table now turned and looked expectantly at Peter.

'Ah, Ms. Benson,' he said, standing up and turning to his dinner guests, 'she's a… sort of writer, you know.'

He was moving towards her now at speed, honed in like a heat-seeking missile.

'Loves to try out her scenarios in real life.'

Sally could see a steely look in his eye she had not noticed before and a slight twitch to the left brow.

'Perhaps we could talk later.' he said, firmly taking her by the arm and steering her towards the restaurant's tinted glass doors, 'Forgive me, Ms. Dupont, Mr. Takishima, gentlemen, I'll be just one minute.'

Standing by the lifts, Peter did not loosen his grip on her arm or divert his gaze from straight ahead, while he jabbed with some violence at the button with his free hand.

'How could you?' he hissed, pressing the button again, 'I'm trying to have a quiet dinner with some very important colleagues and…'

'But,' said Sally, 'you don't understand, I had to come.'

'No,' he said, 'you did not.'

Tears began to well up.

'Sally…' he said, loosening his grip on her arm.

'I'm so sorry,' she said, 'but…'

'I know…' his voice softened.

'But,' she sniffed, 'I did come to apologize to you yes, but… you did lie to me and…'

'And you cheated on me.' said Peter.

'But technically…' said Sally, straightening up and wiping her cheek with the handkerchief Peter proffered, 'we weren't… you said you were married.'

'But I wasn't married.'

'But I didn't know that.' said Sally, 'You lied.'

'But I didn't…'

Peter faltered, he wanted to say cheat but he knew that would be a lie. He may be angry but he was not without blame.

'I told you all about my wife.' he said, instead.

If saying yes to that drink with Karen had been a mistake,

ending up in bed with her had been a disaster. No, he was not without blame, he knew that. He'd behaved badly, but in his defence he had only just started seeing Sally, he didn't know how things would work out, it was before…

'But you didn't have a wife,' said Sally, 'and I didn't know…'

'And I didn't know you were seeing someone else,' said Peter, his anger kicking back in, 'while I was lying in a hospital bed. I could have been dying.'

'But I didn't know that. And you weren't.'

The lift pinged its arrival and Peter turned to face Sally.

'We've had this conversation.' he said.

'Well we need to have it again.'

The doors of the lift opened and they both stood there, looking at one another.

'No Sally,' he said, firmly, 'we don't. Nothing's changed.'

She stepped into the lift. Peter looked at her, standing there, so unhappy, and he felt a huge desire to wrap his arms around her and kiss her. He wanted to put things back to the way they were, make it right, just as he'd wanted to as a boy. He wanted to make Sally better. To kiss away the tears and all the unhappiness and feel her body against his, just to smell her and taste her and breathe her in.

'You're wrong,' she said, 'if you think things are the same, because they're not, they're different. I've been a fool but I'm different now. So don't you think that we could…'

The doors closed and she was gone.

Peering up between her legs and out through the window of Fenella's yoga studio extension, Sally could see the cold, bright sun casting shadows across the rooftops.

'Draw into the hips.' said Fenella, 'drop the chin, release the head… and follow the breath.'

Sally was finding it hard to breathe. Breathing, sleeping, eating, everything was an effort since that night.

'Bring your mind into the room…'

That terrible, awful, dreadful night, why had she thought turning up at Peter's hotel was a good idea? What madness had possessed her?

'And breathe.'

'The thing is,' Sally said, after the class, 'I acted impulsively.'

'Oh no dear, that will never do.' said Mary, pulling on her Wellington boots.

'I know that now.'

Sally pulled on her coat.

'I got carried away, I thought it was the right thing to do. I thought once he'd heard what I had to say he'd understand and…'

'Unreal expectations.' said Mary, 'I met my husband in Ooty, when we were both stationed in India. We both liked hill walking. We didn't have much but we did have a common interest.'

'There's plenty more fish in the sea.' said Joan, 'Although why anyone would want to bother I don't know, I don't bother anymore.'

'Maybe I'm not cut out for relationships.' said Sally, 'I've ended up in such a mess.'

'Like that song,' said Fenella, 'my pulse begins to race…'

'It goes boom boody-boom,' sang Joan.

'Well goodness gracious me.' joined in Mary.

'Boom boody-boom boody-boom,' they all sang along, 'boody-boom boody-boom-boom-boom.'

Despite the rousing chorus from her yoga group, Sally was still feeling low. She settled herself down to watch Barefoot In The Park, one of her very favourite old movies, in the hope that it would calm her troubled mind. She had never noticed before that the mother, the old woman with the hair-do and pearls in sensible shoes, who Jane Fonda tries to fix up with the Lothario in the attic, was only 52 and yet she could barely get up the stairs let alone climb the ladder to the loft of love. Robert Redford jokes that she couldn't possibly be a match for their sixtysomething neighbour because the old goat wears Japanese kimonos and sleeps on rugs, whereas Fonda's mother wares a hairnet and sleeps on a board. At 52 in 1967, a woman might as well have been 62, or 72. Was it better, wondered Sally, to go gently over to the grey side? To accept that once you were past 50 it was game over, time to retire from the fray, step away from the bar and go to sleep on your board? She adjusted her position on the sofa because her hip was now beginning to ache. Wouldn't it be easier if she could just stop fighting for the right to bare arms and wear skinny jeans, and instead reinstate the blue rinse and disgracefully grow old, in dull clothes and comfortable shoes, she wondered?

'*Shama, shama…*' sang Fonda, trying to guide her husband safely in out of the chilly night, '*shama, shama…*'

Someone to help you come in from the cold, thought Sally, that's all she'd wanted. Did she have the stamina to stay in the ring and go round again, could she still climb the ladder to the loft of love? In another time, in another society, her age might have been considered a bonus, she would have been thought the wise woman of the village. Why wasn't she thought the wise woman of the village now?

'And that,' said Sally, 'was that. I went, I tried, I humiliated myself. It's over and I'm fine with it.'

She and Alice had met up at *Cake*, summoned to try out Jaz's potential new Christmas cake recipe. Not her own recipe of course, Jaz was an entrepreneur not a cook, the last thing she'd put in an oven were a dozen Betty Crocker chocolate chip muffins, laced with hashish, sometime in the late 80s. The cake tasting was an annual event and one that Sally usually looked forward to as it often preceded a night of revelry. But this year she was not in the mood for partying.

'So why aren't you eating your cake?' said Jaz, eyeing her thinning friend, 'It's good without all the icing, no?'

The delicious, moist fruitcake, topped with almonds and cherries and candied peel, was proving hard for Sally to stomach.

'You're definitely losing weight.'

'Always a silver lining.' quipped Sally, hoiking up her jeans, loose on the thigh, they hung low on her hip.

Usually she comfort ate during moments of crisis, needing chocolate and biscuits and cake to sustain her in times of need. But not this time.

'The thing is,' she said, 'I mean it would never have worked, he wasn't… he was too…'

'Too?'

'Nothing, I'm good.' she lied, 'I mean even if… I could never have moved to New York, well I suppose I could now Poppy, but… it doesn't matter anyway. None of it matters.' She reached for her tea.

'But if I'd only known why…'

'How many times have you called Peter,' asked Jaz, pragmatically, 'and 141-ed the number?'

'Oh, I don't know, I haven't really… maybe once.' said Sally, moving lumps of cakey dried fruit about the willow-patterned plate with a tiny silver fork, 'Or twice.'

'Don't call him again.' said Alice, refilling the mismatched teacups from a gold lustred teapot.

'If you must call him,' said Jaz, 'call me. I'll be your phone-a-friend.'

'You're too old to waste any more time on him. Let him go.' said Alice, stabbing at a glacé cherry, 'What you need is a rescue remedy. Let's go away, a mini-break.'

'With my finances it would have to be a micro-mini-break.' said Sally.

She knew they were right but she was finding it hard to let it go and leave the pity party.

'Greece,' she said, turning to Jaz and changing the subject, 'you've hardly told us anything.'

'Three men amongst the 30 of us,' said Jaz, 'one with a guitar, one with a ponytail, one with a guitar and a ponytail.'

She was looking remarkably good though, glowing golden despite her holistic holiday not quite living up to her expectations.

'I knew it would be mainly women,' said Sally, 'on a trip like that.'

'The windsurfing instructor and life-drawing instructor were having a shag-fest.'

'Did you pull?' said Sally, sipping her tea.

'I ended up sitting on the beach, under a full moon, talking bollocks to a long haired, old bloke who was stark-bollock naked.'

'Agh.' said Sally, snorting tea through her nose in hysterics.

'More than a whiff of *The Wicker Man*.' said Alice.

'Then the improv woman asked me why I was resisting.' said Jaz, finishing her cake, 'They invited me into the healing circle and told me the talking stick was all mine.'

'Trapped,' Alice, shook her head, 'with the children of the corn.'

'Sounds a bit club-45-to-60-for-fuck-ups.' said Sally.

'So I've decided,' Jaz said, refilling their cups from the pot, 'I'm going to try and make it work with Matt.'

'Really?' said Sally, 'But you said…'

'I know what I said, but I think because Matt was so keen, when we reconnected, I felt like I'd finally won. Then once I'd got him, I didn't really want him. Now I've been thinking, and I think I do want him.'
She took a sip of her tea.

'And he really does want me. I'm done with dating, I'm calling off the search for the soul mate.'

'You mean he doesn't have to make himself unavailable to be for real?' said Alice, 'That's a novelty.'

'It's exhausting is what it is, texting every five minutes: Morning! Sweet dreams!! Love you…' said Jaz, 'Wish he'd stop.'

'But he cares.' said Sally, eager to confirm her friend's newfound feelings for her ex-ex.

'He does.' said Jaz, 'I think it's time to hang up the G-string.'

'All that life-therapy hocus-pocus bollocks must have rubbed off.' said Alice. 'Is he moving up here, to the city?'

'You're not going down there?' said Sally, 'To the country?'
Jaz gave her friend a withering look.

'We're going to do the long distance thing.' she said, 'He can come up here, I can go down there. He's got a really nice house near the sea.'

'And you like the sea?' asked Sally.

'I love the sea.' said Jaz, taking a drag on her fake fag, 'The sea is healthy. I'll go for long walks by the sea. And he's got a dog.'

'A dog?' said Sally, 'You never mentioned a dog.'

'Of course, he's not what I thought I wanted.' said Jaz.
'The dog?'

'No, Matt. But you know, better a flawed diamond than a perfect pebble.'

'Right.' said Sally, wondering how many pebbles flawed or

otherwise were left.

'I just needed to repurpose him.'

'Re what?'

'Give him a new role.' said Jaz.

'I've realised, I'm not really cut out for the whole 24/7 thing.' she said, 'But I'm not really cut out to be on my own either. This way I get to see him when and how I want.'
She shrugged and smiled.

'And like Matt says: if it looks like a duck and it quacks like a duck…

'Right,' said Sally, 'what does that actually mean?'

'Means I'm dating a duck.' said Jaz, waving at one of the waitresses to clear their plates, 'What about you? Why don't you do one of those charity walks? You know, through the foothills of the Himalaya for breast cancer or leukaemia or something?'
She inhaled her fake fag.

'Brilliant idea,' said Alice, 'a week with a captive audience.'

'No make-up, no pretensions, all camped together.' said Jaz, enthusiastically, 'It's intensive speed dating. You can really get to know someone in that situation.'

'And it's for charity,' continued Alice, 'it's the date that keeps on giving.'
Up a mountain, with a bunch of people she didn't know, without make-up. Sally couldn't think of anything worse.

'One word,' said Jaz, 'Mariella Frostrup.'

'That's two.' said Sally.

'Whatever,' said Jazz, 'she walked back to happiness.'

Top tip: to create the illusion of being a proper grown up with a wonderful family and a fabulous home just ask the butcher to butterfly you a leg of lamb.

CHAPTER 27

'Sally.'

Mike popped his head out of his office and beckoned to her.

'Quick word?'

Having realigned herself with her single status, Sally was trying hard to re-engage with her career. This, she thought, was the last thing she needed, as she slid behind the glass door and into full view of the rest of the open plan office.

'Just a catch up.' he said, swivelling left and right in his swivel chair.

When she'd asked him if this new freelance arrangement would mean she would lose work he had said:

'Is it likely? No. Is it possible? Yes.'

And despite his assurance that they would need her, absolutely and definitely need her, to 'run the show and keep an eye on the youngsters' in the office, in reality she had merely written down detailed instructions of what she did and handed over her job to a bunch of unpaid, work placements that would be rotated every two weeks.

'It will ultimately be a fantastic opportunity,' Mike said, adjusting his stripy Paul Smith scarf, the moth-munched holes just visible, betraying Christmas presents from more prosperous times, 'for you, to grow as a writer and widen the long view.'

'It's not going to be the same.'

Tricia said, when she presented Sally with a card signed by a lot of people Sally had never actually spoken to, and an espresso-making, stovetop, coffeepot with two pint sized coffee mugs. Now she was really fucked, she thought, now she needed to phone a friend.

'Not even espresso cups?' said Martin.

'I know,' said Sally, lolling on her sofa, 'I mean that's it, if you get given the gift you're out aren't you?'

'Mmm,' said Martin, 'doesn't bode well.'

'What am I going to do? They're not going to pay me enough just to write *Snacks and The City.*'

'What fucking Chisholm Trail?' Martin groaned.

Sally laughed. It was always his response to a tricky problem.

'I'll lose my home,' she said, 'I can't live with my mother.'

'Actually, I read this article,' said Martin, 'about how we're all going to have to pool our resources, live with our kids and our parents, like a commune and...'

'No,' said Sally, 'stop, I've had enough of this from her. More importantly, how am I ever going to feel better?'

'I told you at the time,' said Martin, 'when you started seeing Guy, it's like rebounding.'

He reached for his mug of tea.

'Bouncing into someone else is fine but it's rarely the real thing.'

'You do it.' she said.

'So I should know. First you bounce one way, then you bounce another,' continued Martin, bitterly, 'then you wind up like an old tennis ball.'

'You were right.' said Sally, 'Now Peter's not speaking to me and... at least Guy's talking to me, I think he was sort of relieved.'

'Ah ha, the cool cuckold.' said Martin, 'Was he going to dump you? Is that what he said?'

'Sort of.' said Sally.

'That's just what we say when we want you to think we don't care.'

'No, he means it. He's moving to the Outer Hebrides, he's got his job, he loves his job. He's all good.'

'How,' he said 'did you get here?'

'Practice.' said Sally.

They both laughed.

'Maybe, you should embrace your singularity,' said Martin, 'that which you are seeking is causing you to seek.'

'What does that mean?'

'Dunno, I read it at meditation class. Did I tell you I'm doing meditation, becoming mindful, learning to take responsibility for my thoughts, I want my life to be more like a life and less like a salvage job. You should come.'

'Maybe.' said Sally.

'It's all here, you need to stop searching and learn to pay attention,' said Martin, 'something like that. I'm going to give a go, stop projecting into the future. Live in the now, it's all we've really got.'

'Any news of Sophie?' said Sally.

His flourishing new relationship had floundered as quickly as it had kicked-off.

'Gone for good this time,' said Martin, 'she tweeted, 'it's not me it's you', so yes, I think this time we're definitely done. She's started seeing someone else, Rebecca.'

'Rebecca?'

'Yes, Rebecca is gorgeous.'

'But… really? Rebecca's a girl?'

'Yes.' he said, 'Even I would pick Rebecca over me and I'm me.'

He laughed a flat laugh.

'Did you know?' said Sally, wondering if she should pursue the enquiry, 'Before? I mean is this a new thing?'

'She's young,' said Martin, 'doesn't want to be defined by her gender.'

With all the trouble Sally'd had just dealing with the opposite sex, widening the options seemed like an unnecessary complication.

'But you'll never guess who Facebooked me?'

'Who?' Sally said, amazed at her friend's romantic resilience.

'Guess.'

'How would I know?'

'Go on.' Martin was insistent, 'Guess.'

'I have no idea.'

'Trey.'

'Trey?'

'Yeah Trey. Remember Trey? LA? Trey?'

Sally would never have guessed Trey, an impossibly good looking boy they'd met in a bar when Sally had visited Martin in LA, a long time ago, before kids and marriage and mortgages, while he was doing some kind of exchange thing at UCLA.

'He's gay now. You should go on Facebook,' he said, 'it's great for keeping in touch.'

'No.'

'Give Peter a poke.'

Sally was silent.

'Or come to LA with me, could be good,' he said, 'we can reconnect with Trey.'

'No.' she said, laughing a little nervously, 'But come for supper, soon, reconnect with me.'

She may not want to delve through her personal back catalogue but she admired her friend's positive outlook. He was right, she must stop living in the future. She needed to start living in the now, and starting tomorrow she would.

Ignoring the mess in her kitchen, Sally made herself a pot of coffee while she pondered her lot: no boyfriend, no work, no prospect of a boyfriend or work. Despite her best efforts, she was struggling hard to break what felt like an endless cycle of sad. Maybe Martin was right, she thought, maybe she was better off single. Maybe it really was time to put away the date knickers. Maybe she should go to LA with him. A road trip across California might be just what she needed. Or maybe not. Maybe Alice was right, a girls' getaway was a much better idea. She would make enquiries at *The Bread House*, a newly refurbed spa hotel on the Sussex coast, she'd read about. What couldn't be put right with two days of treatments, massages, organic cuisine and kale smoothies, for her and Alice and Jaz? A trip with her best friends was, she decided, exactly what she needed.

'Sorry,' she said, looking up at her son who'd lumbered into the room and interrupted her plans to slough off her depression, 'what did you say?'

'I've got a job.'

Max rubbed the sleep from his eyes.

'Cooking.'

'But you can't cook.' said Sally.

'Yeah, well, actually I can, proven by the fact that I've got a job,' said Max, 'as a chef.'

He pulled open the fridge, peered in and started systematically removing the contents, piling them up beside the cooker, getting ready, and steady, to cook.

'Where?' said Sally, still trying to process this new piece of information.

'My friend Jack,' he said, casting a master chef's eye over his assembled ingredients, 'he's got this like van, and we're going to cook food. And sell it.'

'You're going to cook food?' she said, 'In a van?'

Sally looked at her son in astonishment.

'It's a proper thing, his brother was doing catering for… something. But anyway, he can't now.'

'Why?'

'Because he's in prison.'

'Prison?'

Sally put down her cup of coffee.

'Doesn't matter, it's nothing, he put something on Facebook and it all went mental. That doesn't matter.'

'It does matter.' said Sally, visualising her own son handcuffed and dressed in Guantanamo-orange, 'Of course it matters.'

'See, that's my point,' said Max, turning from the onion he was now slicing to look at his mother, 'you're not listening to me. Again. It doesn't matter because he is not my friend and he is not involved in this. OK?'

'OK.' said Sally, flushing the plans for his prison break from her mind and refilling her coffee from the pot.

'Right, now just listen.' he said, waving the sharp knife at her, 'It's Jack MacDonald because he has the catering truck thing, and his friend, Jack Hiney, because he's done chefing at college, and me.'

'Why?' said Sally, confused, 'Why you?'

'Because I have the ideas and I'm good at cooking things too.' said Max, unwrapping a wrap from the packet, 'Is this

235

already cooked?'

He held the flat bread up to the light, looking for clues.

'Yes.' said Sally.

'Yeah,' continued Max, turning back to his mother, 'like my fajita sandwiches. It's dude food.'

'Dude food?'

'Yeah, for dudes which you have no clue about,' he said, breaking an egg into a bowl and whisking it with the knife, 'so don't even try. Do we have any cayenne?'

'Cupboard by your head.' said Sally, surprised her son even knew the word cayenne let alone what it was.

'So, you're going to invent this food, cook it and sell it?' she said.

'Yeah,' said Max, putting the fish finger he'd found in the back of the freezer under the grill, 'outside clubs, at night and down by the Southbank on weekends. It'll be awesome.'

He started slicing up some extra strong cheddar cheese.

'OK.'

'And 'cause they're both called Jack we're going to call it, 'Jack of Clubs @ thedudemobile'.'

'The dudemobile?'

'Yeah, really cool.'

He opened a can of baked beans.

'We thought about Macky Ds, MacDonald and dudes yeah, but the Jack of Clubs thing is better, no?'

'No, I mean yes, and anyway McDonalds might have…'

'And I'm moving out.'

'You are?' said Sally, unable to take it all in.

'Yeah, because Jack M's dad bought this flat for him and his brother to live in and so his mum couldn't have all his money in the divorce.'

'Right.' said Sally, as she watched her son continue to create his bizarre mid-morning breakfast, stunned by his revelation.

'But now his brother's in prison his dad says I can live there for like almost no rent. You got to admit, that is really cool.'

He turned and beamed at his mother.

'Yeah,' said Sally, 'really cool.'

'So don't get at me,' he said, reaching for the jar of Marmite, "cause now I'm weaning.'

The day had started bright but quickly turned to dull and now only a sliver of grey-gold light filtered through the slab of cloud that hung low overhead, a biblical backdrop to their epic road trip. Delighted, and yet strangely saddened by the news that her son had decided to grow-up, Sally was looking forward to her long weekend away with her girlfriends. It was time to get back in shape, mentally and physically.

'I had a chilling thought this morning,' she said, ferreting out the Rhubarb & Custard sweets she'd bought especially for the journey, now somewhere at the bottom of her bag,

'I'm older than the Prime Minister. I've never been older than the Prime Minister before. Now I shall always be older than the Prime Minister.'

'I'd always imagined,' said Alice, 'that the people in charge would always be older than me.'

'What happens when you become older than the people in charge?' said Sally.
She watched out of the window as the cityscape turned into trees.

'Where do you stand on Top Shop for the over 40s?' asked Jaz, putting her foot to the floor and moving into the fast lane.

'Oooh,' said Sally, 'are they opening one just for us?'

'No, but maybe they should.' said Jaz, 'These days when I'm in there I feel like I'm shopping for the daughter I don't have. But I'm a single woman with extensions and biker boots, not married with a blue rinse and sensible shoes. In my head I'm still 24.'

'I feel like I've only just got started and now I'm past the half-way point. It's not fair, why does another birthday have to mean another notch on the ever-expanding belt of middle age? I could still learn French. I haven't even got to tape two of my teach-yourself-French tapes yet.' said Sally, wondering if she still had a tape player.

'Or Spanish?' said Alice, helpfully.

'Exactly,' said Sally, yawning, 'according to my yoga group, once you get through the menopause it all gets better, you get your mind back and your energy.'

'No one said it was going to be like this.' said Jaz.

'That's because the generation who sold us sex and drugs and rock and roll said we'd all be dead before we were 30.' said Alice, 'They lied.'

'So how does a girl proceed into her 50s? Because I may not exactly have had a plan,' said Sally, 'but I didn't plan this. Where's the manual?'

'Don't ask me,' said Jaz, 'I'm a woman of a certain age still trying to dance under the stars.'

Outside, the autumn light burnt umber and orange, as the afternoon drew to a close. Sally stared at the cows dotted across the damp field, she wasn't past her sell-by-date she decided, not yet, as soon as she got home she would embrace tape two of her French tapes.

By the time they reached *The Bread House*, winter appeared to have already arrived, hailed by the roar and crackle of the oversized log fire, burning furiously in reception. They made themselves comfortable in their triple suite with its rolling view of the wide, Sussex sea, chose their beds and began to unpack.

'I'm so glad we did this.' said Sally, tugging off her jeans. She was feeling more relaxed already.

'Yes,' said Alice, unzipping her overnight bag, 'me too.'

Jaz pulled on an enormous white, waffle robe in readiness for her first treatment, and slapped a new nicotine patch onto her toned upper arm.

'Damn.' said Sally, sticking her hand down her knickers.

'What are you doing?' asked Jaz, looking at her friend, now on all fours searching for something under the bed.

'My magnet.' said Sally, 'it's fallen out.'

'You're what?'

'My menopause magnet,' said Sally, 'I read about it in a magazine, supposed to help with hot flushes, bloating, anxiety, tenderness, mood swings, irritability and… fuck.'

'Really?'

'Ow! Fucking hell.'

Sally couldn't reach underneath the bed so was now trying to move it and had bruised her shoulder with an overzealous shunt.

'Shit, ow,' said Sally, stubbing her toe on the leg of the

238

table as she keeled sideways when she stood up, 'it's supposed to help me regain my balance.'

'Not so good with the irritability then.' said Jaz.

'Or the balance.' said Alice.

'It's to do with my negative pole, I don't really understand it but you put one magnet on the inside of your knickers, below your tummy button …'

She pointed at the front of her pants by way of demonstration.

'…and fix the other one on the outside. I got it off the Internet but I lost one half down the loo when I was out for drinks with Will so I'm using the back of an old fridge magnet.'

She looked perplexed.

'Now I've lost that.'

'Is this it?' said Alice, picking something up off the carpet on the other side of the room.

Alice and Jaz watched their friend fiddle with her magnet.

'All you need right now,' said Jaz, tossing Sally a pair of clown sized, fluffy white slippers, 'are these.'

Having been wrapped, exfoliated and oxygenated, hydrated, detoxed and purified, had their meridian points stimulated and their upper thighs pummelled, they were now revitalised, rebalanced and sufficiently relaxed to head for the hotel juice bar.

'This is really quite good,' said Jaz, as they sat sipping their juice cocktails before dinner, 'an excellent treat now I've got the results of that col-whatever…'

'Colposcopy,' said Sally, feeling suddenly panicked, 'and?'

'And nothing,' said Jaz, taking another sip of her Pink Grapefruit Zinger, 'it's all clear. I'm good.'

'You are?'

Sally reached for her Kale and Cardamom Cosmopolitan with relief, Jaz was OK. She had already lost one friend, she did not want to lose another. Mia had been the one who'd got her life sorted out and now she was dead while Sally, the one who was always floundering, had been left behind. Even though she'd told Jaz everything would be fine, she'd been far from certain. She really didn't want to be left behind again.

'It's an age thing,' Alice said, raising her Seaweed Breeze, 'apparently 48 is a very dangerous time. If you can get through to 50 you'll be all right. Till the next wave.'

'When is the next wave?' asked Sally.

'We're all going to live till we're 100 now,' said Jaz, 'apparently.'

'Really?' said Sally, 'You mean I've got to do this for another 50 years?'

They ate a delicious dinner of line-hooked, freshly picked, ethnically marinated, sustainable, seasonal super-food, then retired to their room and another glass of organic fizzy apple juice.

'Hyaluronic Hydra powder, microdelivery triple-acid brightening peel and radiance serum to boost firmness and elasticity,' said Jaz, lining up her newly purchased products, 'and intensive nutritive restorative age-renewal crème with photosensitive technology enhancement.'

'Reduces the appearance of fine lines.' said Alice, scanning the side of a jar.

'Lines are not fine,' said Jaz, 'not as far as I'm concerned. It may have cost me a fortune, but it's an investment.'

'In a cosmetics firm.' said Alice, kicking off her kitten heels, reclining on an adjacent bed and wiggling her freshly painted, Jungle Red toes.

'In my face.' said Jaz, 'Cutting edge products so I won't have to invest in a nip'n'tuck.'

'I don't think I ever could,' said Sally, sitting up to review her reflection in the mirror, 'even if I could afford it.'
She pulled a face, arched her neck and stretched the skin back over her cheeks.

'It is an expense,' said Alice, tapping at her smooth forehead, 'I don't think I'm going to do fillers again.'

'There's another one a friend was telling me about, couple of injections and it sort of re-grows the collagen under your skin.'

'Why do we have to do all this stuff?' wailed Sally, lying beached on her bed amongst the many plump, silk-cased pillows, her glass in hand, 'Why can't we just enjoy getting older, wear our lines as a badge of honour, the mark of a life lived to the full? Why can't we just age like men just age?'

'Serge Gainsbourg may have got away with five days of stubble,' said Alice, 'passed out at the bar…'

'A permanent fag on,' said Jaz, 'and still had women queuing round the block…'

'Try that look as a woman.' said Alice.

Sally checked her phone as she entered the dining-room, she'd been trying to get hold of Martin and despite sending two texts and leaving a voice message there was still no response. Now she was getting a bit pissed off, she wanted to fix a date to cook him dinner, having spent hours with an Italian dictionary translating one of Sophia Loren's delicious pasta dishes. She really hoped he wasn't going through one of his flaky periods that often accompanied his single status.

'Do we have to leave?' she said, sitting down with Alice and Jaz, and pouring herself a cup of Fairtrade coffee from the pot on the table, 'I could get used to this.'

Alice and Jaz were already tucking into a hearty breakfast of seed porridge, fresh berries and yogurt, organic poached eggs and quinoa hash with toasted soda bread and homemade preserves. The trip had been a huge success, Sally thought, looking out of the bay window across the green-blue sea. After two days of freshly squeezed cocktails, pummelling and pampering, she was feeling fabulously relaxed and refreshed, ready to re-engage with the world once more.

'If I had unlimited resources,' said Jaz, helping herself to more toast and homemade chocolate hazelnut spread, 'I'd have weekly facials.'

'Mmmm,' said Sally, reaching for the jar, 'and unlimited chocolate hazelnut spread.'

She spooned up a mouthful and ate it neat. Deep within her bag her phone began ringing.

'Finally.' she said, hoping it was Martin.

It wasn't Martin. Sally peered at the nameless number she did not recognise.

'Hello?' she said, sucking the last of the nutty spread from the spoon.

'Sally?' said the unknown caller.

Top tip: to banish open pours and invigorate a tired face after a hard day, mash half an avocado with one egg yolk and a dessert spoon of honey, apply to face and neck, leave for half an hour and remove with cotton wool soaked in warm water, then rinse.

CHAPTER 28

Standing in the supermarket aisle, Sally studied the wall of snacks.

'Everyone likes Twiglets.' she said, reaching up for a giant bag, 'Maybe we should get two.'

'I don't.' said Alice.

'Really?' said Sally, 'I didn't know that. How come I didn't know that?'

'Get this.'

Jaz, held up an enormous, brightly coloured multi-pack of snacks.

'Twelve individual bags of Hula Hoops,' she read, 'plain, salt and vinegar, cheese and onion, BBQ beef …'

'Nobody likes BBQ beef Hula Hoops.' said Sally.

'Just get crisps.' said Alice.

'We can't just get crisps.' snapped Sally.

'What about Doritos?' said Jaz, 'And dips? Are we doing dips?'

'I don't know,' said Sally, 'where's the list?'

She stared at the piece of paper feeling confused.

'Kettle Chips.' she said, and reached for a large bag, 'Salt and vinegar?'

'I like cracked black pepper.' said Alice.

'Pretzels?' said Jaz, 'They're cheap.'

She picked up a bag.

'No one eats pretzels.' said Sally.

She put the bag back on the shelf.

'Some people might like pretzels.' said Alice.

Sally felt panicked, there was too much choice.

'Shall we get popcorn?'

Jaz held up an enormous candy-striped tub.

'I quite like pretzels.' said Alice.

She picked up the bag.

'And nuts?' said Jaz.

'Really? said Alice, 'I don't think we need to bother with nuts.'

'But you do think we should get pretzels.'

Sally looked blank.

'It's a funeral,' she said, 'not a bloody cocktail party.'

She leant on the trolley, feeling exhausted.

'How much do we need to get?' said Jaz, 'How do we know how many are coming?'

'Twenty?' said Alice, 'Thirty? Fifty?'

'His sister put it on Facebook,' said Sally, 'hundreds could turn up. A flash mob funeral.'

They stood looking at each other, standing in the supermarket aisle, each clutching a super-sized bag of their potato based snack of choice, and burst out laughing, teary, hysterical laughter at the absurdity of the situation; how do you know how many people are coming to a funeral?

'Fuck it,' said Sally, why were they worrying about crisps, 'we'll get it all, it really doesn't matter.'

It really didn't matter. Since the phone call from Martin's sister, Sarah, nothing much had mattered. What did matter was that Martin was dead, knocked down on a zebra crossing. It felt like a bad dream, which, thought Sally, felt like such a cliché, but it was how it felt. Which, she supposed, was why it was a cliché. She didn't want to be in a supermarket buying snacks for Martin's funeral. This could not be real.

'We should get Doritos,' said Jaz, loading the trolley, 'Martin loved Doritos. He'd definitely want us to get Doritos.' The need to do something had been strong and Sarah, who was never close to her brother, had gratefully accepted their offer to help with the food.

'Definitely,' said Sally, 'and he likes Twiglets.'

Martin's death was too surreal to be imagined, too sudden

to be taken in. Not yet. As the nameless days moved towards the funeral everything else melted away. Sally was in that strange period that often follows the news of tragedy, when you feel lucky to have your health, your family, your home; when you feel lucky to be alive. A time when you have a duty to the dead to enjoy living, and ex-boyfriends and unpaid bills all become unimportant. She knew this feeling, she had felt it before, and she also knew it would not last.

Her restless, numb energy kept Sally busy with long to-do lists. She cleaned out the cupboard full of the plates and cups and bowls she never used. Friends pooled names and addresses and she emailed the living to invite them to join in celebrating the dead. She tidied the kitchen drawer stuffed with useful things: string, birthday candles, tea lights, a tube of glitter, a dried-out highlighter without a lid and take-away menus for places long gone. It was cathartic going through the process of sorting stuff, clearing it out, letting it go. She even contacted Trey and he emailed a very sweet reply, sending his condolences and saying he and his new husband would light a candle for Martin.

'He really is gay,' said Sally, who had taken to talking to her dead friend whenever she fancied now, 'you were right.'

The night before the funeral, unable to sleep, Sally stood on a chair in her bedroom and reached up to the top shelf of her closet. There was something else she needed to sort out. She pulled out the red and pink, plaid picnic-blanket, still prickled with dry grass and twig from the summer, and threw it onto the bed, the chequered hunting cap with ear-flaps lined in ratty-fake fur, several old, fat photo albums, Gammy's ancient crocodile handbag with the broken clasp and finally, hidden beneath a plastic bag of unfinished patchwork intended to one day become a cushion cover, the rectangular, silver Marks & Spencer's Special Selection biscuit tin containing the flotsam and jetsam she'd accrued during her affair with Peter, unopened since the day she'd filled it. Now she did open it. She needed to let him go and move on. Life was too short, she thought, as she carefully took out the contents:

a cocktail napkin from the American Bar at the Savoy

a street map of Amsterdam
a salt-shaker stolen from the cafe in the Dorsoduro in Venice
a ticket for a vaporetto
a bill for coffee at Caffe Florian

Sally filled the recycling bag she'd fetched from the kitchen with the pile of paper and card discarded on the bed and wondered why she'd kept any of it:
a cinema ticket for the Curzon Mayfair to see a special screening of *Death in Venice*
a napkin from Harry's Bar
a paper menu from their favourite restaurant in an unknown back street by the Accademia
a Dutch beer mat
the silver and amber necklace he'd bought her.

Once the paper trail of their relationship had been disposed of, she put the necklace into her grandmother's crocodile handbag with the broken clasp and put it back on the top shelf of her closet. She should have thrown it all out a long time ago, she thought. Picking up one of the photo albums she climbed back into bed, peeled apart the plastic pages and studied the pictures of big hair and hooped earrings, laughing faces, craning necks and raised glasses, Glastonbury in the rain, the Empire State Building in the sun, a tiny pink Max wrapped in a huge white towel. She reached for another album, she was looking for Martin. And there he was: a skinny boy with a curly mullet, high-waisted jeans and big sunglasses, pointing at Mickey Mouse twirling a baton, the two of them eating huge ice-creams in the shadow of the Disney castle, Martin leaning against a canal bridge, the sleeves of his jacket rolled up, Sally dancing at a Patti Smith gig, her arms in the air, Martin pushing Poppy in her buggy, Poppy pulling a face, Martin dressed as a vampire poised to bite Sally's neck; so many pictures. She closed the album and went to sleep.

When I am dead, my dearest,
Sing no sad songs for me;
Plant thou no roses at my head,
Nor shady cypress tree:

Martin had been dead for nine days. It was a shocking thought but now the feeling of shock felt normal. The sun shone, bouncing bright off the puddles as family and friends gathered. They nodded and smiled, and remarked on the fine weather, a blessing, they said. Nobody likes to go to a funeral in the rain as if the sun might make the loss any less. Jaz wore a green hat that had always made Martin laugh and Sally wore a dress that she didn't particularly like because she knew she would never want to wear it again. In the crematorium, Martin's coffin wore his red, Liverpool supporter's scarf, a gift from his dad many years ago that Sally knew he'd never worn.

Be the green grass above me
With showers and dewdrops wet;
And if thou wilt, remember,
And if thou wilt, forget.

Flanked by flowers, old friends waved hello at each other across the long benches and laughed at the funny stories about Martin. A group of his mates sang, You'll Never Walk Alone, accompanied by members of his ukulele class and Zac, who had learnt the piece especially, on Martin's uke. Jaz had chosen to read Christina Rossetti's poem, Song.

And dreaming through the twilight
That doth not rise nor set,
Haply I may remember,
And haply may forget.

Sally did not want to speak at the funeral. Instead, she had chosen the music to be played as they said their own goodbyes before leaving the crematorium, the theme from *The Dambusters*. And while she stood with Max she pictured Martin da-daaing along, his arms outstretched like an airplane, as he had once demonstrated to her they did at an England match during the World Cup. She had decided not to do a reading or tell a story about her friend because she was not a natural performer, or as Martin used to say: 'Not without a pint of Merlot.' A quote she used several times that afternoon, as she circulated with plates of sandwiches and bowls of

Twiglets, smiling and chatting to old friends, his dad, Katy. Sophie did not come.

'Do you have to make a joke out of everything?' said Marie, as Sally repeated her one-liner yet again, 'Some things aren't funny.'

Sally smiled but she felt sick. Martin was right, she thought, Marie was a cow. Yes, she did have to make a joke, she had to make a joke and hand out Twiglets because she couldn't make conversation. Because she didn't know what to say. Making a joke was her way of making it not hurt so much, of being in control. She hated Marie.

After all the laughter, and drinking, and promising to keep in touch, upstairs in Martin's sister's bathroom, Sally locked the door. She sat on the side of the bath and peered into the magnified bathroom-mirror, scrutinizing the face of the unknown woman looking back at her: there were no new wrinkles, no new grey hairs, nothing had changed but she did not recognise herself. She felt gaslighted and alone. Where was her friend?

'I still can't believe it,' said Jaz, sitting on the floor in her flat, eating pizza, 'it's like it can't really be true.'

She and Sally were drinking wine. Quite a lot of wine.

'I can't believe he's not here,' Sally said, reaching for another slice, she had not eaten anything at the funeral and grieving was a hungry business, 'he's always been there, somewhere.'

'Did you ever,' said Jaz, refilling their glasses, 'ever, think you might end up with him?'

'No.' said Sally.

'Never?'

'Sometimes… I mean I liked doing things with him, I liked hanging out with him, it was always so easy to be with him but…'

'Why do we have to always be suspicious when it's easy?' said Jaz, reaching for her glass.

'I don't know, I guess I've always thought the course of true love doesn't run that smoothly,' said Sally, 'and I never fancied him. Not without a pint of Merlot.'

She laughed and raised her glass to honour Martin.

'I thought you would.' said Jaz, 'I thought eventually you would. I think he thought so too.'

'Did you?'

'Didn't you?'

'He was always… there for me. It was like he was my champion. I know…'

She toyed with her glass.

'…I knew he would have been up for it if I was up for it but I never was. I only ever thought of him as my friend.'

'Does drama have to be there to make a relationship work? Friendships are a good place to start,' said Jaz, 'don't you think? They can grow into love.'

'I've always held out for that blinding wow-I-want-you-now-and forever-madly-in-love love.' said Sally, 'Maybe that's where I've been going wrong.'

She refilled their glasses.

Finally in bed, Sally wrote down in a notebook all the texts she could find on her phone from Martin, a mobile haiku of memories, and then she cried until she fell asleep.

Top tip: Scarlett O'Hara may have got away with thinking about it tomorrow, but sorting out the deadwood now, can clear the way for new possibilities, both mentally and physically.

CHAPTER 29

Despite everything else that had been going on, Alice had still found time to help Sally get a new job at her friend Anna's art gallery, for which Sally was truly grateful and she was trying hard to be truly excited about. She was also trying hard to be true to her word and embrace her singularity but there were nagging doubts. Why had she been so quick to judge Peter? If she had just confronted him with her discovery right at the beginning then maybe he would have explained about his ex-wife and maybe…

'You're not still thinking about him?' said Alice.

'It is an ongoing thing,' said Sally, 'until it is no longer an ongoing thing.'

'Apparently,' said Alice, 'but it doesn't stop him from being a lying, cheating, loser…'

'We don't know he cheated…'

'We don't know he didn't. Could have had women stashed all over the world. It's done, he's gone, don't over think it.'

The rain poured down outside turning the grey sky as green as the wet grass, gutter-splashing onto the decking and filling the pink, plastic bucket in which Olive had collected the dead leaves from the garden. Inside, the warm glow of the industrial sized, low-hanging lights, salvaged from a French print-works, made sure the sun never set in Alice's kitchen.

'I'd love not to over think it,' said Sally, yawning, it had been another long night of sweats, briefly punctuated with

251

fitful bouts of sleep, 'it's like my brain goes into overdrive, anxiety driven madness in the middle of the night. Another symptom of the menopause.'

She took a sip of her tea. Alice's hand darted crab-like into her over-sized handbag, to fish out her ultra slim cigarettes. She plucked out the last one from the now empty pack of ten, lit it, walked over to the French doors that opened onto the deck and unlocked them.

'Smoking?' said Sally, 'What's happened?'

The damp air wafted the smoke back into the kitchen. Alice turned her back and Sally knew there was something very wrong.

'Ben's having an affair.'

'What?' said Sally, 'Don't be ridiculous. How do you know?'

'Because,' said Alice, inhaling, 'I know.'

Having accompanied her husband to a special screening of his documentary on the slave trade in the 21st century, at the BFI, she had nodded keenly, listened intently, pulled all the right faces at the reception, while a bald headed man with bad breath had gone on and on about the death of the documentary.

'You could make a film about that.' she'd quipped, as she'd excused herself to go to the loo.

Returning, she'd found Ben by the bar, telling his young listening circle an amusing story about an Inuit with a speech impediment, a story Alice had heard many times before but Ben always loved to tell the next generation of filmmakers. And then Summer, Ben's assistant, picked a fleck of fluff from Ben's lapel. And Ben had done nothing. He hadn't flinched, or looked at her, or even noticed and Alice knew beyond a shadow of a doubt, that their intimacy far exceeded the mindless removal of lint.

'You don't know,' said Sally, shocked by her friend's unexpected revelation, 'not for sure.'

'I know how to recognise when someone else is sleeping with my husband,' said Alice, 'as you have pointed out before, it's what I did so I should know.'

Alice had returned to the powder room. Locked inside the cubicle she'd pressed her head against the cold tile and thought, maybe she was wrong. Maybe she was just projecting her own fantasies of infidelity onto Ben. Maybe this was just the insecurities of a fortysomething women, stressed out by having two young children when she was too old. But she knew she was right. Staring into the mirror at the beautiful Armani dress she was wearing, clearly defining the flatness of her twice-weekly pilated-tummy and her arms tightly toned from all that swimming, she knew her body was good for any age. But she also knew there was a lack of elasticity about her fatless frame, her skin now wrinkled and creased at the elbow, was looser at the neck and along the jaw-line. Alice's tired eyes had filled with tears. Ben was sleeping with Summer.

'Do you have proof?' said Sally, 'Actual proof?'

'At the documentary festival,' she said, 'in Manchester, he called me really early in the morning, told me he'd drunk too much, fallen asleep in his hotel room with all his clothes on, watching TV.'

'But…'

'Too much information,' said Alice, 'he spent the night with Summer. He bought me a Marc Jacobs handbag after that trip because he said I deserved it.'

She drew heavily on her cigarette.

'But that doesn't actually prove anything.' said Sally.

'Receipts,' said Alice, 'it's easy to find out once you start checking. Dinner for two, breakfast for two.'

Sally felt sick herself now.

'What are you going to do?'

'Nothing.' said Alice.

'Nothing?'

'I shall do nothing, he can have his Summer fling.' she said, flicking the ash and exhaling a thin curl of smoke, 'If I make a fuss it'll all blow up. Things will be said that cannot be unsaid, he'll seek shelter at her door. And she will have won.' Alice bent to stub out her cigarette in the small pile of butts that had collected in the bottom of an old flowerpot. She closed the door and sat back down.

'If he has really tired of this,' she looked passed Sally, across the open-plan kitchen, it's double-fronted fridge illustrated with drawings by Olive and Stan, magnetised to the doors by so many souvenirs from so many holidays together, and the board pinned down with rotas for school runs and violin lessons and doctors' appointments, restaurant reviews, cinema vouchers and phone numbers for the au pair, 'and of us, then he'll go anyway. But I don't think he does want to lose us.'

'Of course not.' said Sally.

'So I will give him his space.' continued Alice, hardly listening,

'I'm taking the children away to my brother's wood, he makes us all sit round a campfire in deckchairs. Ben can't sit in a deckchair because of his knees. He hates it but I make him come, he will be delighted when I tell him he doesn't have to.'

'But he'll see her.'

Sally was fearful this plan might back fire.

'Exactly, he can see as much of her as he wants.' said Alice, her sleepless blue eyes, greyed with fatigue. 'He can make himself sick on forbidden fruit.'

'Is she younger?' asked Sally.

'She's named after a season.' said Alice, 'Mid-thirties, no children, the deadliest of the species.'

'It's a brave move, giving him his space.'

Sally felt awful that she hadn't seen the pain her friend had been in, so caught up in her self-made madness.

'It's a layer cake of fuck is what it is.' said Alice.

Max was preparing to move out, or at least preparing to pack up his stuff to prepare to move out. This should have filled Sally with delight, this was exactly what she'd wanted. But instead of perusing colour charts and planning the makeover for her new spare bedroom, she felt sad at the prospect. Now she really would be home alone. What would happen if she slipped in the bath? Or died in the night? How long would it be before her decaying body would be found?

'Have you ever slipped in the bath?' said Will, sitting at the kitchen table, looking fit and still tanned from his visit to Italy; a road trip along the Amalfi Coast to see the retired Dr. Annie Barrett, his long-time friend and mentor.

'No,' said Sally, 'not yet. But it's only a matter of time.'

254

She watched her friend twiddle pasta at speed around his fork. She had made him scialatielli con vongole, with the delicious food parcel he had brought her back from his travels.

'Max is leaving the nest,' said Will, 'this is a good thing, and you've got a new job starting, there is much to celebrate, new beginnings.'

'Yes,' said Sally, 'and I am delighted. Really.'

Recent events had taken their toll and she was hoping the good doctor might help her put some perspective on it.

'Indeed you should be, let the past go,' said Will, 'all that messing around, you were behaving like a man.'

The remainder of his gifts littered the table: prosciutto, sun-dried tomatoes, salami made with wild fennel, provola cheese, and a bottle of limoncello.

'I was?'

'Typical male behaviour,' he continued, 'fucking around spreading your sperm.'

'Sperm?'

'Yes,' said Will, refilling his limoncello, 'we have to do it, we are designed to do it, we need to procreate.'

'What? Gay men?'

Sally reached for her drink, she was trying hard to follow her friend's line of thought.

'Same design feature, the need to have sex,' said Will, knowledgably, 'we can't help it, but what's in it for you?'

'I'm hormonally challenged,' said Sally, in her defence, 'my mind isn't working properly. I think I thought what I was doing was OK, I don't think I thought I was fucking up.'

She pulled a very un-smiley face, reached for her glass and drained it.

'Well, don't beat yourself up about it,' said Will, skewering a slice of cheese with the end of his knife, 'it's not that bad, nobody's...'

'Yes it is that bad,' said Sally, biting back the tears, 'and Martin's dead.'

'OK, yes, Martin is dead,' said Will, aware of friend's distress, 'but that is not your fault. A car killed him. You had nothing to do with it, he was on his way to the dentist, you can't own that one.'

'But do you think...' said Sally, refilling her glass, '...was I taking advantage of him?'

'Did he ever make a real move on you, in all those years? No. I think it suited him just fine, being your friend.'

Will grinned and raised his glass to Martin.

'I guess so.' said Sally.

A thin strip of sun poked out through the cloud and momentarily filled Sally's kitchen with a gold glow.

'You know so.' he said, 'You made him happier rather than sadder, you need to lighten up.'

He sliced himself another piece of cheese.

'Focus on your new job, it's a whole new start.'

He refilled their glasses with more of the icy limoncello.

'To new beginnings,' he raised his glass, 'and my new man. He's a lecturer.'

'A lecturer? Oh my,' said Sally, fanning herself in the manner of Scarlett O'Hara, with one of the linen napkins Will had also brought her, the corners inset with lace, 'an academic?'

'Yes, he's a gorgeous physicist,' said Will, reaching for the salami, 'it's all gone very Brian Cox.'

Sally smiled her approval. This one actually did sound like a good match for her friend.

'He's got his own house. And a car.'

Reaching into the fridge she took out two ramekins chocolate pudding and handed one to Will.

'Where did you meet?'

'Well,' said Will, still flushed with the excitement of new love and delighted at the prospect of talking about his new beau, 'it's quite funny really. We met on the bus.'

'Not again?'

'I know,' said Will, and licked his spoon, 'who knew it was the place to pull.'

He took another sip of his limoncello.

'He ran up as the door was about to close and just made it in time…'

'Fate,' said Sally, 'a few seconds later and…'

'Yes, very, Sliding Doors,' smiled Will, 'then he tries to pay.'

'What? With money?'

'And he only had a £20 note, he doesn't have an Oyster…'

'Doesn't have an Oyster?'

'Doesn't have an Oyster,' Will paused for effect, 'he never usually uses public transport.'

'Wow.'

'Exactly,' said Will, as if he's just revealed his new boyfriend was in fact David Beckham, 'and I had change so I offered to pay for him, for once my gaydar was actually working. So we got talking and he said he must pay me back and I said don't be silly and he said he didn't think it would be silly to take me out for dinner and...'

'He paid for dinner?'

'No, we split the bill but,' said Will, 'he paid for breakfast.'

'I see.' said Sally, knowingly.

'And he gave me a book of poetry.'

'Poetry?'

'Yes, I'm dating Shelley.' he said, and laughed.

Sally bit her bottom lip as her eyes teared up with the romance of it all.

'Just one problem.' said Will.

'Alcoholic?'

'No...'

'Bankrupt?'

'No.'

'Drug addict?' said Sally, reaching for the limoncello, 'German?'

'No, and no...' said Will.

'Hairy back?' said Sally.

'No,' said Will, 'his name.'

'What? Not Malcolm?'

'No. It's Will.'

'Oh well,' said Sally, 'where there's a Will...'

She raised her glass to toast her friend's good fortune, it was lovely to see him so happy.

Adjusting her new, now-we-are-fifty, glasses, Sally sat down at her new desk. She was enjoying her new job. The glasses, she believed, at least made her look wise. She had been getting headaches so Will had suggested she get her eyes tested where upon the nice optician had said yes, there was more deterioration, nothing serious, just what you'd expect in your fifties. But Sally had liked her new specs for her new start, so much she had forgiven the rude optician for using the F-word, and had taken to peering over the black frames when answering a question as she sat in the gallery, in what she imagined was an alluring manner. Or removing them completely to ruefully suck the tip of the arm and then run her hand through her hair, in a way that she believed suggested she might well be wearing something fabulous from Agent Provocateur beneath her crisp white shirt, and not a greying M&S full-cup from a 2-pack. She was even toying with the idea of growing her hair longer so she could complete the look with a French pleat, one she could release with a single hairgrip and a shake of her head as she removed her glasses.

The winter sun glared through the glass of the wide gallery window. Sally liked her new job a lot and she liked Anna, who, despite not remembering having ever met her at her party, had said Sally was a 'life-saver' for coming to work in her gallery, because she'd needed a woman of substance, someone older who, in her words, knew what she was doing. She'd even been given her own intern to do the things she didn't like doing. So now, she got to deal with the clients she liked and liaise with the artists, go to private views and write the press releases, while the intern made the coffee and told the public which way Selfridges was when they stumbled in from the cold. She'd completed her first feature for an industry arts magazine, which she'd very much enjoyed. And she was being paid surprisingly well. Plus, she still had *Snacks and The City* and her Top Ten Tips but she didn't have to go into the office and deal with tricky Tricia or Mike the moron anymore. So all in all, things had turned out remarkably well.

This exhibition highlights Marion Enright's innovative approach to light, colour, composition and…
Sitting hunched over her laptop, Sally scanned the artist's bio for more useful facts to pad out the piece she was writing. This exhibition was the first event Sally had worked on since starting at the gallery and she wanted to do a really good job.

…The work has been developed over the last 25 years while she has been living in France with her…

Anna was very excited about this particular upcoming show, partly because she loved the work and partly because she had, many years ago, been at art college with Marion.

...challenging conventional notions of beauty and exploring a range of emotional responses from melancholy and joy, loss and...

Having stepped away from the limelight, Marion had now returned to the art scene with an extraordinary collection of work; a series of prints and paintings charting the evolution of the garden she had created over the years, the corkscrew trees and carved hedges, the vibrant flowers that hid heads of clay amongst their foliage.

...recognisable forms are often fragmented and...

The result was a stunning exhibition, which Anna was very keen to promote. The Private View was going to be a glittering affair followed by a celebratory dinner for twenty or so and although Sally was planning low-key Christmas festivities this year, she was very much looking forward to the opening. And the dinner. She had got on very well with Marion and had been invited to visit her house and garden, in France. It felt good to be back in the world: new friends, new opportunities, a whole new beginning.

When it arrived in her inbox, it had taken Sally a moment to realize that the Peter Jacobs on the list of Anna's personal guests, along with the draft of the Private View invitation, was in fact her Peter Jacobs. Her ex-Peter Jacobs. She stared at his name. It made perfect sense that he would be invited it had just never crossed her mind that he would be invited. That she would be inviting him, she would be the pp. It was ridiculous, she thought, but she just could not do it. She may be moving on, she maybe over him, but she wasn't ready to deal with him, not yet. Maybe never.

'Get me out of this Martin,' she muttered to herself, 'please.'

Since his death, Sally had had many such chats with her missing friend, she found it very comforting to be able to carry on their conversation, even if it was a bit one sided, imagining he might be keeping an angelic eye on her.

'Ooh,' said Maisie the intern, handing her a mug of coffee, 'anything I can do?'

'Actually,' said Sally, smiling, 'there is.'

'Thanks Martin.' she whispered.

Of course, now she herself would not go. She'd come up with some excuse, make her apologies, it would be fine, Anna would understand. She really didn't need to see Peter again.

Top tip: to avoid steamed up glasses when reading in the bath, dip them in the water, like a diving mask.

CHAPTER 30

Staring out of the restaurant window at the snow-wet city: grey, slushed and slow moving, Peter was thinking about Sally. The invitation to the opening in London had not been a surprise. He'd been expecting it ever since Anna had mentioned the show some time ago, when she'd also mentioned the 'great woman' she now had working at the gallery. It had taken him a moment to realize that her Sally Benson was his Sally Benson, his ex-Sally Benson. And the thought of seeing her again had been lurking in the background ever since. Hidden under meetings, obscured by conference calls, buried beneath labour pains and baby gifts, now she had risen to the surface. Of course, he would not go. He'd come up with some excuse, make his apologies, it would be fine, Anna would understand. He really didn't need to see Sally again.

'No thank you.'

Peter looked up as Laura, his date, waved the waiter away and the clatter of the Tribeca restaurant broke through his reverie.

'No dessert.'

'Really?' he said, taking the menu from the waiter, 'You don't fancy anything?'

He scanned the list. She screwed up her face.

'Do you have crème brûlée?' he said.

Oh no,' said Laura, 'dairy and sugar?'

'But…'

'You do not need that.'

'No one needs dessert,' he said, reaching for his glass, 'but it is…'

'So bad for you?'

She smiled across at Peter. He smiled back and handed the waiter the menu.

'You may not care about you,' she said, 'but I do.'

'Just an espresso please.' he said.

Laura winced.

'A double.'

'And an 'erb tea.' she said.

Peter reached for the near empty bottle and went to top up her wine, aware she was yet to finish her first glass.

'I read this fascinating article,' she said, 'about alcohol abuse …'

'Abuse?'

'… in *New York Magazine*, apparently…'

Peter emptied the bottle into his own glass. Maybe it had been unwise to make Max a Facebook friend, he thought, but to be honest he'd been new to the game and thought it too rude to refuse a request to be 'friends', and anyway, he'd liked the boy. Max was an amusing kid, much like his mother. Helping his sister and her boyfriend find a sponsor hadn't been any hardship for him, he was quite happy to help them out, he knew how difficult it was for young people and he'd admired their spirit of adventure, they were good kids.

'…it's an excellent class, it builds core strength and gives me a cardiovascular…'

And that, he had thought, would be an end to it. But Sally's impromptu appearance at his hotel had definitely thrown him. All the pain, all the emotion, all that mess that he'd always associated with love, and worked hard to keep on lock-down, had flashed back again. He'd had to work even harder to forget her.

'… total juice fast and after a week…'

Not speaking to her, not seeing her, had helped him to render her invisible in his head and in his heart. It was a tactic he had employed before and it worked very well. He'd moved on, he was fine.

'…we should definitely go…'

Until now.

'…it really is a fabulous place,' said Laura, 'to totally relax.'

'Sorry darling.' said Peter, he was finding it hard to stay focused.

'The Mount Tremper Detox Lodge.' she said, reaching for her water.

'The what?'

'Up state? Peter have you been listening?' she said, leaning forward and taking his hand, 'You so need to relax. We can take hikes and there's this great Zen Monastery.'

Peter looked round for his coffee.

'They do open-house meditation.' she said.

The restaurant felt stuffy, he was hot, he couldn't breathe.

'It'll be perfect.'

Laura squeezed his hand.

'Just what we both need.'

What he needed right now, he thought, was to get out of there.

Hi Sally
hope all well
would love to see you x

Sally stared at the text. Commuting into London's glittering West End was still sufficiently novel to have her swinging her handbag and humming *Downtown*, every time she emerged from Bond Street Tube. She'd barely come to the end of the second verse, hadn't even taken her coat off yet, when the text came in. A text from someone called Mark. Someone whose name and number were in her phone but whom she could not place. She snapped the lid off her flat white and read the message again. She did not remember knowing anyone called Mark and yet she must do. She racked her menopausal brain for a clue. Nothing. This is how it was these days, her brain was set to some sort of auto-archive, removing all memory of her recent past and the names of everyone, storing it in a locked file for which she didn't have, or could not remember, the password. Unable to recall the name of anyone she had ever seen in any movie, she could hardly hold a conversation anymore without the aid of Google.

'Do I know anyone called Mark?' she asked Alice at lunchtime, when they met for a sandwich and a catch-up.

'What about at Right Stuff?' Jaz suggested, when she popped in to see her for an early evening drink, on her way home.

'Mark?' said Will, 'Wasn't he the one who wrote about words? Remember?'

And then Sally did remember; Mark was the man from the Internet, the cancelled date because of, 'the Big C'. Mark was cancer boy. She may have been quite surprised to receive Mark's text but she was also quite pleased. She may not have been too bothered about him then but she liked the fact that he was still bothered about her now. And he'd put the x. She read the text several times, checking the nuance. She couldn't find any hidden meanings. Her natural response was to call him immediately, have a chat and say... yes, she would love to meet up, in her new spirit of non-judgementalness and because she was lightening-up and trying not to think too much. And keen on new beginnings. But because he had texted her she thought she would follow his lead, so she texted back. And because he'd put the *x* she put the *x*.

He suggested lunch and put the *x*.

She confirmed the date and put the *x*.

He said he'd call on the day to fix the venue and put the *x*.

And although Sally wasn't keen on what she saw as the noncommittal I'll-call-you-when-we're-there mentality of the modern world, she'd replied:

Great

And put the *x*.

'I did exactly what you said.'

Ed's brow furrowed in concentration as he poured Sally a glass of wine.

'And?' said Sally.

'And it was delicious. The lemon, the garlic,' said Ed, filling his own glass, 'really good, just like yours.'

They were sitting in the fairy-light glow of Sally's kitchen while Ed recounted his recent kitchen experience. He had come round to borrow one of her cookbooks having first called to see when it was convenient to pop in.

'Good,' said Sally, 'great.'

It seemed that since her little lecture Ed had had a rethink.

'Playing to our strengths,' he said, raising his glass to toast his culinary success, 'Tam's very busy, like you said, and I have more time so… makes sense I do the cooking.'

'Quite.' said Sally.

'If Max can do it…'

'Exactly.' said Sally.

He drained his glass.

'Can't think why I didn't think of it sooner.' he said.

Sally smiled.

'What about you? How are you managing all your new free time?'

'What free time?' said Sally, reaching for her glass.

'It's the slippery slope you know. First they cut your hours, then you start working from home… '

'I'm busy. Really busy.'

'The next thing they've changed the locks and some spotty youth with a degree in truck-loading is taking over your job.'

'Hello…'

Sally waved her hand in front of Ed's pinking face.

'That was you, this is me. I'm fine, more than fine.'

'Really?' said Ed, embedding himself in his chair, 'good stuff.'

He refilled their glasses.

'Anymore news of whatshisname?'

'No.' said Sally.

'You don't think you were a bit hasty?' he took a sip of his wine and shook his head. 'Have you thought about sending him an email?'

What, thought Sally? Now Ed wanted to give her relationship advice? 'Things might be different now he's had a bit of time and…'

'No.' she said, picking up her glass and draining it.

'But Poppy said he was really helpful…'

Ed refilled her empty glass.

'…sounds like he's a bloody good…'

'Yes, I know,' wailed Sally, now the wine had kicked in, 'he's kind and helpful and he had a ring…'

'A ring?'

265

Ed spluttered wine down his chin.

'Yes, a ring.'

'You saw it? This ring?'

'I saw the box.' said Sally.

'Yeah, but if you didn't actually see it,' said Ed, 'it could have been an empty box.'

Sally looked at her ex-husband.

'It was not an empty box,' she said, 'you think he just walks about with empty ring boxes in his pocket? Just in case?'

'Well…'

'Stupid.'

'It could have been,' said Ed, 'a gesture.'

'Really?' said Sally, 'I don't think Peter does empty gestures.'

She stood up and turned off the pot that had been simmering on the stove.

'Something smells good.' said Ed.

'Boeuf Bourguigon,' she said, 'but now Max is working late so…'

She reached up to the shelf for two dishes.

'…you can have some.'

'Sorry, can't. I'm doing a risotto tonight,' he said, finishing his wine and springing to his feet, 'looks delicious though, maybe you could email me the recipe.'

Sally called Will to see if he wanted to come over for Boeuf Bourguigon but he was doing dinner and a movie with his boyfriend. Who was she going to cook Boeuf Bourguigon for, she wondered, now Max was moving out? Even Ed didn't need her to cook for him anymore.

'Who is it you're going out with?' asked Poppy, standing in the doorway of her mother's bedroom.

'What about this?' said Sally, holding up a dress she never ever wore. Ever.

'New underwear?'

Poppy dangled a champagne pink, satin balcony bra, still adorned with its label, from between her finger and thumb.

'Who is he?' she continued, taking the last of her brother's Jaffa Cakes from the box she was holding.

'A friend.' said Sally. 'A new friend.'

'With benefits?' said Poppy, 'He will expect you to sleep with him, you do know that.'

Sally ignored her daughter and busied herself in the back of her closet.

'How long,' sighed Poppy, 'are we going to have to live with you doing your whole mid-life thing?'

'Those are Max's, Jaffa Cakes, he'll be really fed up if you've finished them.'

'So?' said Poppy, 'It's not like he bought them. You bought them. I can eat them if I want. They're not actually his. He's going to have to learn to buy his own Jaffa Cakes, might as well start now.'

'I know,' said Sally, pleased she'd diverted her daughter away from the subject of her sleeping arrangements, 'but I did buy those for him.'

'Wear that.' said Poppy, indicating a white cheesecloth top reminiscent of something Sally had worn when she was eighteen.

'Really?'

'Makes you look slim.'

Sally beamed.

'Well, not as fat,' said Poppy, wandering back to the kitchen to see what else she could find to eat.

'Thanks.' said Sally to the space her daughter had once occupied.

She looked at the pile of ill-fitting clothes now heaped on the bed and saw the dress she had worn the night she'd met Peter at the party. Why couldn't... she stopped herself, Peter was the past, Mark was the future. New beginnings, she thought, she needed something good to happen.

'It is exhausting,' said Alice, 'I'm exhausted by it.'

Sally had invited Alice to join her at, *The Nail Bar*, named thus because it was once a hardware store. Now it offered cocktails along with manicures and pedicures; a treat, Sally hoped, for Alice, who had just returned from the half-term camping trip with her older brother, Jasper, and his family, in the wood. She could bring her up to speed on the state of emergency that her marriage was now in, while Sally worked out how to turn, 'cocktails and a manicure, it works for me', into 280 words of copy for what was left of her column.

'Before we went to the wood,' said Alice, 'I went out with Angie.'

'Coke-head-Angie?' said Sally.

'Yes, got in at 3 in the morning, completely trashed, just for Ben's benefit.'

'Really?'

'But I can't do late nights anymore,' said Alice, 'partying is painful.'

A handsome youth in tight cords and a full beard replenished their empty glasses.

'Went out again with Anna. Threw a few *Graucho* matchbooks around the kitchen the next day,' she said, 'Ben kept asking me who was there and I just said I couldn't remember and changed the subject. All very nonchalant, infuriated him.'

She reached for her Mojito and admired her In The Pink toenails.

'And' said Sally, 'the woods, how was it?'

'Ghastly.' said Alice, 'It's always ghastly in the wood. She gives us all little jobs to do.'

Alice had issues with her brother and his family: sister-in-law, Issie, always pontificating about the joys of owning their own land and saving the planet, their teenage daughter, Rona, currently practising extreme adolescence and their young sons, Freddy and Felix, who were just weird.

'Jasper made us go to this thing where they taught us how to track badgers and spot deer poo and wield a sharp knife until Fred stabbed Felix.'

'Stabbed?'

'Felix cut off Fred's ponytail with the knife.'

Alice reached for her Margarita.

'Ponytail?'

'Jasper and Iss think it's important to respect his right to choose when he wants to have it cut.'

'Felix obviously didn't.' said Sally, sipping her Mojito.

'Then Fred freaked out and disappeared so we all had to go and search the bloody wood and of course he was just sitting in the car playing with his iPad. Rona refuses to go to the wood anymore and was off with her boyfriend somewhere, threatening suicide…'

'Sounds like fun.'

'Jasper prints out all these rules and laminates them,' said Alice, draining her glass, 'then he pins them all over the trees.'

'Not so good then.' said Sally, surveying the young post-work crowd now filling the long, narrow bar.

'Halfway through Ben turned up, said the house felt empty. He missed us.'
She hailed the cocktail waiter again.

'He hates going to the wood, he hates Jasper talking about sustain-a-bloody-bility and he really hates barbequed food, so he must have really wanted to see us.'

'Excellent,' said Sally, trying to sound as enthusiastic as she could 'seems to have worked.'

'We'll see.' Alice shrugged.

Top tip: when you can't sleep and your brain has gone into overdrive, crush up the seeds from 3-4 cardamom pods, add them to your hot chocolate and enjoy a delicious night's sleep.

CHAPTER 31

'Winter must be cold for those who have no warm memories…'
Peter, still unable to get 8 across, looked up from his *New York Times* at the large screen above the bar, as he heard Deborah Kerr speak the words to Cary Grant.

'We've already missed the spring.'
He had slipped into The Movie Bar, just off 9th Avenue, somewhere in the mid 40s, to escape the snow, which was now falling quite heavily, and to kill a little time before he met up with Laura. They were going to a special charity performance of Art, reuniting the original New York cast, to raise money for the arts project that helped disadvantaged teens, which Peter supported, and then to dinner with Alfred Molina, an old friend.

Popular with tourists, the Hollywood themed bar showed classic movies on several large screens. Peter knew the line from, *An Affair To Remember*, well; it was one of several that Sally had been so fond of quoting. He'd always thought it very cute, her love of old movies, and even though it was a cheesy tourist place he'd imagined he might have taken her there, she would have got a kick out of it, he'd thought. But that was then. As he watched the scene play out between Grant and Kerr, he wondered what the hell he'd been thinking, walking in there now.

It wasn't just the movie or the invitation to the Private View that had made him think about Sally; since the birth of

Jonah, his beautiful, new grandson, he couldn't get her out of his head. Seeing Carrie and Ted rejoicing in their baby boy, his ex-wife so happy holding her grandson, their grandson, all the years of anger, all that animosity he'd held onto, none of it mattered anymore. Sally had unlocked something inside him, a tsunami of emotion, and he was finding it hard to shut it down.

He sat there in the bar, as the slow blizzard spun the afternoon to a close, and remembered how she'd splashed him with Prosecco when they'd first met, he thought about the night in Amsterdam when he'd had to carry her back to the hotel, he remembered kissing her by the Grand Canal in Venice, the way she looked at him, the way she smelt, her laugh. And she ate dessert. He couldn't remember the last time he'd seen a woman eat dessert. Not in New York that was for sure. It was very refreshing to be with someone who showed no prejudice towards dairy, sugar or carbs. And she had really cared about him and he knew that didn't happen very often.

'*There must be something between us, even if it's only an ocean.*' He looked up at the movie and missed her more than he could ever have imagined but he had decided it was over. Absolutely and forever. That relationship was dead. He had planned not to go to the private view but now he was not so sure, would it really be such a crazy idea? His head may be confused but his heart was telling him go; go and put an end to this anxiety one way or another. Isn't that what Dr. Goodfellow's little book had said, deal with your issues, don't let your issues deal with you? Something like that.

He finished his drink, night had come quickly to the city and he would be late. Was he just being foolish, he wondered? Laura cared for him too, cared so much she didn't want him to eat dairy. Or sugar. And she would definitely never be an embarrassment, never end up sitting in a bush or dancing about on a roof under a full moon, she would never... Peter looked down at his paper, eight across still undone. He was lousy at crosswords, he only did them because they reminded him of his father. He wished his dad was there now, he missed him too; he would have known the answer. Outside on the street he saw Laura smiling as she walked towards him through the snow and he smiled and waved.

No more Americans, thought Sally, she had let go and moved on. She was looking forward. Looking forward to seeing Mark. Maybe this was the right time, like for Jaz and Matt, a second chance, a sign, a gift from the gods, another...
Yoga wow!!
Sally read his text on her way to her class.
Call me when you're done x
She tried hard to 'be in the room' and 'stay in the now' but she was mainly back in her bedroom, going through her wardrobe again planning what she would wear to lunch.

Once at home she re-read his text again and made the call. Sally couldn't really remember Mark's voice but she knew instinctively, when he said:
'I thought you were still in South Ken.'
that all was not well.
'No.' she said, her mind still catching up with her mouth, one leg in, one leg out of a pair of control top, silhouette defining tights.
'Really? But I thought...'
But now Sally was thinking, as she lay beached on the bed.
'You don't know who I am,' she said, 'do you?'
'Of course I do,' he said.
There was a pause.
'... you're Sally.'
But Sally knew she was right, he'd got the wrong Sally.
'So how are you Sally?'
'I'm good. Fine. Great.' she lied, half laughing now, imagining how they would joke about this over lunch and he'd see how brilliant she was anyway and it would be a perfect Richard Curtis moment, 'How are you?'
'Oh you know,' he said, 'work's not so good... did a piece about Christmas books for the loo, that sort of thing and... well... the thing is... um... I don't seem to have as much time today as I...'
Oh my god, thought Sally, hardly able to take in what he was saying.
'The thing is, I'd love to see you, of course I would...'

She was being dumped before the date.

'But… it would be better if we had more time and…'

He spoke with the calm reassurance of a Dignitas salesman, he didn't want to see her, he wanted to see South Ken Sally.

'Right, you know what? I didn't even know who Mark was when you texted. I had to ask my friends. I had to ring people up. It took me ages to work out who Mark was. I really wasn't bothered about seeing Mark, I only said yes to lighten up and not think so much. I only put the *x* because you put the *x*. I would never ever have put the *x* if I was texting you, and I would never ever have texted you anyway, because I didn't want to see you.'… is what she would like to have said. But if age had taught her nothing else, it had taught her that things rarely get heard the way you would like them to be. And so instead she said:

'Right, you take care Mark.' in her most I-know-you-got-the-wrong-Sally-and-couldn't-even-see-it-through-you-arsehole-so-fuck-off voice. And hung up.

'The thing is,' said Sally, still laying on the sofa in her sitting-room where she'd been all day, 'I didn't even fancy him. But he doesn't know that. That's the thing.'

She was enjoying a range of bar snacks and a bottle of red wine, kindly supplied by Jaz who'd said she and Alice were coming over. And would bring dinner.

'Wanker.' said Jaz, fingering out another Hoola Hoop from the near empty packet, 'Complete bloody tosser.'

She reached for the bottle.

'Yeah, but I put the *x*.' said Sally, shaking her head.

'Forget him.' ordered Alice, refilling their glasses, 'Now.'

'I was dumped before the date.'

'He is not worth another second of your time.' said Jaz.

Sally glumly nodded as she devoured the last of the Twiglets.

'I thought he was going to be…'

'History,' said Alice, 'delete him.'

'But I was dumped before the date,' said Sally, draining her glass, 'again.'

Jaz reached for her bag and pulled out dessert: a large bar of fruit & nut chocolate.

'Harsh, I know.' she said, 'But maybe, it was for the best.'

'Yeah,' said Sally, 'd'you think?'

She snapped a square of chocolate.

'Bastard.'

'It was a lucky escape.' said Jaz.

'It's alright for you.'

Sally reached for the wine and refilled her glass.

'You've got it all.'

She raised her glass to toast her friend

'You're living the dream.'

She hoped Jaz was living her dream, somebody ought to be living the dream.

'Matt is not exactly my dream,' said Jaz, refilling her own glass, 'it's just that I made adjustments to my wish list.'

She took a sip of her wine.

'Maybe you need to re-think too. What about adult education classes? The ones in that prospectus you had looked really…'

'No.'

'You could try Spanish. Don't give up on love. What about Home Maintenance?'

'No.'

'Woodwork? Got to be loads of blokes in woodwork.'

'I don't want to do woodwork. Or Spanish. Or go out with anyone,' she said, 'ever again.'

'Really?' said Alice.

'Really, I'm fine, I've got friends. I've got stuff to do. I'm good. It's all good.'

'And Peter?' said Jaz, 'You don't want to…'

'What?'

'If he's coming to the show, I just thought…'

'No,' said Sally, reaching for the Fruit & Nut, 'absolutely not. That ship has sailed. I've already humiliated myself enough. That relationship is dead.'

'The thing about losing face,' said Alice, 'is it doesn't matter. You always wake up with more face. There's always more face to lose.'

'Have you decided where you're going?' said Sally, firmly changing the subject.

'San Sebastian,' said Alice, 'just the two of us. No kids.'

'Good,' said Sally, 'sounds great.'

'I hate it there,' said Alice, 'but Ben loves it.'

'Going away is always a good idea,' said Jaz, 'change of scene, change of perspective.'

'Do you think it's over?' said Sally, 'Do you think he dumped her or…'

'I don't care who did what,' said Alice, suddenly looking drawn, 'I'm still checking his pockets but so far he's clean.'

'But,' said Jaz, 'is it getting better?'

'Yes,' said Alice, 'and no. I still feel hurt, still feel full of rage, but you can choose to deal with it… or overlook it.'

'Can you get over the obstacles in act two,' said Jaz, 'and make it through act three, to the happy-ever-after?'

'I hope so,' said Alice, 'as long as I don't drown in my own tears.'

Sally looked at her friend and nibbled her chocolate as she thought about what she had just said. Usually so strong and self-possessed, she looked fragile. Would any of them make to the to the happy-ever-after, she wondered? She emptied the bottle into their glasses.

'What's that smell?' said Jaz.

'I've been burning sage.'

'Why?'

'It's cleansing,' she said, 'I'm cleansing the house of Peter and Guy and… bad energy.'

'Smells like you've been smoking pot,' said Alice, sniffing the air.

'It's to rebalance my life, realign and get rid of negativity.'

'Sounds like you've been smoking pot.' said Jaz, 'Maybe we should smoke some pot, do you think Max has got any?'

Although Sally had said she was most definitely done and dusted with relationships, and completely fine about it, her punchy bravado did not truly represent how she was actually feeling. But her mind was made up, to avoid risking the wrath of Peter and any further humiliation she had come up with what she believed was a very credible story about the unfortunate need for her to head out of town and minister to her frail mother who had flu, and underlying health issues, just as soon as the show was hung. She would make her apologies and she hoped Anna would understand.

'Etre bien dans sa peau.' said Sally.

'Oh god,' said Will, 'you've been doing those French tapes

again.'

'Mais oui,' said Sally, 'it's a much better way to spend my evenings, non?'

Concerned about his friend after the disaster that was the non-date, Will had asked her to join him for a Saturday lunch in Brixton Village.

'Oui,' said Will, 'but if you're so 'happy in your skin...'

'I am, I feel great, I'm happy, happy by myself. Happier by myself.'

'Then how come I've eaten twice as much as you and you love this stuff?'

The café where they sat was cornered in the old south London market, now a warren of world eateries tucked, pig's cheek by fish head, amongst the vintage boutiques and stalls selling bolsters of bright African prints, fresh guavas and cooking implements. Cool it was, quiet it was not as the hip and hungry jostled for a seat.

'Because you're a pig. Honestly,' shouted Sally, 'I'm good.' She smiled to prove it. And, despite the dreary weather, wet with little sign of love on the horizon, she was feeling much better and really enjoying her job at the gallery. She hadn't had a single fight with Max, now he'd finally moved out, and even Poppy had been pleasant to her, since she and Habib had booked the registry office.

'But you're not going to the Private View,' said Will, 'or the dinner and you were really looking forward to both. You said...'

'I've decided,' said Sally, 'it's better not to be there.'

'Why,' said Will, prodding a prawn ball, 'if you're so fine with it all?'

'I've said what I wanted to say to Peter, he feels the way he does and that's that. I've moved on.'

'Quitter.' said Will, popping the last spicy ball into his mouth.

'So,' said Sally, sipping her *White Monkey Paw Green Tea* and keen to change the subject, 'how's it going with the boyfriend? Give me everything.'

'He's still gorgeous,' said Will, stabbing a slippery prawn and egg dumpling with his chopstick, 'it just keeps getting better.'

He smiled.

'And better.'

'Wow.' said Sally, grateful the subject was now Will's new boyfriend and not her ex-boyfriend.

'He's doing a lecture tour in Span,' he said, 'in Spanish.'

'Tres bien, he is a proper grown up.'

A bearded young man with prematurely thinning hair, wearing a lime green T-shirt, *The Empire Strikes Back*, emblazoned across the front, squeezed onto the table next to them.

'Exactly,' said Will, raising his chopsticks to shovel in a mouthful of sesame noodles, 'a proper, proper grown up. I don't know why I never tried one before.'

The waitress, a Scarlett Johansson look-alike in a scoop neck T-shirt that revealed the lacy, cerise edge of her balcony-bra, presented them with more small plates of Beijing street food: pork and Chinese-leaf dumplings, sticky chicken wings, and a big smile.

'Enjoy.' she said.

'These are really good.' said Sally, biting into a dumpling. Her appetite was coming back, that had to be a good sign.

'We're planning a weekend away,' said Will, taking a swig of his Tsing Tao Beer, 'a road trip. To Manchester.'

'Why?'

'He's a bit of a Chelsea fan,' said Will, not usually known for his love of football, 'season ticket holder actually. Home and away. Big game.'

He beamed. Sally took a sip of her tea and marvelled at the magic of love. And then she remembered how amazing it had been that she and Peter had ever met at all, how she hadn't wanted to go to the party, how…

'Brilliant,' she said, snapping herself out of it, 'that's so good.'

'Yes, let's hope it's not too good,' said Will, his brow furrowing as he took another swig of his beer, 'to be true.'

Sally shifted to make room for the bearded man's girlfriend, who had now arrived. Styled by Julie Andrews, she was modelling a waistcoat apparently made from old curtains, her hair in two loose madchen braids. They briefly acknowledged one another and then busied themselves with his and hers iPads.

'Give him a chance,' she said, gnawing gingerly on a chicken wing, 'everyone deserves a chance.'

She licked her sticky fingers.

'But you're not going to go to the Private View,' said Will, 'and give Peter a chance?'

Sally dropped her dumpling into the sweet, dark vinegar Will had poured into the shallow dish between them.

'We're done.' she said, reaching for her tea.

'You work at the gallery,' said Will, finishing his beer, 'you've got a perfect right to be there, it's not like you're stalking him at his hotel. Again.'

'I know that. But…'

'But what? I thought you said you'd misjudged him.'

'I did, but...'

'You've forgiven him.'

'Yes, but…'

'Now forgive yourself.' said Will, 'Life's too short. And it's your job to be there.'

'OK,' said Sally, trying to curb Will's enthusiasm, 'I know what you're saying, but…'

'Get over it and go to the opening.' said Will, 'What do you think is going to happen?'

'Nothing…' she said, 'but it's not that simple, just because you're feeling all loved up and…'

'The path is smooth,' said Will, waving for another beer, 'why do you throw rocks before you?'

'Shut-the-fuck-up.' said Sally, throwing her screwed-up napkin at her friend instead.

'We all make mistakes,' said Will, 'that's why pencils have rubbers.'

'Ahh,' said Sally, 'did you just make that up?'

'No,' said Will, 'I saw it on a poster at the nurse's station at work.'

She laughed and finished her tea but Will did have a point, life was too short. And she had been looking forward to it. And it was her job. And Anna was expecting her to be there. She had planned not to go to the Private View but now she was not so sure, would it really be such a crazy idea?

'OK,' she said, 'I'll think about it.'

'Great,' said Will, 'what are you going to wear?'

Top tip: to clear a path before you when walking down a busy street, always looking just above the heads of those coming towards you. They will think you're not looking where you're going and scatter.

CHAPTER 32

The snow had settled overnight and lay deep and thick and streaked with black as the cars slushed through the un-shovelled streets. Sally couldn't remember ever having seen so much snow in London, certainly not before Christmas. Inside the gallery, the heating turned up high, the exhibition was almost ready, just a few minor changes and they would be all good for tomorrow night. Anna was delighted. Marion was delighted. Sally was delighted.

Having continued her conversation with Will over a bottle of Malbec back at his flat, they had finally decided to settle the issue of whether she should or should not go to the Private View by consulting the doctor's Medicine Cards. A bit like tarot but drawing on the 'healing power of animals', they had been given to Will years before, by an ex-boyfriend from Santa Fe. Sally had shuffled the cards and drawn the armadillo. Then Will had read out the meaning while she had listened carefully.

'... and you may think the only way to win in your present situation is to hide or to pretend that you are armour-coated and invincible...'

'See,' Will had said, 'you're acting like an armadillo.'

'... open up and find the value and strength of your vulnerability. You will experience something wonderful if you do...'

'Really?'

Sally had not been convinced.

'…The only real rejection is in not trying to break out of the armour you have used to protect yourself…'

'What does that mean?' she'd said.

'Means you roll up in your armour, like the armadillo, to protect your vulnerable, soft underbelly. You need to expose your soft underbelly.' Will had said, 'If you want to grow.'

And so, Sally had decided to stay in London and attend both the Private View and the dinner, and not be an armadillo.

Sitting in her office, at the back of the gallery, Sally felt emboldened by her decision and her thoughts had now turned to her closet; she wanted to look good. Very good. The Private View was the next day and frankly, she had nothing to wear. She went to see how Maise was getting on stuffing the coming soon leaflets into catalogues with a view to nipping out to see if she could find something fabulous in the pre-Christmas sales.

At first, she did not recognise Peter through the steamy porthole of finger-wiped window, bare-headed and hunched under the December snow, but it was definitely him. Muffled in his familiar mustard coloured scarf, he was emerging from the back of a black cab that had pulled up across the road followed by a woman: tall with long auburn hair, she was pretty and probably, to Sally's expert eye, in her mid-thirties. She watched as Peter's dark overcoat dusted quickly with snow. They stood on the other side of the road facing one another, their heads bent against the chill breeze, talking. She was smiling, listening and nodding as he gesticulated excitedly. He clamped his gloved hands on her arms and drew her towards him, kissed her quickly, and hugged her before they crossed the road towards the gallery.

In the stifling heat Sally froze where she stood. She thought she might be sick, Peter was seeing someone else and now they were both coming into the gallery. Together. He must not, on any account, find her there. She dropped to all fours and crawled at speed towards the counter where Maisie was sitting on the swively chrome stool, inserting flyers. She looked down at her boss.

'Shhhh.' Sally hissed.

'Sally?'

The voice was warm and deep, like salt caramel over toasted pecans, the accent American, east coast, dry-witted, cultured and confident.

'Is that you?'

Sally looked up to see Peter peering down at her over the counter.

'It's not here,' she said, to Maisie, grabbing a handful of flyers from the shelf as she stood up, 'must be in the office.'

She shuffled the pile of papers she was now holding and turned to Peter, standing quite alone, in front of her.

'Sally,' he said, again, 'how are you?'

'Peter?' she said, arranging her eyebrows like a couple of exaggerated exclamation marks, 'Wow! Peter!'

Where was the woman, she wondered?

'Hello.' he said, smiling his slightly lopsided smile, turning a tiny scar at the corner of his mouth into a dimple.

'Wow,' she heard herself say, again, 'what are you doing here?'

She scanned the gallery behind him and then the pavement outside, the woman was nowhere to be seen.

'Didn't you know I was coming?' he said, giving her a quizzical look, 'I did RSVP.'

'No.'

'But you work here,' he said, 'I thought...'

'Yes, I do. I do work here,' said Sally, her throat achingly dry, 'of course I do and yes, of course I knew you were coming. I knew you were coming... to the show.'

'You did?'

Peter looked a little confused. He felt uncomfortable, more uncomfortable than he'd imagined when he'd made his plan to come and see her, to talk to her. To tell her everything. Absolutely everything.

'I did, of course. I mean...'

What did she mean, she wondered?

'I meant, what are you doing here... today?' said Sally, wondering if she might just fake a faint, being rushed to A&E would get her out of this, 'that's exactly what I meant.'

She smiled, fainting was too risky on the hard tiled floor, what if she really hurt herself? Had to spend her life in a neck brace?

'I came to see you.' he said, and touched her arm.

Peter looked at her, her smile was still the same beautiful smile he'd always found so beguiling.

'I assumed you'd be really busy tomorrow evening and I…'

'Absolutely,' said Sally, 'I will be. Busy. Busy. Busy.'

She gave a little shrug and rolled her eyes but did not pull her arm away.

'Rushed off my feet.' she said, in a strange, squeaky, comedy-mouse voice.

What was she doing?

'I am… rushed off my feet right now actually.'

'I thought,' said Peter, tightening his grip on her arm, 'we might go for a coffee and…'

'Oh dear…yes, no.'

Come on Martin, thought Sally, get me out of this.

'Ooh,' said Maisie, 'anything I can do?'

Sally turned to her assistant, thank you Martin she thought.

'Go and get a coffee,' said Maisie, beaming helpfully back at her, 'I'll text if I need you. It'll be fine, they're nearly done. Go on, go.'

Maisie's white-blonde bob shook back and forth as she nodded violently at Sally.

'Go. Go. Go.'

'OK.' said Sally, 'If you're quite sure?'

Outside, darkness was already in the air, as they silently crossed the road to Luigi's Trattoria. Sally pushed open the door of the café and the hot air, heavy with the aroma of baked lasagne and cappuccino, almost choked her.

'Shall we order coffee?' said Peter, smiling nervously, a sort of bare-toothed grimace.

He had hoped Sally might have been a little more pleased to see him.

'Or would you prefer tea?'

His face was pinched by the cold, his brow furrowed and his nose almost comically red. At another time she might have made a joke about it. He would have given her one of his quizzical looks, raised an eyebrow as if he were annoyed, and then laughed. And then they'd have kissed. But not anymore.

'I haven't really got much time.' she said.

Bitter disappointment hardly covered what she was feeling.

Tears were beginning to well up as she sat down at the table, had she forgotten to take her HRT? She was an hormonal time bomb, how could she speak to Peter now? Get out of here, she heard the voice in her head instructing her, don't look back, keep moving, he's an arrogant, mean, American …

'Black coffee.' she said.

On the other hand, she wanted to tell him she was fine, he needed to know just how fine she was and that she didn't care about him. Or his girlfriend. Who the hell was that woman?

'Thank you.' he said to the waitress, after she took their order.

'So?' said Sally, her voice as crisp as the thickening snow outside.

'Well…' said Peter, clearing his throat, he was there to talk about them, to explain everything to Sally. He wanted to say sorry, to apologise for his part in their downfall. And he wanted to ask her if they might perhaps have dinner. If they might, perhaps, start again, 'I wanted to see you because…'

Sally sniffed, to underline just how much none of this mattered.

'To talk to you on your own because…'

This was not going as well as he had hoped. Through the Dutch courage of a single malt in his hotel room the night before, it had all gone rather well.

'I don't want to hear it.' said Sally, as she rolled herself up in her armour.

'I don't think you quite understand.' said Peter.

'Oh really,' said Sally, the anger now rising through the nausea, 'you don't think? I think you do think. I think you think you can do whatever you like. Say whatever you want. Married, not married. You thought about that alright didn't you?'

The waitress stood by the table holding the coffees, looking first at Sally and then at Peter.

'No thanks.' said Sally, standing up and heading for the door.

This, she thought, is what happens when you expose your soft underbelly.

'Great,' said Peter, thrusting a fist full of pounds at the girl, 'just great.'

He followed her outside.

'You know what?' he said, the snow flecking his hair, 'Maybe you're right. Yes, I did make a mistake, the worst mistake of my life but…'

'What?'

'I came here today to apologise to you.'

'Really?' said Sally, 'I thought it might be to introduce me to your girlfriend.'

Peter gave her a quizzical look.

'What?' he said, 'What are you talking about?'

'Peter,' she said, 'I saw you.'

Sally did not want to give him the satisfaction of knowing she felt jealous, that she felt anything at all. But now she'd started.

'I saw you with her.' she said.

She couldn't stop.

'Across the road from the gallery. Through the window.'

Peter arched an eyebrow as the penny dropped.

'You saw me just now?' he said, 'With my niece? You saw me saying good-bye to Sinead?'

'Sinead?'

'Yes, my sister Ruth's daughter.'

But,' said Sally, trying to understand her misunderstanding, 'I didn't know you…'

'No, there's a lot you don't know, like how she happened to be visiting London from Dublin, where she happens to live.'

'Right.'

'Right, and how she brought her parents' Christmas presents over to my hotel so I could take them back to New York.'

'Ah.'

'Ah ha.'

Peter was relishing his position on the moral high ground. Sally had got it all wrong.

'Yes,' he said, 'and I took her out to lunch.'

'Oh.' said Sally.

'No,' said Peter, 'you didn't know that, did you?'

'No.' said Sally, now feeling stupid and sick in equal measures.

'Not my girlfriend.'

Peter looked at her, so forlorn standing in the snow, and was stricken to see her so sad.

'Sally, you didn't think…' he said, his voice softening, 'Oh that's just stupid, I…'

'Well, men your age can be pretty stupid, ever thought of that?' she said, and she began to cry fat, salty tears.

'I was seeing someone,' he said, 'briefly, but… would it matter to you if I was?'

The snow started to flutter across her face, mixing and melting in her tears.

'No…'

'Does it matter to you?' he said, wiping the snow from her cheek.

'Yes, I don't know.' she said.

'I have made some mistakes,' he said, 'a lot of mistakes but I don't think you're one of them.'

'The thing is…'

'The thing is Sally…' said Peter, 'I never took the ring back.'

'What?'

'Because I'm still in love with you.'

'But… what…'

'Will you give us another chance?'

She looked up at him through the salty wetness, open mouthed.

'I think you should. Whatever happens,' said Peter, 'one thing I do know, even if you say no, I will always be in love with you, but I think you should…'

'Yes.' said Sally.

'I think you should say yes.'

'I said yes.'

'You said yes?'

'Yes.' said Sally, 'I said yes.'

Top tip: much like a small child, use your (old) age to get away with anything. So annoyed by a man on the train shouting:

'I'm on the train.' into his mobile phone at his wife, my friend lent over and in her most breathy voice, said:

'Don't believe a word of it, he's with me.'

At seventysomething she does just whatever she likes.

287

ABOUT THE AUTHOR

Jo Gardetta is based in London but still on her journey. This is her first novel.

joanna006@googlemail.com

Printed in Great Britain
by Amazon